HOLDING SMOKE

HOLDING SMOKE

ELLE COSIMANO

HYPERION
LOS ANGELES NEW YORK

For information address Hyperion, 125 West End Avenue, New York, New York 10023.

First Edition, May 2016
10 9 8 7 6 5 4 3 2 1
FAC-020093-16046

Printed in the United States of America

Library of Congress Cataloging-in-Publication Data
Names: Cosimano, Elle, author.
Title: Holding Smoke / Elle Cosimano.
Description: First edition. | Los Angeles; New York: Disney-Hyperion, 2016. |
Summary: John "Smoke" Conlan risks everything to clear his name of the two murders he did not commit while he cultivates his supernatural ability of traveling freely outside the concrete walls of the dangerous juvenile rehabilitation center known as the Y, helping himself and his fellow inmates have a chance at redemption.
Identifiers: LCCN 2015030628 | ISBN 9781484725979 (hardback) |
ISBN 9781484728147 (trade paperback) | ISBN 9781484729007 (ebook)
Subjects: | CYAC: Juvenile detention homes—Fiction. | Supernatural—Fiction. | BISAC: JUVENILE FICTION / Social Issues / General (see also headings under Family). | JUVENILE FICTION / Love & Romance.
Classification: LCC PZ7.C8189 Ho 2016 | DDC [Fic]—dc23
LC record available at http://lccn.loc.gov/2015030628

Reinforced binding

Visit www.hyperionteens.com

THIS LABEL APPLIES TO TEXT STOCK

For Tony

HOLDING SMOKE

ONE

It's been weeks since the last yard brawl, and every one of us is twitchy, ready to jump out of our skins. I check out the scattered pockets of orange jumpsuits under the guard tower, listening as Six screws with the new kid. The concrete walls are smooth, twenty feet high, and looped with razor wire. The guard posted in the tower scans the grounds, his head moving in slow rotations you could set a watch by. I crack my knuckles in my pockets while my breath curls in and out to the beat of an internal clock—the only kind I own.

No denying it's the perfect opportunity. And opportunities don't happen much inside the Y.

I cross the yard, one eye on the tower guard. When he turns in my direction, I take up a quiet place behind Six's back, eye level with the infected hash marks carved in his neck, one for every life he claims to have taken. The number is just talk. Inside the Y, everybody's got big numbers and big stories. All of us building ourselves up just to keep from being knocked down.

His cellmate cuts his eyes at me. I stand a little taller, waiting for Six to turn around, but he's distracted with the new kid—a skinny black boy with a fresh buzz cut and crisp folds in his jumpsuit. He's young.

Maybe fifteen if I had to guess. He picks at what's left of his tight curls, looking like he might cry.

Six stares at the name inked in the orange fabric over the kid's chest and laughs. "Fff... aggett?"

"It's Haggett." The kid's wide, wet eyes dart everywhere but to Six's face, looking for someone to save him. But there aren't any saviors in the yard. And I'm no exception.

Six spits on the ground close to the new boy's feet, and the boy flinches. Six's buddies cackle with laughter.

The sound draws the attention of the tower guard. He locks in on me, and I smile a little, just enough to confirm that something isn't right. He reaches for the mouthpiece of the radio hooked on his vest. I planned to say something to piss Six off. Something I haven't managed to come up with yet. Instead, I put a hand between his shoulder blades and push.

Six turns around slowly—the only way we're allowed to move in the yard. He sizes me up while his boys zero in. The new kid shrinks in on himself and backs away. I don't bother to look at his face to see if he's grateful. All my attention is on Six. On his angry eyes and his narrowed brows. They're dotted with acne and small red holes where his piercings used to be. Behind him, a line of orange jumpsuits takes shape, shifty and eager.

"You got a problem?" Six asks. It doesn't feel like a question.

There's a hum through the yard, an undercurrent that makes my hair stand on end.

Walkie-talkies squawk, and guards push through clogs of curious inmates.

"Nothing I can't handle." I squint up at Six's face, past it, to the tower guard already in position with his rifle tip up. I know exactly what will happen next. Six'll roll his shoulders, his body language unmistakable, while he tells me what he thinks of my mother. Then I'll tell him where I fucked his.

That's when all hell'll break loose.

This is usually the part when everything plays out in slow motion. He'll come at me with everything he has, every blow bouncing off me like an echo. I'll take the hits until my body throbs and my blood sprays in time with my heartbeat, proof that I'm still alive. That I can feel anything. Then, for the sake of self-preservation, maybe I'll throw a few.

And it does go down just like that. At first.

See, I count on the guards rushing in, waving batons and shouting through their masks for us to get on the ground facedown, hands where they can see. And I count on Six's boys tightening up the knot, slowing the guards while Six gets in a few good hits.

But that's a few more than I get. The first and last thing I see is his fist coming at my face and a burst of light behind my eyes before it all goes dark. Six actually likes his mother—maybe even loves her—and I guess I never counted on that.

TWO

I come to in an empty cell. Not empty like the cells in general population would be empty. I blink against the fluorescent lights and look around. A metal toilet reaches out from the wall—no seat, no hardware. No footlockers. None of my personal baggage. Even the bed I'm lying on is a single metal piece.

One piece. One bed. I'm in the hole—Segregation.

I smile. My face hurts like hell. I run a hand over my left cheek, tracing the soreness, grateful for once for the metal plates that hold me together under the jagged, smooth scar at my temple. I hope Six gave it all he had. Hope he broke every bone in his hand. My head is a metal shell. Indestructible.

I follow the scar with my fingertips, from the distorted corner of my left eye up over the side of my head, where the blond hair barely conceals the thick, raised ridges. I grit my teeth, gently at first, testing my bite. Then run a hand along my jaw, feeling the inside with my tongue. Just a couple of loose teeth and a bruise that probably doesn't feel nearly as bad as it looks, but I'll never know. There are no mirrors in the Greater Denver Youth Offender Rehabilitation Center, known more commonly as the Y. Mirrors are dangerous. Easily broken and made into weapons.

I rock my jaw back and forth, shaking off the ache. I don't need to look that closely at myself anyway. I know exactly why I'm here. Why every single one of us is here. We're already broken. Already weapons. We don't need mirrors to show us that our outsides are as ugly as the parts we can't see.

I sit up slowly, stretching, my joints popping and my muscles tight. Everything's sore, like I was knocked on my ass and dragged around by the guards. They have no sympathy for me. Judging by the stiffness in my shoulders, I've probably been out cold for hours, but there's no way to tell for sure how long. Time isn't the same in Segregation. The points of the clock are marked by Lights On, three chow trays passed through the slot in the steel door, and Lights Out.

I rub at a copper-brown smear on my jumpsuit and wonder if there's blood on the basketball court. Or brains on the sidewalk. A stunt like mine could have had the entire yard in a riot. It could've meant smoke grenades and rubber bullets and a hospital wing of busted bones. Today I'm lucky. I made it back to Segregation. Hopefully no one else got hurt. I don't let myself wonder about the new kid. He was probably overlooked in all the chaos. Probably made it back to his cell okay. Not that I was trying to do him any favors. All I wanted was to be alone.

A loud bang rattles the door, and the rectangular slot in the middle slides open.

"Conlan," says the voice on the other side. "You awake?" Officer Brooks doesn't need to ask. The small eyeball in the corner by the ceiling gives him a closed-circuit shot of the bed. All I can make out through the small opening are Officer Brooks's hands around a set of cuffs. "The warden wants to see you."

I pull my forehead from my hands and stand up slowly, then walk backward to the opening, offering my wrists through it. Better to get my ass-chewing out of the way so I can get the hell out of here tonight.

If the warden is in a hurry to get home, I can be back in Segregation by chow, then downtown before Lights Out.

Officer Brooks hums quietly to himself as he clamps the cuffs around my wrists. They're still warm from the last kid who wore them. He opens the cell door, and another officer watches to make sure I don't do anything stupid while Brooks shackles my ankles. Like any one of us would dare to mess with a guy like Brooks. When he stands up again, he towers over me, a wall of muscle. It's hard to tell his age. He shaves his head clean to his smooth black skin, and the only wrinkles on his face happen when he's smiling or thinking. The guys in the pod say he's a retired Marine. That he taught hand-to-hand combat and did two tours in Iraq and came home with a Combat V—a medal for valor—but he doesn't like to talk about it. He's one of the only guards in the Y who doesn't bother wearing Kevlar. Oscar asked him once why he doesn't wear a vest. Skivvy joked that they probably didn't make them big enough. Brooks just smiled and said he'd been to war. Said he knew what evil looked like, and we weren't it.

"How are you feeling?" Brooks asks, doing a survey of my face. He's used to my scars and doesn't linger on them. Doesn't give me hell about them like Officer Monetti does. "You don't look too bad off."

I shrug. It hurts to smile. "Been through worse."

Brooks laughs and shakes his head. He's got one of those grins that splits his whole face in two, revealing every one of his straight white teeth and making his eyes shine as brightly as the polish on his boots.

Officer Brooks speaks into the mouthpiece on his shoulder and stands singing, his rich baritone belting out behind me while we wait for the control room to let us through. I brace for the buzzer. When it finally comes, every muscle in me jumps even though the sound is as familiar as breathing. I've been in the Y for four months. I'm used to hollering guards and slamming doors and the overhead speakers used to keep us in line. But I'll hate the sound of that buzzer for the rest of my damn life. I wonder if Brooks knows. If maybe that's why he's singing, to drown out the sound so I won't flinch. Or if he hates the sound of that buzzer, too.

We have to pass through my pod to get to the warden's office. Pods, the warden calls them, instead of cell blocks. Young people, he calls us, instead of juvenile felons. As if small tokens of political correctness might change what's incorrect inside us, or inside this place. The kinder officers—ones like Brooks—have adopted the warden's vocabulary. But when you're on the other side of the bars, it's harder to be optimistic. Semantics never did much to change our situations anyway.

For the most part, C pod is reserved for the most violent offenders. Kids like Six and his cellmate, Bumper, who were tangled up in gangs. Kids like Oscar, who endured so much abuse at the hands of his stepfather that he eventually snapped and burned him alive. None of the curious faces that peer at me through the Plexiglas windows look like they can be fixed. And they're all pissed. Whatever happened in the yard after Six knocked me out probably cost everyone in the pod a few privileges. I ignore the jeers and finger gestures, and keep my eyes straight ahead, resisting the urge to look in my own cell as we pass. All my shit's probably sprawled over the floor, pillaged by my cellmate in my absence. It's a small price to pay for a few nights alone. And it's not like I've got much worth taking.

A few guys gather outside their open cells in view of the control room. Bumper cusses at me under his breath.

"Keep it cool, gentlemen," Brooks reminds them quietly. Rico looks away and crosses himself in a small, nervous gesture as I pass. He's superstitious and the only kid in the Y who's afraid of me, probably for the right reasons. Oscar acknowledges me with a small nod. The rest keep a respectful distance, fearful of the unspoken connections they think I have outside.

The squeaky wheels of an approaching cart break the silence as Officer Brooks and I near the end of the cell block. Martín's library cart makes the rounds every afternoon, just before third chow, and it's my favorite sound in the Y. His short, square frame pushes steadily through the pod, and the cons who can read grab his attention, calling, "Hey, Libro."

Martín doesn't look at me, but we both slow our pace as the cart passes. Out of the corner of my eye, I see him tap a finger against a stack of books. Their worn spines are bound with a rubber band over a piece of paper that reads, *HOLD for SMOKE.*

I staunch the beginning of a smile that wants to bleed warm over my face, nodding once as he shuffles past. I count Martín as something more than a podmate or a friend. Friends can't be trusted here. But as much as I hate to admit it, I've grown to like him almost as much as I need him. He's smart and, most important, quiet. I can count on him to approach the right people, to be discreet about taking jobs. When he does, he knows how to place them in just the right books so their meaning is clear when he hands them off to me. I'm glad Martín is younger than I am—maybe sixteen at most. He'll be here a long time. And since I don't plan to be released anytime soon, that's probably how long I'll need him.

The rubber band is stretched to near breaking. By the looks of it, at least half a dozen new jobs are waiting, and I'm already behind on last week's. I needed that fight, because I need time alone to catch up. Reputation—that respectful distance that keeps the Sixes off my back—is everything in the Y, and mine is going to hell in a library cart if I don't get out of here tonight.

I start toward the administration offices in the East Wing, but Brooks pulls me up short.

"Not today," he says, steering me gently in the other direction. "The warden wants to meet with you in private." He's not singing when he buzzes us into a secured room full of narrow cages, like maybe this hurts him as much as it hurts me. The room is a remnant of the old maximum-security prison this building used to be before it was repurposed as a juvenile rehabilitation center. The cages are just tall enough to stand in, but not wide enough to do much more than that. Equally spaced in neat rows, they look like headstones, and I feel cold all over at the sight of them.

I've been here before, four months ago when I was as green and orange as Haggett. Warden Somerville calls it the old counseling room, where high-risk convicts meet with government-issued therapists and caseworkers without immediate supervision of a correctional officer. Up close and personal, with enough steel mesh between us to keep us from pocketing their dollar-store watches or strangling them with their cheap-suit ties.

I plant my feet just short of the first empty cage. I've been stuffed in them before, the first few times I met with my caseworker after my conviction. Then again with Dr. Manning, when she churned up the years of fucked-up-ness that landed me here until she was satisfied I wasn't a threat to myself or anyone else. I was moved from the cage to individual and group sessions, and haven't been back since. Warden Somerville doesn't like to use this room. He says it's barbaric. That he prefers more civilized methods of encouraging communication. A cold sweat beads under my jumpsuit, and I wonder if I've gone too far this time. My head pounds and my scar's burning a hole in my temple, like it's trying to bury itself under the skin.

I cuss myself as Brooks closes me inside, then put my hands and feet backward against the openings in the cage so he can remove my restraints.

"I told Warden Somerville you were just sticking up for the new kid," Brooks says, keeping his rich, deep voice melodic and slow, like he's trying to soothe me. "The warden's a fair man. Maybe he'll go easy on you. Either way, you'll be all right." He bends to release my shackles.

It's tight in the cage. When I manage to turn myself around, Brooks is already gone. I exhale a long string of quiet swears and drape my fingers over the bars while I wait fuck knows how long until the warden decides to show up.

He's taking his time, no doubt on purpose, giving me a few minutes to think. My jumpsuit is itchy and hot, and I shift as best as I can in the small space. The longer I wait, the more the unease seeps in. Not because of the cage. I'm okay with cages. Cages are safe. Safer than the yard. Safer than general population. Safer than outside. It's the in-private part that's bothering me.

We usually meet in the warden's office. Officer Brooks or Officer Monetti or whoever else is on duty is usually there, and usually I'm shackled, but that's all right. Warden Somerville has a big leather chair in front of his desk. It's warm, with soft, round arms and a back that's wide enough for three of me. He has floor-to-ceiling mahogany bookshelves that smell good, even if all the books are about law and punishment—the business of human containment. I sink into that chair, breathe in those books, and steal glances at his pictures while he lectures me. I like the pictures framed on his desk best of all.

The largest of the photos is mounted in a thick gold frame. The warden is in the middle, wearing swim trunks and sunburned cheeks and a smile as wide as the lake behind him. His arms drape over the shoulders of a woman and a girl, the same ones who appear in the collection of smaller frames that seem to dot every corner of Somerville's office. The girl in the photos looks about my age, maybe seventeen, with long blond hair. Not the bleached kind that's dry and broken and dark at the roots, like the girls from my neighborhood. This is pretty blond. Strawberrylike. It hangs in glossy curls down to her shoulders and matches the freckles on her cheeks. Her eyes smile through the glass, and I wish I could get close enough to see what color they are. To see who might be reflected inside them. To know who's making her smile like that. But I don't dare reach for the frame. I would never dare touch her. She's too good to be wasted or stolen or busted up, like everything I've ever tried to hold on to.

I shake the cage, releasing some frustration, cursing the small part of me that probably picked that fight just to sit in the same room with those damn pictures. Lot of good it did me this time.

The buzzer jolts me and I straighten when Warden Somerville comes through the door. I clear my head of his daughter's face, grateful he can't read my mind, but he leans against the wall just beyond arm's reach, staring at me like he might be trying to. He gives me a long, tired look and loosens his necktie before checking his watch.

He massages his eyelids. Then he pierces me with a pale gray stare. "You know why you're here, John."

I wonder about the gray. Wonder what those eyes might look like on a face with strawberry hair. If they'd look anything like my own. "Yes, sir," I say.

"So maybe you could explain it to me, son."

We're both quiet. Me thinking of all the places I need to be right now. Somerville probably thinking the same.

"You're a bright kid. Doc Manning says your head's on straight, which must be a damn miracle after all you've been through. You know," he says on a weary sigh, "I've always thought that if you could stay out of trouble, successful completion of the rehabilitation program here in the Y might be an option for you."

I can't tell if he's staring at my scar or at the fresh bruises from the fight I picked in the yard. Either way, it feels like he's passing down some kind of judgment. So maybe, if I could stay out of trouble, I'd make it through the program. Maybe, if I behave myself, they'll let me stay here until I'm twenty-one and cut me loose. Successful completion, he calls it. Like it's some sort of graduation to something better. But it doesn't make any difference. Eventually, most of us'll wind up in an adult offenders facility anyway. It's nice of him to think I might make it out someday. All those books in his office about reform—about preparing us to live outside these walls. Well, I died out there once already, and I've got no plans on leaving.

When I don't answer, he says, "I can't help wondering why you keep gambling away what little future you might have left. Dr. Manning says impulse control problems and anger management issues are common in patients with head injuries like yours . . . something about frontal lobe damage. But I don't think that's what we're dealing with here. Officer Brooks and Officer Rickers think you're picking fights, hoping you'll get thrown in Segregation. Buying yourself some time alone."

I don't say it, but Brooks and Rickers are pretty sharp.

"I can't help you unless you're willing to tell me what's bothering you, John. Are you having trouble with anyone in particular?" His forehead creases, and he inclines it toward me, not close enough to reach, but closer, like he's waiting for me to confess a secret.

"No, sir."

"Is it your roommate, son? Because if you're not getting along with Dale Crenshaw, we can talk about it."

Truth is, I can't stand my cellmate. He talks too much, he's got BO, and he can't keep his hands off my stuff. But that's nothing I can't deal with, and there's no sense wasting favors. "No, sir."

The warden's quiet for what feels like a long time. Then he straightens and folds his hands behind his back as if he's come to some decision.

"Son, Segregation isn't the solution to your problems, whatever they are. So you've got one night. I want you to do some thinking. Tomorrow after breakfast, I'm moving you back to your pod."

One night. That's all the fight with Six bought me. One night to do three jobs spread over half the city of Denver. Pain shoots through my bruised jaw as I clench my teeth against all the arguments boiling up inside.

"Next time," Warden Somerville says sternly, "and I sure hope there won't be a next time, I'll send you back to district court for revocation proceedings."

My jaw falls slack. "Revocation?" But I don't need to ask what this means. I grip the wire until it digs into my skin.

"You're almost eighteen, John. Keep breaking the rules, and I'll have no choice but to ask the judge to move you to an adult facility. They've got a handful of openings at Supermax."

Supermax. My father's doing time in Supermax for attempted murder, because semantics doesn't have a special name for killing someone if that person comes back to life. According to my doctors, I was dead when the EMTs found me, but according to the law, he only *attempted* to kill me, because they resuscitated me six minutes later. It was one of the reasons my public defender fought so hard to get me into the Y, so I wouldn't have to live under the same roof with him again.

"I'd hate to see you end up there, John." The warden looks genuinely apologetic, like he's failed me as much as I've disappointed him, which only manages to make me feel worse.

I nod, numb. No more fighting. No more Segregation. I can still travel, but it'll be risky. I've done it before—traveled away from my body when it wasn't alone, when I wasn't there to protect it. And it cost me the rest of my life.

"Give it some thought, son." Somerville turns and raps on the window, getting Officer Brooks's attention. I twitch at the sound of the buzzer. "You've got until tomorrow."

"Warden?" I start to say, even though I feel bad asking. He turns toward me, looking worn as hell. His hair's silvering around the edges, and his middle's going soft, and the haggard lines on his face make him look older than the diplomas behind his desk suggest he is. Older than the man in that photo at the lake.

"Can I take my books with me?" I ask anyway, even though I know the rules.

The warden pinches the bridge of his nose, like I'm giving him a headache. "You know you're not even supposed to have those hard-spined books in here, John. I've already made an exception. Given your behavior today, I'm not inclined to make one more."

"Please. Just for tonight?"

Somerville gives a small shake of his head. "No personal property in Segregation." But the way he says it feels pliable and soft. As he turns away, my mind gropes for something to barter, an exchange worth bending the rules over. I need those books tonight, or tomorrow morning I'll be back in general population with three pissed-off customers.

I call out, "Six's got a shank hidden behind a false panel in his footlocker." The warden pauses halfway to the door. I don't like being a rat, but I don't like Six more. And I need those books. "And you'll find a soup can in a sock inside Bumper's mattress."

Somerville hooks his thumbs in his belt, staring at me sideways.

"How'd you come by that information?"

I don't answer. He strokes the late-afternoon stubble on his chin, assessing me with a curious expression.

"Officer Brooks says people call you Smoke. He says you have a lot of connections outside." He arcs an eyebrow as if it's a question.

I want to laugh. I have no connections. Not inside. Not outside. Hell, half the time I can't stay connected to my self. But reputation is everything, and if people think I've got eyes and ears outside, and they're willing to trade for it, so be it. Ever since I got here, people've been speculating. Wondering how I'm able to know all these things I know. They cling to the most logical explanations, even if they can't prove them. Most everyone in the Y thinks I'm connected to a gang and I get my information from bangers on the outside, even though I don't identify with any of the local colors, and no one in any of their circles knows who I am. Others think I've got a sugar daddy—some rich pervert trading favors for favors, even though that kind of visitation isn't permitted in the Y. A few assume I must have a private investigator or a cop in my family, which almost makes me laugh, since I probably wouldn't be stuck in here if I did.

I've never confirmed or denied anything. It wouldn't matter anyway. People only see what they're conditioned to believe.

Somerville heaves a sigh and looks at his watch again. Information like this calls for a shakedown of the cellblock. He'll probably miss dinner with his wife and daughter—the ones in the pictures. One look at his tired face confirms it. He'll have to toss half the cells in C pod for contraband tonight while the inmates are at chow, and then he'll spend all day tomorrow justifying the overtime he spent to the deputy director and the other white-shirts he reports to. I've given him enough information to make it worth his while—he'll confiscate a couple of shanks and soup cans—but this is his house. His rules. He doesn't have to give me anything in return. I hold my breath.

The door opens and Officer Brooks steps inside.

"Mike," the warden says quietly, rocking back and forth on his heels. When he finally plants his feet, he says, "Take John back to his cell. He can take a few books to Segregation tonight. If anyone has a problem with that, tell them to talk to me."

The door slams shut after the warden, blowing in the familiar smells of the Y and the predictable reek of overcooked broccoli from the mess hall. I rest my head against the bars and breathe.

THREE

Brooks is kind and waits till my asshole cellmate leaves for chow before taking me back to my pod. He removes my shackles and locks me inside my cell, giving me a minute to scrape my belongings off the floor. I gather up my own books first, carefully inspecting the pages. I'll kill Crenshaw in his sleep if he's torn a single one of them. When I came to the Y four months ago, these five books were all I had. Everything I owned. Even my shirt wasn't mine. On close inspection, some of the bloodstained pages are bent, but the bindings seem fine, so I stack them gently back inside my footlocker, honoring my deal with Somerville to be discreet and keep my contraband books out of sight. These aren't the books I came for tonight anyway.

Instead, I carry three of the books from Martín's library cart to Segregation. Once I'm settled in, Brooks passes a dinner tray through the opening in the door.

"Night, Conlan," he says through the opening. Which means it must be precisely six o'clock.

"Night, Brooks."

His deep voice carries back to me as he sings on his way down the corridor, ready to check out for the night. It's getting late. I eat quickly, barely tasting the food, which is a mound of yellow rice and taco meat and a side of wilted broccoli. I set the empty tray by the slot in the cell door for the night guard, Officer Rickers, to pick up. Then I spread the three books on my cot and give each one a cursory inspection.

Rickers lowers his face to the opening and peeks inside, close enough that his ruddy cheeks and blue eyes are the only things visible. "What do you have in there with you, Smoke?"

A bubble of worry surfaces inside me. The guards never call us by our nicknames. The warden doesn't like it, since a lot of the kids bring their gang nicknames into the Y with them, like Skivvy and Bumper, whose names are tattooed on their faces. Bad baggage, the warden calls it. But Rickers is pretty new here. Newer than me. There are still a lot of things about the Y he doesn't know. Like my deal with Warden Somerville. "The warden said I could bring my books," I reply.

Rickers's blue eyes search the cell and find nothing else of concern. His face creases with a smile. "Okay. I'll be back to check on you before Lights Out."

I exhale a relieved breath, collapse onto my bed, and open the first book.

Martín has marked each one, careful not to make the notations too obvious in case the guards ever get it in their heads to check them. Usually, he dog-ears a page or two, calling my attention to words, phrases, or names. He lightly circles the numbers in a table of contents or on a copyright page to tip me off to an address. I open the first book and fan through the pages. None are folded down, and I wonder if Martín missed something, until I close it. The name on the cover jumps out at me. It's a self-help book by an author named Rickers. I hope like hell it's a coincidence. But I turn to the title page, and there it is—the name *Rickers* circled lightly in pencil.

Rickers. The only Rickers I know is Officer Rickers, the guard who poked his face into my cell and said he'd be back to check on me. I've never done a job for a guard before, and for a second, I think about returning the book and telling Martín to be more careful. But maybe Martín didn't have a choice. It didn't take long for word to spread through the cellblocks. *Smoke has connections. If you need information from outside, Smoke can get it.* I tell inmates what they want to know about their friends and families or enemies on the outside, in exchange for things that make life inside the Y more bearable for me. Comfortable, even. It stands to reason that the guards would eventually start hearing about it.

I hold the book in my palm, judging the weight of it. This particular job is valuable. The kind that might come in handy if I ever find myself on the outs with the guards.

Curious, I open the book to the table of contents, scanning the numbers circled lightly in pencil and Martín's notes. An address on South Pecos Way. I recognize the street name from my old pickup route when I worked for Highland Waste. Somewhere in Athmar Park. It won't be hard to find. I commit the house number to memory and flip to the back cover. The library books all have pockets with index cards to keep track of previous borrowers. My name appears last with a due date beside it. Tomorrow. A rush job.

You've got one night.

I cuss under my breath and ignore that part. The name printed above mine reads *L. Driggs.* No one working in the Y's library looks close enough to notice the extra names Martín writes in and pencils through when I return the books, or the erroneous due dates, or that there aren't any convicts named L. Driggs. Lucky for me, I guess.

I thumb the pages from front to back, searching for the lightly circled letters that come together to form a question: *Is she cheating on me?*

I slam the book shut and toss it onto the bed. Some nights I feel like Maury fucking Povich. I sigh deeply and rub my eyes, then check out the other two jobs. The next one is a simple request from a quiet kid named Matthew Simpson in B pod. I don't know much about Simpson. Only that he's in for armed robbery and mostly keeps to himself. Word around the Y is that he was busted stealing for his mother, who couldn't hold down a regular job, so I'm not surprised when the letters in the book ask, *Is my mom ok?* I know the address. A run-down apartment building, not far from Rickers's house. It'll be an easy job, and worth the trip. Simpson works in the mess hall. He'll ration out a little extra on my tray now and again, like last night, when the meat loaf was sliced a little thicker, and had a little more gravy on it than usual. It was a gesture of good faith. A taste of what I can expect in return. So I memorize the apartment number and move on to the last book.

It's a Sherlock Holmes mystery containing an address off East Colfax Avenue in Capitol Hill. Judging by the location, it's probably a bar. There isn't a name printed above mine on the card, but the job is clear enough: *Is Panagakos giving freebies?* I pick at the edge of the page, considering the payoff. Holmes is a convicted drug dealer in my pod with a lot of connections. Rumor is, he's got a phone hidden in his cell, but the guards have never found it. Because it isn't there. I'm probably the only one who knows that it's hidden behind a loose tile in the showers. I've never told anyone. Not even the warden. I keep that little nugget locked away. Holmes is dangerous. Everyone in the Y seems to know his name. People say he has pull, both inside and out. That his older brother is a well-known supplier with a private attorney. I guess that attorney comes in handy, because Holmes has been in and out of the Y doing jobs for his brother since he was fourteen, which makes him sort of a veteran here. He's older than most of us—too old to still be hanging around in the Y with his record—and if he's offering protection, which is the only favor Holmes is known to deal in, I'd be an idiot to pass on the trade.

I pile the books neatly on the floor, then ease my bruised body down onto the bed and wait for Lights Out. After a while, Officer Rickers opens the slot in my door.

"Got everything you need, kid?" Our eyes lock through the opening. His slide to the pile of books beside my bed.

"Yes, sir."

Officer Rickers nods and shuts the slot, hopefully for the rest of the night.

I cross my arms over my chest, ignoring the headache under my plates and the stiffness in my jaw.

"Lights out!" calls the overhead speaker, just before the room goes black.

Eight hours. I close my eyes, tamping down the exhilaration that steps up my pulse. I focus on breathing, deep pulls in and out through my nose. I flex and relax each muscle, top down, until I feel the first lightening, the cord that connects me to my body loosening its grip, rendering me buoyant, until I am as shapeless as smoke.

There's a pins-and-needles feeling in my belly as a few threads snap. Then nothing. The absence of pain and discomfort—of all physical sensation—as I drift up and away and watch myself sleep. These threads . . . this cord . . . isn't something I can see. It's something I feel—a constant, gentle pull at my gut—like a stretchy anchor line that guides me home. But the line is thinner than it was last week, and even thinner than the week before. I feel the broken threads float up around me like spider silk—more now than there used to be. It's becoming easier and easier to let go, and harder to pull myself back. I try not to wonder how many more trips I have left, before the line that keeps me tethered snaps for good. For now, these small escapes—and the alliances they buy me—are all I have. I give my body one last look. And then I'm gone.

FOUR

I step through the concrete wall as easily as taking a breath. Walls, razor wire, locked doors—none of them matter, so long as I can picture what's on the other side. Once I'm outside the Y, I take off running. I don't feel the wire mesh of the perimeter fence pass through me, but I feel the ground underneath. Not on the soles of my feet, but inside me, the resonance of a memory. I remember the crunch of my sneakers against icy pavement and the way the cold air burns inside my lungs. I recall every turn of the road ahead of me and I push myself forward.

I run north, orienting myself against a recalled landscape of snow-capped Rockies behind the neighborhoods and highways to my left, and endless brown plains beyond the city to my right. I can't see them. Not from this street, which cuts through the congested belly of southeast Denver. But I know they're there, images of them clear in my mind, making this city navigable to me, even in the dark.

I stick to the sidewalks, pausing at the intersections. I'm not afraid of them. Not really. Theoretically, I guess a car should pass right through me, the same way walls and fences and people do. But it doesn't feel good when something barrels through your core like you're not even there, leaving you with a million busted pieces to put back together... or worse, like broken threads that you can't put back together at all.

two at a time, still feeling heavier than I should. No flesh to slow me down, no lungs to worry about, I remind myself. But places like this make me forget that sometimes, stirring memories that make it hard to breathe. I find the door to 3B, cracked slightly open. There's an eviction notice taped to the frame, the same as all the other doors. A red paper sign on the wall warns of an upcoming demolition date. I was right. The building's been condemned.

The tabby hisses and runs between my legs, pushing the cracked door open and disappearing inside Mrs. Simpson's apartment. I peer through the narrow opening into an empty room. No curtains to keep the streetlight from drifting in. No shadows of furniture inside. No sound but the shuffle of the cat. Her tail bobs through an open door in the hall, shaking with repetitive jerking motions like she's working on something. I ghost into the vacant apartment. The cat pokes her head out of the bathroom and turns to look at me. As I get closer, she bristles and scurries down the hall, a low growl coming from her throat. I hate cats. Almost as much as they seem to hate me.

The bathroom door is partway open, and I peer inside, half expecting another cat to come scrambling out. The sink cabinet is ajar, its contents spilling onto the floor, and I jump when I catch sight of my reflection in the mirror. I turn away, blinking away the darkness. A narrow window over the bathtub carries in the dull glow of a streetlight, and as my eyes adjust to the dimness of the room, I see her.

A fully clothed woman is sprawled in the bathtub. Flies circle her head, her nostrils and ears. They land on the corners of her lips, then disappear into the black space between. Her arm is ashen and rail thin, lined with tracks where it hangs over the edge, almost brushing the floor. One finger is gnawed to the bone, the others chewed to fleshy stumps, the blood licked clean. I choke back the overwhelming urge to be sick, a physical reaction tangled up so tightly in fear and disgust that my soul seems to forget my stomach isn't here.

The cat watches me impatiently, licking her lips between growls as I dry-heave into the sink. She's thin. Hungry. I'm standing in her way. But I can't let her do this to Simpson's mother. I straighten up tall and curl my fingers. My eyes are black holes in the mirror. I peel back my smoky lips, turn toward her, and charge. Her claws shred the carpet as she bolts for the apartment door.

I draw in a deep breath and let it out slowly, not because I need any air. I just need a minute to think. Maybe I got the apartment number wrong—the doctors said things like that might happen—but my memory's never failed me. I don't forget things. And Martín doesn't make mistakes.

I head to the kitchen, searching for anything that might prove I screwed up. That I'm in the wrong place. That this woman isn't Simpson's mom. There are no photographs stuck to the refrigerator. No monogrammed dishtowels beside the sink. Just a pile of junk mail resting on the counter. I squint and make out the name: *Francine Simpson*. That mail could have been mis-delivered. Maybe a neighbor brought it in.

I head back down the hall toward the bedrooms. They're empty, except for a short stack of cardboard boxes, and some knotted trash bags on the floor. And then I see Matthew Simpson's name. In the smaller bedroom, horizontal pencil lines climb the wall, forming a ladder of uneven rungs, each line pointing to a handwritten date. A growth chart. At the top, the name *Matthew* is written in messy script. And for a moment, it feels like he's standing right in front of me.

I turn away. Simpson hired me to tell him if his mother was doing okay without him. But he already knew the answer or he never would have felt the need to ask.

On my way out, I give the decomposing woman in the tub one last look. I wonder what it must smell like in here, in this place where Simpson grew up. I wonder if it's more terrible to know your mother rotted slowly, consumed in her own home. Or if the taste of loss this'll leave on Simpson's tongue is any less bitter than if his mother had disappeared overnight.

Do I tell Simpson straight up that his mother is dead, or make up some lie he can live with for a while? I can't risk trading bad information. Simpson'll be out soon, and he'll come home looking for her. I can't let him find her bones picked clean in a bathtub.

Forgetting myself, I reach to shut the door, to keep the cat from eviscerating what's left of her, but my hand only passes through the knob.

"I'm sorry," I tell the dead woman. A shadow creeps across the corner of my eye, but when I turn, it's gone.

Damn cats.

I materialize through the gap in the front door, no choice but to leave it cracked. Two more cats skitter in behind me.

I head north to South Pecos, running the whole way. But no matter how fast I run, I can't shake the image of Simpson's mom. I spend the entire trip hammering out the best way to tell Simpson his mother either starved or OD'd while squatting in their condemned apartment. Wondering if it's better to tell him she's gone in some vague, noncommittal way, or tell him all the gory details and save him the pain of wondering if she'll ever come back. A phantom ache throbs in my jaw where Six hit me. Mothers are a sticky subject. You can't talk about them in the Y without someone getting emotional. Like they're the only bright spot in the universe. The city lights shine ahead of me, but when I look up, I can't see a single star in the whole damn sky.

When I finally get to Officer Rickers's neighborhood, every house looks exactly the same: short, rectangular boxes set back from the sidewalk, elbow-to-elbow; their tiny porches sticking out with tacky welcome mats. Like the cliquey girls I remember from school, hard to tell apart because they spent so much time trying to look like everyone else. I cut through the front yards, tight against the front of them, counting off the house numbers until I find the one written in Martín's book. A flashy yellow Camaro with a thick black stripe down the hood is parked in Rickers's driveway. Probably not Rickers's car. Everything about this car shouts, from the loud paint job and the vanity plates, to the big-mouthed chrome exhaust pipes. Rickers doesn't seem the type. He's quiet, too low-key.

And he works nights.

I creep up to the front window and look inside. An attractive blond, presumably L. Driggs, stands in the kitchen with her back to the sink and her hands and lips and legs all tangled around some guy. He's tall with dark hair, which rules out Rickers. When they come up for air, he pulls away and turns for the door. I recognize him before she catches him and jams her tongue back down his throat. It's Officer Monetti, the asshole who works day shift with Officer Brooks. Which sucks, because this means he's also the asshole working Rickers's girlfriend.

Christ. Nothing is easy tonight. I have enough dirt on Officer Rickers's girlfriend to make a trade and keep him off my back, but it won't do me any good if it puts me on Officer Monetti's shit list. And if Monetti doesn't kill me for ratting him out, I'll starve to death anyway. Because Simpson's going to be pissed when I tell him about his mother, and he'll probably take it out on me in the chow line for the next four years. Just because people know the truth doesn't mean they like to hear it.

I stomp down the driveway and kick a piece of gravel at Monetti's car. The gravel doesn't move, and my foot blows apart. I stand in the middle of the road, swearing a string of cusses so long and loud the neighbors should be peeling back their curtains. Nobody hears me. Nothing changes. And Officer Monetti and L. Driggs keep kissing like nobody cares.

I'm exhausted when I leave Rickers's neighborhood, not because my feet hurt or I'm out of breath—I don't get that kind of tired. It's more like I'm tired inside. Like I've been jumping to catch the bottom rung of that ladder all night. When I make it to Colfax Avenue, it takes me a while to find the address Martín wrote in the Sherlock Holmes book. The numbers are half hidden under a neon sign that's barely working, and the door and only window are blacked out. Whatever information Holmes hired me to dig up for him is inside this club, so I wait on the sidewalk listening to the thump of the music on the other side of the wall.

I have no idea how long I've been standing there when a man in a three-piece pulls up to the curb. He locks his Beemer and heads right toward me. When he reaches for the door, I lean in close, trying to see the time on his watch, but he moves too fast and I make a quick grab at his hand without thinking, as if I could still it long enough to read it. My fingers pass right through him.

The man pauses in the open door, letting the music spill out into the street. The hair on his wrist stands on edge, goose bumps hardening to alert little peaks. He's still. So still I could probably read the time if I weren't so busy trying to read the expression on his face. He shivers and glances over his shoulder, toward me, and for a split second, I wonder with a creeping thrill what he'll see. But he shakes me off like I'm just a cool breeze, letting the door swing shut behind him.

I trail in before the door closes, clinging to the narrow slices of detail I can make out through the opening. Mirrors line the longer walls, making the place look bigger and more crowded than it is. A repetitive techno beat pulses the walls, loud enough to support the illusion. But it's not hard to see through the thin veneer of smoke from the colored lights. It's not a big club. Just a couple of worn-out pool tables, a forgotten dartboard, and clusters of small, circular tables and chairs skirting the room.

A long bar runs the entire length of the one wall. Waitresses bounce through the room in brightly colored wigs and spiky heels, their barely there shorts and crop tops revealing more than they might in your average sports bar, but far less than in the men's clubs, like the one next door. I've been in a few of them. In my first weeks in the Y, before I started trading, I visited some. But the novelty wore off quickly. All the guys on their bar stools, numbly watching. All the girls looking through them like they weren't even there. It was just sad. Like finding out a scratch in a mirror is actually a broken piece of yourself.

I move through the room looking for signs of Panagakos, the one Holmes wanted me to check out. I hover beside the pool tables and outside the men's room, then listen in on conversations at the bar, looking for his name on open tabs and credit cards, and doing my best to ignore everyone else.

Until a short waitress with a bright pink bob pauses midstep and looks at me.

The slow turn of her head as I walk by is almost too precise to be a coincidence. Her eyes seem to trail me as I slip through the room. I watch her over my shoulder, hardly paying attention to where I'm going when I collide with something solid—a blue-haired waitress—and burst into pieces, leaving bits of me mingling with the smoke in the air. By the time I collect myself, the oblivious waitress I just crashed into is already across the room. She ruffles Pink's hair to get her attention and points out the suited man where he sits, waiting for a drink. Pink swats her away. Her cheeks flush to match her hair, and she smooths it back in place as she heads toward the suited man's table, never once looking in my direction. She maneuvers easily through the crowd in a pair of purple sequined Converse. There's less bounce in her step than the other two waitresses, more determination in her stride. Her uniform looks different, too. Not just the shoes. Her shirt isn't as clingy as the others', and it hangs lower around her waist, as if she's intentionally stretched it out to hide the fact that her shorts are sitting looser and lower on her hips, covering more than Blue's do.

She stands beside the suited man's table, taking drink orders and a ration of shit from the group of guys he's joined up with. They're loud and drunk and sloppy, stripping her down with their eyes, and her face is redder than it was a minute ago, even under the colored lights in the room. She bats away a clumsy hand before it can graze her thigh. Then she grits her teeth behind a hard smile and collects the empty bottles like she can't get out of there fast enough.

She makes a beeline for the bar and dumps the empties, shouts an order to the bartender, grabs her tray, and spins back toward the room. She makes it halfway across before her eyes find mine, and she stumbles. She scrapes a stray lock of hair from the corner of her lip. I could almost swear she's staring at me.

At me. Not through me.

I take a few steps to my left, and her eyes follow. On a hunch, I step toward her. She backs into a table, knocking over someone's beer.

Holy shit.

I get closer. She turns her back to me and rushes to clean up the mess. She's offering to replace the spilled beer on the house, wearing that same plastic smile she wore a few minutes ago. I step up beside her, close. Real close. I lean in slowly, stopping a breath from her face, and her smile melts away.

"Can you see me?" I whisper, almost to myself, still not sure that I'm not imagining the strange tension between us. A thread. A connection. An awareness.

She backs up, nearly losing her tray.

"Hey." One of the guys yanks at the hem of her shorts. "You gonna get us another round or what?"

Her glossy lips are pressed tightly shut, eyes glued on the tabletop. Her arms are covered in goose bumps, and the hair on her neck is standing on end.

"You can see me, can't you?" I say into her ear.

She flinches.

"Wait! Can you hear me?" I move with her, following her like a shadow around the table as she clears it with hell-bent focus. Her tray rattles, and the empties waver. "Answer me! You can hear me, can't you?"

She clenches her teeth and barks, "Back the hell off!" making every head at the table turn.

They all fall silent. She could have been talking to any of them, but I know she was talking to me. A hand shoots out and grabs her wrist, making us both start.

"What did you say?" He's got long hair, a lanky build, and hands big enough to circle her wrist twice. I'd give anything to do the same. To grab her and make her look at me. Maybe that's why I want to break every one of his fingers.

She balances her tray one-handed as the bouncer lumbers toward us. The suited guy peels a twenty from his wallet and mutters, "Leave her alone. You're going to get us kicked out." Pink's eyes flick to the cash, then back to her wrist. She twists out of his grip, snatches the bill, and tucks it into her apron. Giving the bouncer a stiff nod, she turns on her heel for the bar.

I start to follow. If I follow her around talking all night, maybe she'll keep talking back.

"You owe me twenty, Panagakos," says the Suit.

I pause. My eyes follow the pink-haired waitress, but my ears are focused on the conversation behind me.

Is Panagakos giving freebies? That was the message inside the book from Holmes. The lanky guy who just grabbed Pink is my last job of the night.

I stand behind Panagakos, trying to listen in on his business while I watch Pink make her rounds. The drinks on her tray ripple with the heavy thump of the bass. She slips in and out of pockets of drunks, balancing her tray over her head to dodge crowded tables. She moves easier through all this chaos than I do, taking drink orders without writing down a word, reading her customers' orders on their lips. No way she can hear them. I can't hear a damn thing over the vibrating subwoofers, and I sure as hell can't read Panagakos's lips, but after a while, the suited man nods, slips cash into the leather check folder, and slides it across the table as if they're all contributing to the bill. Panagakos deftly extracts the money, and they shake hands, passing something between them as the suited man stands to leave.

Not a freebie.

I could leave right now. Follow the Suit right out the door, get back to the Y, and still have a few hours to crash before sunup. I glance at his watch as he passes. It's late. I find Pink and catch her glancing in my direction.

I should stay. I should watch one more transaction, just to be sure. I can't risk dealing in bad information, so I stick around, watching, waiting for Panagakos to make one more deal. Waiting for Pink to look at me one more time . . . I feel like I'm back at some crappy high school party, holding up the walls, waiting for a girl to notice me. I don't drink. Always hated the smell of the stuff on my father's breath. But as Pink crosses the room toward Panagakos's table, I reach for one of the bottles on her tray, just to have something to hold, as if that might make me look like I belong here, instead of feeling like some kind of out-of-place creep. But the bottle, and Pink, whoosh by. The bottle doesn't move, and she doesn't acknowledge me in the slightest, and as I pull myself together, I'm starting to wonder if I imagined the whole thing.

Panagakos makes another quick cash deal. I should just leave, but I don't. Pink's heading my way again, shoulders back and chin pushed out, all focused and defiant. At the last second, I throw my foot out in front of her. She falters, almost tripping through it. She glares at it, like she might will it out of her way, but I leave it there, waiting to see if she'll step around it. Waiting to see if I'm right about her.

Her head snaps up, and she looks hard at me. Me, not the customer behind me. I prickle under the weight of that stare, but I can't stop the smile from tugging up the corners of my lips. I wave at her, a casual two-finger salute. She scowls and swipes at her eye makeup with a stiff middle finger. I bark out a surprised laugh, and I know she can hear it. She grits her teeth and sets her drinks down too hard, sloshing the short glasses and making the bottles foam over, her cheeks glowing as bright as her hair.

She doesn't walk by me or look at me again. Instead, she circumnavigates the room. I'm empty of any doubts, teeming with a million questions instead. And even though part of me feels guilty for bugging her, there's an exhilarating lightness inside me, like I'm tethered to her by a fistful of threads.

Panagakos makes two more deals, and cash changes hands each time. The waitresses and the bartender all seem to turn a blind eye to the fact that he's closed four tabs in less than two hours. It's near closing when he's finally alone, and no one's asking him to go. Pink looks tired. Her eye makeup creeps below her eyes, and her lipstick's worn thin. She gathers the empty glasses from Panagakos's table and collects his tab. Her cash apron hangs low on her waist, heavy with tips. He watches her go, turning in his chair to look at her. I don't realize I've been smiling all along, until I feel it slide from my face. Something doesn't feel right. How he's still here sucking on a bottle as she's closing out her tickets. How he checks to make sure the bouncer has his back turned before he finally sets his drink down.

I step between him and the narrow hall where Pink just disappeared. Panagakos pushes off his stool and walks right through me. I scatter into a million cussing, pissed-off pieces while he ducks past the EMPLOYEES ONLY sign, following close behind her.

I pull myself together and rush after him, just in time to see him grab her. He spins her around and backs her into the wall hard enough to make her grunt. Her eyes are wide-awake now. She looks back toward the bar, like she's hoping someone might come. Someone other than me.

"Candy," he says in a gentle tone that doesn't match the way he pushes her. "All the other girls are nice to me. We're all friends here, aren't we? They give me something. I give them something. When are you gonna let me give you something?" Panagakos waves a small bag of pills in her face, one hand gripping her arm and a knee planted between her thighs.

She takes one last look down the hall, but no one's coming. Panagakos takes her face roughly in his hand and makes her look at him. She doesn't look scared. She doesn't seem chilled by the same premonition that crawls over me as Panagakos's drug-addled pupils glass over with want. Her eyes land square on me, tracking me where I pace.

Until he presses himself against her and sniffs.

Reflex takes over, and I reach for his shoulder before I remember I can't. I clench my hand at my side, feeling myself shrink under the critical cut of her eyes. "What the hell am I supposed to do?" I can't grab him. Can't hit him. Can't call out.

She lifts her chin. Her eyes swing to the bag and then to Panagakos.

I shake my head. "Don't do this." I know she can hear me, even if she wants to pretend I don't exist. I point at Panagakos's back. "If this guy's boss finds out you're taking free product, you're as dead as he is." And I don't want to have to tell Holmes about her. She's the only person outside the Y who can see me, and I have too many unanswered questions. Even if she doesn't want to talk to me, I'd rather she live to flip me off another day.

I tell her as much, but she doesn't offer the faintest clue that she hears.

She grins at Panagakos instead. "You want to give me something?"

He swallows hard, relaxing his grip. "Never thought you'd come around. Anything you want. I got it all."

"How about you start by giving me some space." She brings her knee up hard into his groin, and I feel my own balls scream even though they're twenty miles away. Panagakos drops, twisting on the floor. Pink stomps down the hall and shouts for the bouncer. Then she steps over the writhing, groaning puddle that was Panagakos and slips into a back room. She starts to shut the door.

At the last second, she looks at me and leaves it cracked.

FIVE

Pink snatches an oversize hoodie from a wooden coatrack beside an emergency-exit door and throws her arms through the sleeves. For a second, I worry that she's leaving, but then she kicks off her Converse, peels off her sweaty socks, and drops barefoot onto a stool. She's sitting in front of a lighted mirror over a small counter that's mounted to the wall. We're in some kind of break area or dressing room. It's small, just big enough for a worn-out love seat and an old, beat-up coffee table, both covered in magazines. A tall bank of five lockers stands against the wall, all but one padlocked shut, and I wonder if Pink's the last one here. The rack by the door is empty except for one coat.

"That was pretty hard-core," I say when I'm sure we're alone. I watch her face in the mirror, waiting for a reaction. She peels her eyelashes off and sets them on the dressing table. They look like spiders with long, fuzzy legs, and I crane my neck to see over her shoulder, curious as she dismantles herself. She plucks a tissue from a box and wipes off her lipstick, never once looking at me. The tissue crumples, smeared red, leaving bits of fuzz on her lips. She looks like a kid at Halloween. "You missed some," I say, trying to be helpful. I wipe a smoke hand over my own lips to show her what I mean.

She makes a big show of looking in the mirror, pretending to notice the fuzz herself. Pretending like I'm not standing here at all. The clock on the table says 4:00 AM, and the inevitability of morning is a nagging tension that seems to tug at my threads. I don't have much time, and it's a long run home.

"Talk to me," I urge gently, trying not to piss her off. I like my spectral balls right where they are. "You've been watching me all night. I saw you."

Color floods her face, and I inch over her shoulder until our eyes are level in the mirror. She wraps the sides of her sweatshirt tightly around her.

"Come on, Pink. I know you can see me."

She snatches a handful of pink hair and pulls. Her natural hair, brown and chaotic, tumbles around her shoulders, and she slams the wig on the table, startling me quiet.

I'm getting somewhere. I know it.

"You can hear me, too, can't you?"

Her shoulders rise and fall with her short, agitated breaths.

"Candy?" I whisper, plucking away at her nerves. She looks like she's ready to jump out of her skin. "Is that your real name?" I goad louder. "Your mom couldn't come up with something better than Candy? So fucking cliché."

And that was the last straw. She spins and looks me dead in the eyes. "I am *not* a cliché!" Then she shakes both hands in the air and curses at the ceiling.

I step back from the familiar slope of her nose and the recognizable curve of her cheeks. All the pieces of her—the frizzy brown curls and brown doe eyes, the square chin—snapping together to form a face I've seen before.

The ache sharpens. "No! It's not like that—"

"Whatever happened, you can't stay here." She turns back to the mirror and flips the light on, and my reflection fades. "Here's a tip, John Conlan. Follow the light. Not this one. The big one with the angels and the harps and shit."

"I can't. It's not like that—"

"Why? You have unfinished business with that creep in the bar? I saw you watching him. Fine, make peace with whatever the hell happened to you. Have at him, Casper. Just stay out of my way. And keep out of the break room. It's girls only." She points at the door and turns back to the mirror.

"I'm not dead," I tell her.

"If I had a dollar for every time I heard that . . ."

"I don't understand." The clock flashes 4:15. I'm running out of time, and I have more questions now than I did when I got here. "How come you can hear me?"

"Because I'm a medium!" She drags a brush hard through the knots in her hair, making it frizz. "You're giving me static. Quit standing so close."

"A medium?" I step back just enough to keep her talking while she smooths it down. "What's a medium?"

"Someone who can talk to people who are . . . you know . . ." She waves her hairbrush around, like she's searching for the right word. "People who aren't people anymore."

"Well, how come you can see me and nobody else can?"

"I don't know," she says with a frustrated roll of her eyes. "It's like male pattern baldness or something. It skips a generation, and I'm the one who got screwed." She sighs, and all the fight slips out of her. She

"I know you." I feel like I've been sucked back in time, hugging the wall at that same school party. She's my age. From my neighborhood. We might have had a math class together freshman year. Or maybe English . . . No, it was definitely English. My eyes fall away, and I feel a little sick at the idea that she might remember me, too.

She stands up slowly and steps closer with a grave expression, squinting up at me like she's searching for someone. Someone she hopes she won't find. She reaches behind her and switches off the lights over the dressing table. The room dims, and my reflection brightens in the mirror. For a long tense moment, neither of us moves.

Then Candy . . . Candace Something-or-other . . . slumps back on the stool as if she's relieved. "You scared me," she says through a sigh. "For a minute, I thought you meant we knew each oth—" She pauses, then narrows her eyes at me. "Wait. You're the Conlan kid from those crappy apartments behind Navajo? The one who . . ." Her forehead crumples as if she's trying to make sense of something. "But that can't be right. They said you were alive. It was all over the news. That you killed that teacher, and they convicted you and put you in the Y. . . ." Her brows shoot up and she shakes her head defiantly. "Oh no." She thrusts one hand righ through my chest, like she's trying to push me away. When she pul her hand back, a cloud of me trails with her, and she shakes it off wit disgusted look. It shouldn't hurt, but it leaves me with a dull ache insi

"You want to know what's cliché? I'll tell you what's cliché! All dead people showing up on my doorstep, wanting someone to talk Well, I'm tired of it. How am I supposed to get any work done you following me around and talk-talk-talking in my ear all nigh enough to make someone crazy. I bet that's what happened, is Your cellmate probably got sick of all your yapping and shanke What can I say, karma's a bitch."

slams down the brush and slumps on her stool. "Look, I'm really sorry you died. Again." She cringes at her own choice of words. "I mean, no one should have to die twice, right?" I flinch. She's talking about my father. About all the other stuff she saw on the news, about the miracle boy who came back from the dead.

"I only died once," I correct her. "I'm not dead. You can come to the Y and see for yourself. There's a woman who works at the visiting desk on Saturdays. If you slip her a twenty and tell her we're cousins, she'll let you—"

"Fine." She holds up a hand to silence me. "I get it. The gravity of your situation hasn't quite sunk in, and you haven't figured out what you are yet. Whatever. You'll figure it out soon enough. I'm tired and I've got a long walk home. You can come back tomorrow and haunt Panagakos. He's here just about every night. But I have to go." She stands up and wraps her sweatshirt around her, pulling it down to cover her shorts. She stares at the lockers behind me.

"I can't come back tomorrow." I'm standing in her way, which feels like an asshole thing to do. She doesn't owe me anything. I look around me, trying to figure out what I can trade. What information she might need. What would give her a reason to talk to me? But I come up with nothing, and she pushes past me. "I've got to be back in my cell before sunup, and I only have this one night. Please—"

"Right," she mutters. "Back in your cell . . . Don't let me stop you." She turns her back on me and digs around in her locker, plucking out a pair of jeans and a thermal top. She's holding her sweatshirt close, waiting for me to go. She doesn't believe me. And I guess I can't blame her. Frustrated, I exhale a long, slow breath, and I'm sure it's my imagination when her pink wig shivers on the table.

"Go!" she says sharply.

"I'm going." I back to the door, a million unanswered questions racing through my head. I'm scared I might not see her again, and I can't make sense of this urgency I feel to make her believe me. It's a Hail Mary pass, but I blurt out, "There's a dead woman rotting in a bathtub in apartment 3B of a condemned building behind the Jack in the Box on South Federal. I don't want to cause you any trouble, but maybe you can make an anonymous call?"

"Did you kill her, too?" Pink snaps.

The accusation is a fist to the gut, and it takes me a minute to pull myself back together. "I didn't kill her."

Pink wraps her sweatshirt tighter around herself. She won't even look at me. "I liked her. She was nice, you know, that teacher they say you . . ." She presses her lips together like she's afraid to finish. But I know the rest. Everyone knows the rest of the story, but no one wants to hear the truth.

"I liked her, too."

Pink doesn't answer. Doesn't turn around. I feel the only thread connecting us snap, so I turn to go.

"Hey," she calls after me. "If you were in the Y, then how'd you get all the way to that apartment on South Federal? And how'd you get here?"

Hope anchors me halfway in the room. "I walked."

"That's impossible." Her tone is caught somewhere between derision and surprise. "My grandmother said we only haunt the places where we die."

"I told you already, I'm not dead." I sift through the door, more exhausted than I've felt in a long, long time. She'll believe what she wants, and the sun's going to rise in a couple of hours whether or not I stay here trying to prove myself.

Outside the break room, I reach for my threads, wondering how many this night cost me. I feel the broken ones waver in the air around me like the strands of Pink's wig, and I hope I'll get the chance to come back.

SIX

I return to the Y just before dawn and find myself in Segregation. I drift close to my body and pull myself back inside. My skin feels heavy, like the lead drapes the radiologists used to put on me before they scanned my head. I slide in awkwardly under the weight of it, my body still half-asleep and disconnected from my mind, the muscle and bone not quite conforming to me yet.

I'm barely settled into myself when the overheads flicker on, and I wince at the shock of white light. My eyes are crusted shut, reluctant to wake, and my stomach is queasy with a familiar burn I used to get after pulling an all-nighter before an exam. I blink myself fully awake, feeling my threads contract until everything is back snugly in place.

Close. Too close. I barely made it back to Segregation before Lights On.

Clang, clang, clang. The handle of a Maglite bangs against the cell door. "Get up, Smoke. Time to go home."

I ease out of bed, bracing myself on the rim of the sink. Slowly, I stretch my arms over my head, roll each shoulder, and crack my knuckles. I'm in complete control of my body when I walk backward to the opening in the door and offer my wrists to the guard on the other side.

Time to go home.

Home. The Y is home now. As much as any other institution has ever been. My bunk here isn't all that different from the gym mat I stashed in the boiler room at school. Or the sofa in the office at the waste management company where I worked. Or the hospital bed I slept on for weeks before my bunk in juvenile detention. Just a safe place to weather a storm.

The "crappy apartment" I shared with my dad had never been home.

I hold my breath and wait for the buzzer. I wonder if there will ever be a time when I won't have to remind myself that, here, the buzzer means I'm alive. That a door is opening. That someone is coming for me. When it sounds, I fight back the flinch. This isn't my dad's apartment, I remind myself. Ms. Cruz isn't leaning on the button and screaming to get in. But no matter what my head tries to tell the rest of me, every muscle remembers. Eleven months later, that buzzer still rattles me.

I shake it off and carry Martín's books with me out of Segregation for what is probably my last time.

Officer Rickers calls out to the duty guard. "My shift's over. Conlan's cell is on my way out. I'll take him." The Segregation guard turns me over to Rickers, and I fall in step beside him. My gut growls as we round the corner by the mess hall. The salt-and-oil smells of runny eggs and greasy potatoes are thick in the corridor. I clench my stomach, wishing I could clamp down the hunger by sheer force of will. Simpson's waiting to hear something about his mother. He'll pile a mountain of hash on my tray with those damn hopeful eyes. All I want is to sleep through chow. Really sleep. Projecting myself across town probably burned more calories than a yard brawl, but just thinking about last night strips me of my appetite. I don't want to see Officer Rickers's face when I tell him his girlfriend is screwing around with Officer Monetti.

I don't want to think about Simpson's mom in that bathtub. And I don't want to keep picturing the way Pink's eyes crinkled up when she asked me if I'd killed her, too.

I drag myself down the corridor to the beat of Rickers's boots. He moves stiffly under all that Kevlar, like he's been walking these halls all night. His face is drawn and his eyes are rimmed red, and I wonder if he's itching to get home and climb into bed with L. Driggs.

He slows before we get to my cell. When we're out of the view of the control room, he pulls me to a stop, darting quick glances in both directions.

"What do you know, Smoke?" he asks in a low voice, his tone slightly skeptical.

"She's seeing someone else," I say, hoping he'll make good on a trade without making me name names.

Rickers searches my face like he's trying to catch me in a lie. "Who's your source?"

The answer to that question isn't part of our deal. Rickers casts an anxious glance down the corridor. "If you won't tell me your source, then how do I know your information is good?"

I pitch my voice low and do my best to keep it steady. "You asked me if your girlfriend was messing around. I gave you the answer." But Rickers isn't going anywhere. His blue eyes are intent, calculating, looking for a way to tip the scale. And we don't have time for renegotiations. The Y is awake, guards buzzing in and out of the pods and kids laughing and shouting insults as they move in small groups to the showers, just a few yards away. Neither one of us wants to get caught having this conversation. "Fine," I say. "You want to know if my information is good? I'll tell you who your girlfriend's fooling around with and you can check it out for yourself. Take it or leave it."

His expression is hard, but not angry. More like he's braced for the truth. And as much as I don't want to tell him about Monetti, it's the only hand I've got. I can't tell him the name of my source, and even if I could, he'd never believe me.

"Monetti" is all I say. It's enough. Rickers rolls back on his heels, his ruddy cheeks pulling down like a painting left out in the rain. No shock. No anger. He already knows. He just didn't want to believe it.

Rickers is quiet, long enough to make me wonder what he's thinking, and I hope I haven't made a mistake. "Monetti'll kill me if he finds out I told you."

Rickers nods. We both know this. Monetti isn't the kind of officer who negotiates. Monetti is cold-forged, the toughest officer in the Y. He's been here longer than any of them, having been handpicked by Somerville when they relocated him from North Carolina to rid the place of corrupt officers four years ago. My life is in Rickers's hands.

I let out the breath I've been holding when he says, "This conversation never happened."

I follow Officer Rickers to my pod. It's too late to grab a shower, and too early to head straight to chow, but at least I can drop off the books. I stand in front of my cell, shut my eyes, and brace for the buzzer, waiting for Crenshaw's BO to hit me. Waiting for him to mouth off and say something that might otherwise get his jaw broken if Rickers weren't still standing behind me, unlocking my cuffs. But when I open my eyes, something is wrong.

"What are you doing here?" I say as the steel door clatters shut behind me. The new kid—Haggett—is sitting on my mattress on the lower bunk. He jerks to his feet so fast he hits his head on the bed frame, then winces, rubbing the spot. I step slowly around him and survey the cell. Crenshaw's stuff is gone.

The new kid clears his throat and extends a skinny hand. "I'm your new cellmate." His voice wavers. "Name's Haggett. Benjamin Haggett. But you can call me Ben." He stands there, this stupid, dumb look on his face, and I stare at his hand until it withers. My eyes drop to the name marked on his jumpsuit. Then to my bunk, at the ripples in the neatly made sheets where Haggett was just sitting.

"I didn't sleep in your bunk—I swear." He eases out from beside the mattress, talking fast. "Some officers came through last night and searched a bunch of cells. But they didn't come in here. No one touched your stuff. I promise."

I open my footlocker. My books are all there, stacked neatly where I left them. Stupid. Warden Somerville should have had them search my cell, too. I hope they made it look like a random cell toss, or people might start suspecting a rat in the pod.

I turn and stare at Haggett, still wondering what the hell he's doing in my cell. His eyes grow wide, and he stares at the scars on my face until they burn, making something inside me snap tight.

"Jeeesus," he whispers. "What happened to your—"

"What are you doing here?"

He stammers. "I just got here yesterday. They were gonna make me sleep in a cell with some other kid, but he scared the shit out of me, so I asked Officer Brooks if I could be with you."

Haggett's looking at me like he's regretting that decision.

"What'd you do?"

Haggett's confession is too quiet, like it isn't anything he's proud of. "Breaking and entering, possession of stolen property, resisting arrest . . ."

"And?"

Haggett glances over his shoulder to make sure Rickers is gone. "Assaulting a police officer," he says quietly. "But that was an accident," he rushes to add.

The rubber bands inside me relax, but only by a fraction. The kid isn't much of a threat as far as cellies go, and I can't figure out what Warden Somerville was thinking, putting him in C pod. Unless this is Somerville's way of punishing me for yesterday's fight, making me share a cell with a kid with an easy target on his back.

Officer Brooks raps on the door. "If you boys are done with introductions, it's time for chow."

Benjamin Haggett and I just stare at each other, neither one of us willing to turn our back. He hesitates, then steps sideways toward the cell door. I brace for the buzzer, staring hard at the imaginary target that's going to be sleeping in the same cell with me until Somerville decides I've paid my penance. "You want to survive in C pod?" I offer quietly.

The goose bumps on his arms stand at attention.

"If anyone asks, you're in for assault. The only thing you possessed was intent with a deadly weapon."

"But there wasn't a weapon. It was an—"

"An accident? You really think anyone in here is gonna believe you?" Haggett stares at his feet.

I clench my jaw, awakening bruises from yesterday's fight. "Look, you want people to leave you alone or not?"

Haggett nods, head tucked tight to his shoulders.

"Then for Christ's sake, toughen up a little. And stand up straight. You're too tall to hide in your goddamn jumper."

Haggett cringes. Then he pulls his head out of his orange shell, slowly stretching upward. Even hunched, he's got three inches on me, a withering six-foot-two green bean, maybe taller if he'd get his head out of his ass. The kid looks like a poster boy for scoliosis.

He shrinks again as we enter the mess hall. Orange jumpsuits fill the room, carrying plastic trays and shoveling in their breakfast with spoons. Officer Brooks ushers us straight to the mess line, and I do a quick scan of the room. Another officer has taken a post right behind Six's usual table. It's uncharacteristically quiet, and a quick inventory of their faces tells me Six isn't there. Probably still stuck in Segregation after yesterday's fight.

Bumper's lip curls. His buddies laugh and point at us.

"What are they saying about us?" Haggett asks, moisture creeping down the pits of his jumpsuit.

I don't bother to answer. He doesn't want to know. And no one is paying me to tell him.

In the mess line, he sticks close enough to be my damn shadow. The two guys in front of me are complaining about last night's shakedown, and I move closer to hear.

"I never got a chance to thank you," Haggett says over what I can make out of their conversation. "For sticking up for me yesterday."

I'm only half listening. I inch forward with the line and drop my eyes to avoid meeting Simpson's. He's standing on his toes behind the serving station, looking for me while he slops eggs on the trays ahead of mine.

"That fight had nothing to do with you."

Haggett falls back a step. Relieved, I think maybe he's done talking.

"It was my first day. I guess they do that to all the new guys?"

He wants me to say that no one will try to kill him or fuck with him today. I can't say that. Won't give bad information. So I say nothing at all.

I can almost feel Haggett pale. Day two won't be any different from day three or day one hundred and three, except that I won't stand up for him next time, and now he knows it. Hell, that's probably why Somerville had him moved to my cell. Because Officer Brooks and everyone else thinks I was protecting him. And now the kid's stuck in C pod with the worst of us. He still hasn't figured out that I didn't do him any favors yesterday.

I take a breath before pushing my empty tray in front of Simpson's station. His ladle is overflowing, hovering between us, heavy with expectation. I wait for him to dump the contents onto my tray, payment for services rendered. Then I make myself look in his eyes. He must know. They're like two giant ladles about to spill over.

"I'm sorry," I say, and move down the line.

Simpson stares blankly at Haggett's tray. Agitated voices rise from the back of the line. Simpson snaps to, dipping his ladle back in the warming pan, coming up half-full. He isn't crying. No one cries in the Y. None of us are full enough for that.

SEVEN

I pick at my eggs, and Haggett seems to know better than to speak to me. He eats silently, hunched over his tray beside me, careful not to make eye contact with Six's friends. After chow, I manage to stay upright just long enough to grab a shower. Sleep is supposed to be a time for the mind to rest, but mine has been awake and running all night. I waver a little on my feet, and even under the hard spray of ice-cold water, I can't seem to stop yawning. Haggett follows me through my morning routine, never more than two steps behind me, but he's quiet—quieter than Crenshaw was—and after a while, I start to consider that he might be an improvement. When personal hygiene time is up, Haggett crashes out in his bunk with a magazine. Twenty minutes to kill before they'll come get him for orientation. And I have the morning to myself. I consider grabbing a little rec time, maybe a run in the yard if it isn't too cold, but exhaustion wins out, pulling me into my bunk. I throw an arm over my face, and sleep sucks me down into the mattress. I don't worry about Haggett. I'm not going anywhere without my body for a while. Candace Whatever-Her-Name-Is didn't believe me anyway, and there's no sense wasting my breath and whatever threads I have left to go back and try to convince her otherwise.

The pages of Haggett's hot rod magazine turn over and over, rustling from the bunk above me in a steady rhythm that makes sleep come easy.

I don't know how long has passed when someone starts banging on the cell door.

"Conlan," says Brooks.

I blink to see him peering in at me before the control room buzzes him through. The sound scratches against the plate in my head and makes my bones itch. "Get up. You've got a visitor."

I'm groggy and still half-asleep and trying to wrap my brain around what Officer Brooks is saying. Ms. Cruz's is the first face to cross my mind, the only visitor I had when I woke up in the hospital. But that can't be right. Ms. Cruz is dead. I know, because I'm the one convicted of killing her.

I roll onto my side and curl up my knees. Maybe I'm still asleep. In four months I've never had a visitor. I blink at the wall, eliminating possibilities. My mom left town when I was eight. She didn't bother to come back at all when I was laid up in a hospital bed, when every news channel in the country was probably running the story, so I can't see her coming back now. It's easy to rule out my father. He's got fourteen years ahead of him at Supermax. Maybe only nine if he's lucky.

I close my eyes, sleep still tugging at me, and pretend Brooks isn't still standing there, tapping his foot.

"Get your ass up, Conlan! I don't have all day."

He might not have all day, but I've got thirteen hundred and thirteen of them left, and I'm not going anywhere. I blow him off and throw an arm back over my face. I think about what Pink said about karma and wonder if karma gives a shit about semantics. Six minutes in hell doesn't seem like a very long time.

Brooks bangs on the cell door again.

"Must be a mistake," I holler, just to shut him up. "I don't know anyone out there, and my caseworker isn't due back for two months."

"Well, that's too bad." I can practically hear him smirking. "She *says* she's your cousin, but I'll tell her she's got the wrong John Conlan—"

Come to the Y and see for yourself. There's a woman who works at the visiting desk on Saturdays. If you slip her a twenty and tell her we're cousins . . .

"Wait!" I stand up too fast, and the cell wobbles a little. I scrub a hand over my face. I'm hollow and tired. I gave Haggett what was left on my tray at breakfast. Let him take my double portion because I was too sick over Simpson to swallow it. Fatigue and hunger are catching up to me. I walk to the cell door and shut my eyes against the buzzer, but pulling them back open again is hard. My mind isn't sharp. It feels dull and jumbled like someone stuck it in a blender.

Officer Brooks directs me to the East Wing. On the way, we pass a few kids being escorted back to their cells. Saturday visitation is busy, so I hear. I've never been to family visitation before. We pass the warden's office, then a big, wide-open room full of long tables, and stools that are affixed to the floor. Through the window, I see rows of jumpsuits inside, sitting across the tables from their families, and I search the faces of everyone who's not wearing orange, looking for Pink. Officer Brooks nudges me along before I can find her.

"Sorry, Conlan. You know the rule. You spend time in Segregation, you lose your contact visits for the week."

Truth is, I didn't know that rule. Or maybe I just never had a reason to pay attention to it before.

Brooks directs me into a long room with small stations that remind me of the carrels in the library at my old school. Except each one has a phone receiver hanging from a partition that offers about as much privacy as the Y allows—next to none. A half inch of clear plastic separates the inmates from the visitors. I peer inside each cubicle as I pass, catching glimpses of hands touching, like mirrors through the glass. Some of the faces are crying on the other side, and I wonder if that's a reflection, too.

The thought dissolves when I pass a thick neck with six angry hash marks in it. Six leans close to the window, whispering into the receiver. A rough-looking thug with a messed-up eye listens on the other side, nodding and concentrating hard. His knuckles are covered in scars and homemade tattoos, and I wonder if they're actually related or if Six's buddy got in the same way I'd heard so many other unauthorized visitors did . . . making trades. I pause, as hungry for secrets as everyone else. But the guard nudges me to an empty stool two partitions down.

I falter when I see Pink waiting on the other side of the glass, belying that voice in the back of my head that was certain she'd never come. I ease onto my stool. She leans back on hers.

She watches me with wary eyes, and her puffy blue ski jacket looks like it's swallowing her whole. Under it, she wears the same shirt and pants she pulled from her locker a few hours ago.

Pink's mouth moves, but there's no sound. I reach for the receiver and bring the phone to my ear, angling my knuckles forward to hide the scar beside my eye. She stares at it as she picks up her phone.

Her lips stop moving. All I hear is the soft sound of her breath.

From the back of the classroom, I watch Ms. Cruz write a poem on the whiteboard. I recognize it after the first line—Robert Frost, "The Road Not Taken"—and I write the rest of it from memory in my notebook so we finish at the same time.

She turns back to the class and adjusts her glasses. Her warm smile skips over the faces in the room, finds mine, and her smile falters. I look down at my notebook, tracing over the lines of poetry with my pen, hoping I'm slouched low enough to hide the bruise on my cheek. But she already noticed.

She pretends she didn't. "We'll continue our poetry unit this week." There are a few groans from the class. "We're going to be talking about 'sense of place.' Your assignment tonight is to read Frost's poem and identify three techniques Frost uses to create a sense of place. Then I'd like each of you to write a highly descriptive paragraph about a place that is special to you, using at least three of the types of imagery we discussed last week in class."

"What do you mean, special?" someone asks.

"It should be a place you feel a strong connection with. Someplace that makes you feel something on an emotional level."

"Does it have to be someplace we've been before? Because that would be really boring." A few students laugh.

"I'll make you a deal. If you can visualize your special place clearly enough to convey a strong sense of place, you can use it. But I want descriptive language and imagery. I want to be able to close my eyes and listen to your paragraph and feel myself in this place."

"What if it's a place we're not supposed to be?" asks the girl sitting in front of me. A few heads turn, and it feels like their eyes are on me.

My pen pauses on the page, and I'm waiting for the answer. I can't see Ms. Cruz's reaction, because I'm still hunkered low, hidden behind the girl's huge blue parka. I peek around her frizzy brown curls. Ms. Cruz is leaning on the edge of her desk with her arms folded.

She thinks about that for a minute. "This a journaling exercise, Candace. I won't ask you to share it with the class, or anyone else, if you'd rather not."

The girl in front of me leans over her notebook and starts writing. Curious, I sit up tall and try to look over her shoulder, but she's hunched over the page. After a few minutes, she tips her head back and shuts her eyes, like she's concentrating hard on something. Or maybe just daydreaming. It makes me wonder about this place where she isn't supposed to be.

No one's sitting behind me, looking over my shoulder, so I start writing, too. I write about the old boiler room at school.

Bauer. Her name is Candace Bauer. "Hey, Pink."

She shudders and twists the phone cord anxiously between her fingers. Her blue nail polish is picked almost to the cuticles.

"Why'd you call me that?"

Same as Simpson. Same as Rickers. Inside her, she already knows the answer, but she has to hear it from someone else to believe it. I draw the phone closer and whisper, "Because that was the color of your hair last night."

The color drains from her face, like she's seeing death for the first time. Not like last night, when she was all brave and bold and full of herself.

She shakes her head, some of that sureness coming back. "That's not possible."

I let the truth sink in, spreading my fingers over the glass and pressing until my fingertips turn white. Pink watches with a look of sick fascination.

"You were right about that woman. The one in the bathtub. How did you know?"

I straighten on my stool, surprised she listened last night when I told her about Simpson's mom. Or at least that she was curious enough to go to the apartment and check.

"Because I was there. I found her."

She studies my face, like she's dissecting it for lies. Remnants of her thick eye makeup still shadow her eyelids and purple rings sag beneath them. I wonder if she ever went home.

"That's not possible," she says again, as if saying it over and over might make what I'm telling her any less true. "How did you get there—and the club—if you were in here?"

I lean in to the phone, in to her. "You tell me. You seem to know more about this than I do." She said things last night. Things I haven't been able to get out of my head. Things we can't talk about here.

Pink bites her lip.

"Did you do it? Did you kill Ms. Cruz?"

I pull my hand from the glass, old wounds opening at the mention of her name. "No."

She doesn't believe me. I know that look. I saw it on every face in that courtroom, every lawyer, every counselor, every cop. But the blood on my hands was never Ms. Cruz's.

"What about the boy? Cameron Walsh?"

This time I don't flinch. "Yes." My prints were on his knife; my hands were covered with his blood. But I didn't kill Ms. Cruz.

She swallows hard. Something big. Something she hadn't wanted to take in. When she finally speaks, it's still stuck in her throat. "Did you mean to do it?"

I think about the advice I gave Haggett. That no one believes in accidents in here. That the best way to get people to leave you alone is to make them think you hurt someone on purpose.

"It was an accident," I say.

I wait through the silence that follows, wondering how long it'll take her to call me a liar and walk out of here.

Her eyes drift to the guard behind me, and she leans closer to the window.

"Can you come back to the club?"

I don't answer right away. I can't put myself in Segregation again. Warden Somerville made the consequences clear. I'd have to leave my body alone with Ben Haggett. "Come back next Saturday. I'll stay out of trouble so we'll have more time."

"We can't talk here. Not about this. And definitely not if it's gonna cost me twenty dollars every time I come see you. My shift is early tonight. I get off at ten." She's different, sitting here in the daylight without the fake eyelashes and phony hair. More curious than cynical. Even if she's not ready to believe me yet, I'm sure she's ready to deal.

"What's in it for you?"

"Let's just say I wouldn't be sitting here if I didn't have questions, too."

Six's visitor rises and crosses the room behind Pink, drawing my attention as he heads for the door.

“I’ll be there,” I say quickly. “But I need you to do something for me. See that punk getting ready to leave?”

Pink looks over her shoulder and watches as Six’s visitor signs out.

“I need you to follow him. Don’t talk to him. Don’t get too close. I just need an address. If you can do that, I’ll tell you anything you want to know.”

She turns back to me, mouth half-open and ready to argue.

“Time’s up, Conlan,” says the guard behind me.

Pink stares at him and chews her bottom lip. Then she nods and slips the phone onto its hook. I stand up slowly, watching her brisk steps to the visitation desk. She looks like a kid in her thin-soled tennis shoes, her small frame dwarfed by her oversize coat. Standing behind Six’s friend, she looks even smaller. She barely comes up to his shoulders, and for a second, a niggling regret worms its way into me. I back out of the cubicle at the same time Six does. When I look over at him, he’s watching her, too.

EIGHT

My insides buzz as I follow Officer Brooks back to my pod. I have to get to the club tonight, but I can't risk another yard fight. Not if it means getting transferred to Supermax. As a minor, I'd be put in protective custody until my eighteenth birthday. And then they'd throw me to the wolves in general population. It would be just like the months I spent in jail after I was arrested, before I was transferred here. Even in my body, I'd never be safe. There has to be another way.

When we arrive in C pod, Haggett isn't there, and all the doors are slung wide. The duty officer leads me out to the yard, and I blink against the brightness of the day. Orange jumpsuits huddle in warm patches of late November sun, avoiding the shady corners where dirt-gray snow holds tight to the ground. All except for one. Haggett's neon-bright jumper clings close to the recreation guard's shadow, his Y-issued beanie pulled low against the cold.

On instinct, I turn away. Weakness is a magnet in the Y, attracting attention I can't afford right now. I squint into the sun and find Holmes across the yard. We meet halfway, and his buddies hang back, close enough to watch but not close enough to hear.

"What do you know, Smoke?"

I keep my voice low. "Panagakos is giving freebies to the waitresses in the club in exchange for personal favors."

Holmes scratches the black crow tattoo on his neck. No hash marks. No numbers to show off. A guy like Holmes probably lost count a long time ago. But the crow is a gang tattoo I recognize, and it carries a message of its own. "My brother's gonna be pissed. He and Panagakos go back all the way to grade school. You're sure about this?"

I shrug. "I have a witness."

Holmes swears quietly and angles his face to the sun, like he's apologizing to the universe for something he hasn't done yet. Panagakos is probably as good as dead, and something inside me is happy about that.

"You're all right, Smoke," Holmes says, holding his tattooed knuckles out for a tap. "Consider yourself a friend." But he isn't offering friendship. More like shelter under a vulture's wing.

The timing couldn't be better.

"Actually"—I incline my head toward the shadows where Ben stands shivering with his back to the wall—"I'm thinking Haggett might need a friend more than I do."

Holmes raises an eyebrow. But I'm not asking him to amend our agreement. We had a deal—I provide him with information, and he watches my back. Protection is protection, no matter whose ass you're covering. Seems like a reasonable trade to me.

"You sure about that?"

I glance at Haggett, scrunched up in the shadows, blowing warm air into his cupped hands. "If it's all the same to you, I owe him a favor."

"After yesterday's fight, I figure it might be the other way around."

"Nah. Six had it coming regardless. Ben and I have other business." And I need Ben in one piece for that.

"If you say so." Holmes shrugs and slips on his beanie. "Consider it done. But watch your back, Smoke. Six has it out for you."

I check the yard for signs of Six for the fifth time since we started this conversation, but he's nowhere in sight. "Maybe next time," I say. I hope I live long enough to see a next time so I can get around to covering my own ass. For now, Ben's is more important.

Ben straightens a little as I cross the yard. He reminds me of a giraffe I saw once at the zoo. I wave him over. He ducks his head and shambles out of the shade on wobbly legs, his knees practically knocking together. His nose is running from the cold, and he wipes it on his sleeve.

"Didn't I tell you to stand up straight?" The kid isn't doing much to make Holmes's job any easier, and I'm beginning to understand Holmes's hesitation in accepting the deal. Keeping Haggett out of trouble is going to be a full-time job. At my insistence, he pulls up his shoulders, shuffling anxiously from foot to foot.

"That's better. See that guy I was talking to? The one with the crow on his neck?"

Ben nods.

"He's your friend now. It cost me, but he's going to make sure nobody messes with you."

Ben's throat bobs up and down, and I hope like hell he isn't going to cry. Just in case he is, I put a hand on his shoulder and turn him to face the wall.

"Why'd you do that?" he asks, practically hyperventilating.

"Because you're going to do something for me, and this whole arrangement'll work out a lot better without anyone's foot up your ass."

A small noise comes from somewhere deep in Ben's throat.

"For Christ's sake, Haggett. It's nothing like that." I move my hand off his shoulder. "I just need you to keep your eyes and ears open after Lights Out. I don't trust people not to mess with me when I'm sleeping."

"When you're sleeping?" Haggett wipes his nose, looking confused. "We're locked in a cell."

My first thought runs to Monetti. How easy it would be for him to get in if he finds out I ratted about his affair with Rickers's girlfriend. Or worse, how easy it would be for Monetti to let Six and all his buddies in while he turns the other way.

"If you're right," I say, not wanting to scare him, "then it's real simple. Holmes keeps an eye on you. And you keep an eye on me."

"What do you mean, if I'm right? You mean there's a chance I could be wrong? That someone could come in and try to . . ." Ben trails off, his breath coming too fast. I push him down so he's sitting against the wall and press his head between his knees. Better people think he's got a nosebleed than a panic attack. He sputters, dripping snot and tears into the dirt. "I can't protect anybody, Smoke. Hell, look at me!"

He's right. There isn't a thing about Ben Haggett that's fit to survive here. His eyes are too wide, his arms are too thin, and his baby-smooth skin doesn't have a single scar or tattoo on it. But I don't have a better option.

"You don't need to protect anyone. All you need to do is wake me up if something's wrong." Even across town, a hard shake of my shoulder and a shout in my ear can yank me back into my body. As best as I can figure, I'm like one of those dollar-store ball-and-paddle toys. My threads are elastic and my consciousness is the ball. If someone jerks the paddle, I'll come slamming back into it. Hard. It's painful, and disorienting as hell. But a few seconds' warning is all I'd need to get back in time to take care of myself. Better than waking up to a knife in my gut. Or not waking up at all. I hope Haggett can manage this much. "But if you don't think you can handle it, I'll tell Holmes the deal is off—"

"Wait..." Ben's head snaps up. He reaches for my arm, but thinks better of it. He looks around, sweat beading on his lip. Across the yard, Six's buddies are watching us, and Holmes is watching them. "I'll do it."

I don't get a chance to think much on my new plan.

Or to grab another nap, either.

Saturday afternoons are my court-ordered group sessions with Dr. Manning. The usual suspects file into the classroom. It smells like commercial disinfectant and sweat, and the fluorescents make all of us look a little green. We each claim a seat in the tight circle, drawing our chairs back and farther away from one another as we sit down. Officer Brooks takes up his usual post just outside the door, watching us through the Plexiglas window. Dr. Manning smooths her pantsuit and the tight knot of black hair at the base of her skull. Her closed-lipped smile looks more artificial than if she'd painted one on.

"Good day, gentlemen." She crosses her legs at the ankles, folding her unadorned hands over her knees, modeling everything she expects us to be. Stripped down and modest. "I'd really like this to be the week we make progress. As a group." She pauses long enough to look into each of our hard, uninterested faces. She still hasn't figured out what each of us knows instinctively. That our tough exoskeletons can't be stripped without killing us. That poking holes in them only makes us curl deeper inside.

Bumper fidgets with the hole in his earlobe, a nervous tell he has difficulty hiding. Rico shoots me wary glances and massages the cross tattooed at the base of his throat. This group will never make progress. Sharing is dangerous. It's also the whole point of group therapy. But exposing and exploring weaknesses isn't something I want to do with the convicted felons I eat, sleep, and shower with.

We all stay quiet, angled back in our chairs, feet planted firmly on the floor. Except for Skivvy. His bony knee bobs up and down like a piston. He's twitchy, always shifting in his seat, struggling to repress impulses the rest of us don't quite understand.

"Next Thursday is Thanksgiving. For some of you, this may be your first Thanksgiving away from your families, and the holidays can be difficult when we're separated from loved ones. So I thought we'd spend this week talking about gratitude. At one point or another, we have all had someone or something to feel thankful for. I'd like us to share some of those memories today and also to talk about the relationships and people we're grateful for here inside the Y. By opening ourselves up and sharing, I'd like to see if we can help each other feel less alone."

Bumper snorts. "Bend over, Rico. Help me feel less alone, man." Whoops erupt. Rico flips him off.

Dr. Manning suppresses a smile and makes a quieting gesture. "I'd like us all to close our eyes for a moment—"

"Keep your hands to yourselves, pussies," Skivvy mutters.

"—and think back to a time when someone paid you a kindness."

Oscar scratches his head, exposing the trail of cigarette burns that climb up his wrist. "Paid us a what?"

"I ain't never been paid nothing but minimum wage." Skivvy and Oscar slap hands.

"Maybe if you assholes would pay attention in class and learn how to read—" Rico starts in.

Oscar jumps to his feet. "I know how to read!"

"*Hustler* don't count."

Oscar narrows his eyes at Rico and folds himself, red-faced, into his chair. He darts anxious glances at Officer Brooks, who's taken a step closer to the window, reminding us all to settle down. "I don't know what you're talking about, man."

"All right, gentlemen." Dr. Manning smiles tightly, giving the okay sign to Officer Brooks. "Let's try to stay on track today. I'd like us all to close our eyes and think back to a time when someone did something nice for you."

We're all quiet. Bumper smiles to himself. He makes a lewd gesture and works the inside of his cheek with his tongue. "Her name was Angela." The rest of the circle bursts out laughing until Officer Brooks raps on the window, looking stern. He has zero tolerance for "ungentlemanly behavior," and he's looking like he's ready to throw one of us in the hole.

We all eye one another as the laughter dies, arms crossed, none of us trusting enough to follow Dr. Manning's instructions, even if we are probably all considering the question she posed, answering it silently in our own heads. All the trash talk and joking is just a layer of scale. An armor that gets thicker every day we're here. Dr. Manning doesn't notice. Her eyes are closed.

It would be too easy to close mine, too.

To remember kindness. To remember Ms. Cruz.

Some days, like today, it's hard not to.

I remember that she smelled nice. Like the lemon polish on Somerville's bookcase, and the leather tang of his chair reminds me of her boots. She wore glasses with thin gold frames, and I saw my reflection in them when she smiled. Her hair hung over her face on one side, smooth and dark like a curtain curling under itself. It made her seem shy. But she wasn't at all. She was braver than every thug in this place. I wonder how long I'll be able to remember the smaller details. The warm walnut color of her eyes or the dimple in her right cheek that always appeared when she smiled. I lost those bits and pieces of my mother years ago, all those forgotten birthdays and missed holidays whittling away at the planes of her face, eroding the sharp memory of her promise to come home into something pointless and indistinct.

It's been over a year since Ms. Cruz handed me those books in my footlocker. They were a present, she said, and she wouldn't let me give them back, even though I told her my father wouldn't let me keep them. She insisted, saying I'd earned them, that I'd take those books with me to college someday. I almost believed her. I cracked the stiff leather bindings and trailed my fingers over the crisp pages. There were five of them—Shakespeare, Poe, Twain, Hemingway, and Dickens—a start, she called them. I'd read some of them already. Had checked out and devoured the battered library copies with a million other people's names inside. But these books were mine, brand-new and trimmed in gold. She'd written my name in the covers in permanent ink, as if she'd known I wouldn't believe they were mine otherwise.

The books were heavy, and I was light carrying them home.

But I'd been right. All that brightness—those gold-dipped dreams about college and a future—bled out of me that night, all over my kitchen floor.

"John." Dr. Manning's voice drags me back to myself, into the circle of faces all turned toward me. "It's your turn to share. Tell us about a time when someone paid you a kindness."

Everyone is quiet, waiting for me to empty my pockets of secrets. They'll steal them. Trade them. Carve them up like hash marks and brag about them to their friends. In their hungry eyes, I see Ms. Cruz cut up in the hallway. I picture Pink, bleeding puddles on the floor. I weigh my words carefully and make sure Bumper is listening. I make sure the lie I'm about to tell about Candace Bauer will get back to Six.

"Some chick from my high school came to see me this morning. Turns out it was on a dare. I've got no memories of kindness, doc. Hell, I don't even remember her name."

NINE

Holding your insides in when someone's trying to rip them out is exhausting. After group sessions, I feel sluggish. Empty. Like all my beating parts have shut down and are hibernating somewhere deep in some last-ditch effort toward self-preservation. My feet drag, sneakers squeaking on the slick tile floor, waking me from a daze. I'm vaguely aware of the clatter of trays and the warm, thick smell of Salisbury steak and beans. I follow the rhythmic stride of Bumper's shoes, only looking up when I'm in the mess line. I check out the row of servers in smeared white aprons and hairnets, looking for Simpson. He isn't working today, and I'm grateful. I pass through the line without a word, my tray just as full or just as empty as everyone else's.

"Smoke." Martín jerks his chin toward the open seat in front of him as I emerge from the line. I set my load down, sinking heavily onto the cold metal bench, and poke around my beans and mashed potatoes, waiting for him to say something. He doesn't. I'm not really sure what he wants from me. His square brown hands rest facedown on the table beside his empty tray, like the hard cover of an open book I can't read.

I raise my good eyebrow. "No books today?"

Martín has a way of smiling without moving his face. His mouth is a straight line, neither lip curling one way or the other. The kid's down on the man he shredded as impassively as he's looking at me now. I down my pint carton of milk and stare at him over the top. Set it down with a hollow thunk and toss my napkin onto my half-eaten plate.

"If you've got something to say, say it."

"You told me you'd have someone check in on my sisters. That was two weeks ago." He studies my face, my bunched-up shoulders, my arms folded tight across my chest. "You're falling behind, is all." No judgment. No concern. No one said Switzerland is warm.

"I've got a lot going on."

"Orders are piling up."

"Warden's on my ass." I run a hand over my patchy stubble, dragging it back and forth against the grain. "I just need some time. A few days to take care of something." I rub my eyes. "I'll catch up next week."

Martín sits stone-still for a long minute. I try to hold eye contact, to offer a mental handshake, but I can't fight back the slow, aching yawn crawling through my jaw. My eyes squeeze shut, mouth stretching wide of its own will. By the time I blink it away, Martín's rising silently from the table.

"Woman problems." He nods. "Get some sleep."

His jumpsuit cuts a steady, even swath down the center of the chow hall. A few heads turn, but no one messes with him. We all hold a quiet respect for a balanced blade. Or maybe we're all just too afraid to test it.

I tense at the heavy fall of boots and the rustle of polyester against Kevlar behind me. Cautious, I set my hands evenly beside my tray and turn to look slowly over my shoulder. Officer Monetti chews hard on his gum, breathing down spearmint, his thumbs hitched in his belt. His jaw is strong and sharply cut, and brags a dark shadow even when he's clean-shaven. He isn't much older than most of us. Maybe mid-twenties. He unwinds a slow grin. A bright purple hickey flaunts itself like Switzerland. It isn't easy to be neutral in the Y, but nothing see to throw him off-balance. Not the guards. Not the inmates. H Dr. Manning probably couldn't dredge an emotion to Martín's surfa And yet something about the set of his smooth, round cheeks and t small crease at the edge of his eyes tells me he's smiling.

"What?" I finally ask, amusement twisting a weary grin out of n I hide it behind a spoonful of processed meat. "What's so funny?"

"What's her name?" His lips barely move, and his eyes are impenetrable as the yard wall, but he is definitely laughing at me.

My smile sucks back into my head. I chew slowly, swallowing har salty gravy leaving a trail all the way down. "You're full of *mierdo*."

"It's *mierda*. Your Spanish sucks. I might have a book that can he you with that."

"Your books are what got me into this mess."

"I'll bet you your mashed potatoes that this has nothing to do wi the jobs. You've got woman problems written all over you."

I give him a derisive look. "Yeah? What do you know about woma problems?" He was barely fourteen when he got here.

Martín shrugs. "I've got four older sisters. You show all the cla sic signs."

I shovel into my mashed potatoes hard enough to scrape my plat "I've got no woman," I grumble. "No woman. No problem."

Martín shakes his head.

I down another bite, careful not to taste it. Martín hasn't move It's hard to picture those paper-soft hands cutting a man to pieces. I' never seen them as anything but featherlight on the spine of a boc Have never seen his face betray the rage or fear it takes to jam a bla between a man's ribs. I wonder if he'd babbled and cried and called c to God when he saw the blood on his hands, like I did. Or if he'd look under his collar, too proud to stay hidden. Might as well flash a neon sign that reads, I LAID RICKERS'S GIRL IN HIS OWN KITCHEN.

"You need something?" I say too sharply, hoping like hell this has nothing to do with the news I shared with Rickers.

His grin hardens, teeth grinding back and forth like he'd like to chew me up.

"Warden Somerville wants to see you," he says, and my shoulders sag with relief. He puts his hands on his hips, resting his fingers on the blunt end of his Maglite while he waits for me to dump my tray.

All eyes turn to watch as he escorts me from the mess hall, a few tables calling out bets on the reason. Bumper's table is a little too quiet, and a premonitory knot tightens in my gut. Bumper's and Six's chairs are both empty.

"What's this about?" I ask when we're in the corridor.

The only sounds are the steady pulse of his boots behind me and the rattle of cuffs on his hip. We pause at the sally port—a series of controlled-entry doors at the end of the pod. Monetti cuffs my wrists in front of me and waves at the guard in the control room, signaling him to let us through. The buzzer saws at my skull, and I flinch, catching Monetti's attention.

"Jesus, Smoke," he says, shaking his head as the locks slide home. "Your old man really did a number on you." He unrolls another stick of gum and whistles low between his teeth. Something that'd be a lot harder to do if he didn't have any. I imagine my hands at his throat. Imagine beating him with his Maglite.

"You know, I heard about your little stunt in the yard yesterday," he says, matter-of-fact, taking the hall slow and easy, like we're just two guys strolling. "Funny, I've got a buddy working over at Supermax. He says your dad was doing real good. A model inmate. That he was reading the Bible and going to NA meetings every day." My hands fist at my sides until I feel my pulse pounding inside them. "Then last week he tells me your daddy lost it in the break room. Flew off the handle about something and shanked some poor bastard in the eye. And all I can think to myself is, like father like son.

"The way I see it, they should have let you bleed. A kid like you can't be fixed. All this shit about reform . . ." He shakes his head. "It's a waste of perfectly good tax dollars, if you ask me."

I'll never tell him he's right. That all those stitches and metal plates are only holding my outsides together. Instead, I bite out, "Nobody asked you."

Monetti's hand flies to his belt, his fingers twitching over his Mag. He steps in front of me and leans into my face. I keep my eyes to the floor. "Nobody asked that pretty schoolteacher you cut, either."

I'd rather he'd just hit me. "She'd tell them it wasn't me," I say, even if it's only to myself. You can only repeat yourself so many times before you realize no one's listening. I keep saying it anyway, to remind myself that I'm not the one who killed her. Otherwise I might start believing it, too.

"The dead can't speak for themselves, kid."

I look up at him with eyes cold as corpses. "Tell me something I don't know."

Monetti smirks around a mouthful of gum. "You think that makes you special? That the big man upstairs felt sorry for you and gave you a second chance? Well, guess what, kid. Your six minutes of fame are over. You blew it. In here, you're nobody, just like everybody else."

But he's wrong. I'm not like any of them. I can walk right through him and out of this place whenever the hell I choose to. He'll never see me coming. Never see me lurking in his living room, watching every move until I catch him doing something worth trading for. He can take his fucking handcuffs and choke on them.

Monetti shoves me toward the warden's office. Conversation's over, and it's back to business as usual. Monetti waves at the control rooms and makes small talk with the guards in the corridors as we pass. When we come around the corner into the East Wing, we bump headlong into Officer Rickers, and my heart, still racing from my conversation with Monetti a moment ago, freezes in my chest.

Our eyes lock, and I think maybe he can see the flash of panic in mine. "Hey, kid," he says. Rickers steps around us, his tone neutral, his eyes barely flicking over me as though just to be polite. He nods at Monetti. If he notices Monetti's hickey, he doesn't let on. He keeps walking, and I breathe a quiet sigh of relief. Rickers's poker face is as good as any I've ever seen, and if I wasn't sure I could trust him before, I like him just fine right now. He could have lost his cool or whispered some threat in Monetti's ear as he passed. I glance over my shoulder to make sure Rickers is gone and catch Monetti, grinning to himself like a fool. He gives me a hard shove to the shoulder. "Eyes forward on the floor, Conlan."

But it's only a matter of time before Monetti figures it out—I can see a lot farther than that.

TEN

Monetti spits his gum into a wrapper and tucks it in his pocket before he raps on the warden's door. Warden Somerville's door is made of wood. The sound is gentle and earthy, absent of a buzzer. It feels out of place in this big steel-and-concrete box. It whispers against the carpet and shuts quietly behind us.

I stand beside the big brown leather chair, breathing it in. The lighting in the room is incandescent, soft and shaded, casting the bookshelves in quiet relief. Their spines are a landscape of color, and they smell alive and musty, like old trees.

"John." Warden Somerville's voice is as peaceful as the room. "Welcome. Have a seat." He stands and gestures to the big brown chair, watching as I ease down into it. The scent of leather whooshes out like a breath.

The warden frowns at my cuffs. "The restraints aren't necessary," he informs Monetti.

"But Conlan was in Seg last night—"

"And this morning I released him." The warden's tone is firm. Monetti kneels in front of me, his back to the warden as he uncuffs my wrists. When his eyes cut up to mine, there's a warning in them. He stands and steps out from between us, but I can feel him close, like a shadow behind my chair.

"I'm glad you're here, John." A file rests neatly in the center of the warden's desk. My name is printed on the tab. There should be a stone in my stomach—a cold, hard foreboding of the conversation to come. But his bristled gray eyebrows aren't pointing at me, like they do when he's disappointed. They lie smoothly against his forehead and arc with his slight smile.

I hold that smile discreetly up against the photos mounted in polished frames on his desk. The girl in the pictures smiles, too. Not the quiet, cautious smile her father wears now. Hers is careless and wide, eyes crinkling with laughter and shining with possibilities. I've never known anyone who smiles like that, too happy to notice her picture being taken and too perfect to care.

Warden Somerville reaches behind him to his printer and removes several sheets of paper from the tray. He spreads them over the surface of his desk, turning them so I can see. They're a collection of photographs, the images enlarged and marked with reference numbers. Pictures of soup cans and razors, toothbrushes melted down and whittled to dagger-sharp points, packs of chewing gum, bits of scrap metal molded into lockpicks, tiny mirrors, and slender metal tubes.

And a knife.

I know this knife.

I know the feel of its black bone handle and its thick, short blade. The slicing force of it sliding home, warm and slick and sticky in my palm, buried to the hilt. The wet, sucking sound it made when I jerked it from Cameron Walsh's belly.

I swallow hard, the leather chair creaking as I shift. For the first time, I am uncomfortable in this room.

Warden Somerville reaches for the photo of the knife and holds it toward me, giving me a closer look. There are fresh nicks etched deep into the bone. Hash marks. Six of them. I raise my eyes to the warden's, careful not to reveal my racing thoughts.

"Your tip was good, John." He collects the photos and tucks them inside his desk drawer. "Officer Brooks found that knife in Tyler Garrison's cell."

Tyler is "Six" Garrison to the boys in the pod. How did Six end up with the same knife I'd used to kill Cameron Walsh? The one Walsh's friend had used to kill Ms. Cruz. Last time I saw that black bone handle was in court, in an evidence bag, dangling from the crooked finger of the prosecuting attorney. That knife should be in a cardboard box, stowed away in some police department records room. So what the hell is it doing in the Y? And more important, how did it get in Six Garrison's cell?

"Still no clue how all this contraband got in," he says as if reading my thoughts. "Some of it . . . the toothbrushes, the razors, the cans . . . those are easy to figure out. But the knife is worrisome, John. A weapon like this could only come from outside the Y, which means somebody went to an awful lot of trouble to smuggle it in." He shakes his head. "I don't know how you get your information, John. Not sure I want to know, to be honest. But if you have any idea how a weapon like this made it inside my house, I'd like you to tell me."

He's asking, as if I have some kind of choice. But there's a subtext—an expectation I'm reading in the forward lean of his posture and the earnestness of his eyes. My mind is running faster than the conversation.

Three leaps ahead. I don't have the answers Somerville's looking for. In fact, I probably have more questions than he does. How did the knife get here? Who does it belong to? If I trace it back, would it prove that I never hurt Ms. Cruz? That I killed that boy in self-defense?

Somerville steeples his hands on my file and waits. When I don't answer, he glances at Monetti over my shoulder.

"I understand if you don't want to say anything, given your history with Tyler. Officer Monetti will look into it. You don't need to be involved in this anymore."

He looks down at my file and sighs. "I don't blame you for being distrustful. Maybe that's partly my fault. All this time you're spending in Segregation—it's not the solution. I think we're failing you, son. A young man with your background might just need a little more supervision. More interaction with adult authority figures."

"Sir?" What does this mean? Is he sending me back to court? Is he kicking me out of the program?

Cold, wet trails slide from my armpits. He looks at me thoughtfully, one hand drumming the desk. My skin feels heavy and my head feels light, and I wonder if an out-of-body experience is possible while I'm awake.

"You know what I think? I think you're a good kid who's stepped in some rotten shit, and you think you'll never shake it off." He flips open a pair of wire-rimmed glasses and slips them on. Then he opens my file. "Says here you were a solid student. Above average. Advanced Placement in English." He shoots me a quick sideways glance, a hint of admiration on his pursed lips. "You scored high enough grades in school to get into a good college. Up until the day you were hospitalized, you had a perfect attendance record. And if my math is right, you were an exemplary employee of the Highland Waste and Recycling Company since before you were old enough to legally hold a job."

He taps the page lightly. "I'm going to take an educated guess and assume you were hauling trash before school to save money for college. Tell me I'm wrong, son." He looks at me over his glasses. His eyes are wide like Simpson's, waiting for me to tell him what he wants to hear. But I don't deal in bad information.

"No, sir," I say quietly.

"What were you doing with the money?"

"I bought groceries. Paid for my clothes. Sometimes I paid the rent."

"For your father?"

"Yes, sir."

"And what was he doing?"

I think about that a moment too long. Long enough to let the memory of him settle painfully into my thoughts, like an arthritic ache in a once-broken bone.

Until the warden's office all but disappears.

I know my father's messed up the minute I open the door. The sudden silence is thick with a pressure I feel but can't see. I know he's on the other side of the wall, and I listen as I brace the door with my foot, peel the key slowly out of the lock, and let it shut with a soft click.

My backpack is heavy. It cuts into my shoulder, but I don't set it down. I grip it, pull it closer. Listen to the slow drip of the sink faucet in the next room. I hold my breath. The apartment smells like anger burning, and it sucks all the oxygen from the room.

I flinch as a bottle flies through the opening of the kitchen and crashes into the wall. I take a slow step toward the doorway, shards crunching under my shoe.

A cabinet door slams. Then another. The rapid fire of cans and boxes being hurled across the room.

"Where is it, John?" My father's voice is so strained it's breaking.

I peer into the opening just as he throws open the freezer door and tosses the contents onto the floor.

"Where the fuck is it?"

His eyes are wide and bloodshot and crazy. His hands shake and pull at his hair. I can't stand the sight of him like this, so I look everywhere else. At the cabinet doors slung wide, the refrigerator oozing its contents onto the yellowing linoleum. I shift the weight of my pack tighter to my body. Farther from him.

"Is that where you're hiding it?"

"I'm not hiding anything." I angle my shoulder away from him slowly, trying like hell not to attract his attention to the bag any more than I already have.

"I know you got paid on Friday. Don't lie to me. Where's the money, John?" He smiles at me, his lips twitching, peeling back over a mouth full of teeth discolored by abuse and neglect. In one quick motion, he grabs the handle of my pack and rips it from me. He tears open the zipper, flips it upside down, and dumps out the contents. I swoop in, grasping for the heavy books, but I'm not fast enough, and they thunk down like logs on a fire. My father shoves me back hard against the counter.

"What the hell is this?" He snatches Mark Twain off the pile. My insides break as he takes each side of the cover in one hand and shakes the book upside down until the spine groans. The smell of leather and ink bleeds from the sagging pages, and I panic.

"They're mine!" I push off the counter and grab for it, but he jerks the book out of reach.

"Where'd you get them?" He glares between me and the pile, forehead creased as if he's calculating their worth against mine—and I'm coming up short.

I don't answer, and his face twists with disgust. "Take them back where you got them and get the damn money back."

"I can't. They were a gift."

"Bullshit!"

*I bend down and throw open Poe's cover. I show him my name—*my *name—penned permanently inside.*

He winds back and hurls Twain at my face, his unbuttoned shirtsleeves falling back to reveal a few angry red tracks, some fading to green-and-yellow bruises.

"You're just like your mother," he says, shaking his head like he's shaking off the memory of her. "Keeping things from me." His hands are trembling. Not the fine tremors I'm used to. Now he's shaking and red all over, and he spits when he talks, the way he used to right before he hit her. Right before she left. For the first time, I think maybe I can forgive her for not coming back. I bend down slowly, never letting my eyes leave his face. I reach for my backpack with one hand and feel blindly for the nearest book with the other, but he swings out his foot and kicks it away.

"You're gonna leave now? Just like her . . ." he mumbles, squeezing his head and pushing out hot, angry tears. I see myself in the shine of his eyes, the way he must see me. My blond hair all tangled in hers, falling over her gray irises and curling around her ears. "You're just like her!"

The door to our apartment buzzes from the plastic box in the hall, followed by a faint knocking.

"John?" I freeze at the muffled sound of Ms. Cruz's voice. "I've been thinking about what you said. About the books. Can we talk?"

I scramble for the last book. I have to get out of here. Get her out of here. I swing my pack over my shoulder and bolt for the hall just as the buzzer rings again.

"Where the hell do you think you're going, you little shit?"

My right leg buckles where he kicks it, and I fall on my hands and knees onto the kitchen floor. The sickening crunch comes from inside me. I barely hear the buzzer over the ringing in my ears. I blink, open my eyes. They're wet, burning, and the room swims as I hold the counter and pull myself to my knees. He's standing over me, winding the wrench back again. My head shatters and my vision explodes in a spray of dying fireworks against a black sky.

"John? Son?" The warden speaks softly. "I asked you about your dad."

I mask my shudder with a shrug, fighting the urge to scratch the burning scar at my temple. I don't want to think about my father anymore. Besides, the answer is right in front of him in my file. The night my father was arrested for killing me, he was so high on meth it took four officers to subdue him.

"The warden asked you a question," Monetti growls somewhere behind me.

Warden Somerville holds up a hand to silence him. He waits for my answer, like he knows he's pulled me back from someplace dark, and I need a while for my senses to adjust. When he speaks, his voice is quiet, padded soft with something that might be sympathy.

"When was the last time you had a real meal, John?"

I wipe my hands on my thighs, half expecting to see them spattered in blood. I swallow back my nausea and glance at the cherry-and-brass desk clock, the Salisbury steak and reconstituted potatoes insoluble in my belly.

"About half an hour ago, I suppose."

The warden chuckles gently. "No, son. When was the last time you had a *real* meal?"

I start to open my mouth, trying to remember whatever had come before forty-two days of Jell-O and applesauce, and Styrofoam cups with plastic lids and bendable straws.

He shakes his head. "Not hospital food, either. I'm talking home-cooked, John. Served on a real plate, at a real table with people who care about you."

The silence between us is total and complete.

"That's what I thought." He drags the spectacles from his face, letting them fall to the blotter.

"Next week is Thanksgiving, son. I'd like you to come home for dinner with me."

A shadow falls over me, Monetti emerging beside the chair in which I sit speechless.

"Warden Somerville, I don't think—" he manages before the warden silences him with a look.

"I've cleared it with the deputy director. Mr. Conlan will be released for four hours into my custody on Thursday evening pending Dr. Manning's approval. The director has also requested an officer remain with John at all times, so Officer Rickers will be joining us for Thanksgiving dinner. Officer Rickers can return John to the Y after dessert. He's on night shift anyway."

"Rickers?" Monetti practically spits on himself, and his hickey turns a deep shade of violet.

"You have a question, Officer Monetti?" Warden Somerville spreads his palms on the desk, poised to stand even though he doesn't have to. He's the tallest short man I've ever known. Monetti clenches his jaw and resumes his post behind my chair.

"It's come to my attention that Officer Rickers will be alone for Thanksgiving. I'm sure he could use the company. Vivian and I have plenty of room, and there's no sense spending the holiday by ourselves. My wife's family has other plans, and mine are all back in North Carolina, too far to join us." The warden sighs deeply. "We haven't had company for dinner in a long time, and it'll be good for Vivian and me to have a full table. I could use a real meal myself." He mumbles something about being sick of charity casseroles from the women's group at church, and Monetti casts his eyes to the floor.

"Besides, John and Officer Rickers will be spending a lot more time together. This will be a good chance for them to get to know each other a bit."

I lean forward, not sure I heard him right. "Sir?"

The warden smiles. "Officer Rickers came to see me after his shift this morning. He likes you, son. We both do. I think we both share the same concerns... that you're a good kid who's fallen off track. After our conversation, I spoke with Dr. Manning. We all want to see you complete the program, so we're going to try coming at this from a different angle. Dr. Manning suggested you might respond well to an adult mentor. Someone you can talk to. A big brother, if you'd rather think of it that way. I think it's a fine idea."

"But, sir—" Monetti mutters.

"It's all arranged," the warden says definitively. "John will be excused from morning chores to spend a few minutes with Officer Rickers at the end of his shifts."

Neither Monetti nor I move, both of us too shell-shocked. I figured Rickers would be true to his word—to keep an eye on me in exchange for checking up on his girlfriend—and maybe cut me a favor now and then. But extra one-on-one time with him isn't exactly what I had in mind. And Thanksgiving dinner at the warden's house just seems wrong.

My eyes skip to the pictures on his desk, then to my sweating hands and my numbered jumpsuit. I rub my scar to relieve the headache blooming behind it. I don't fit inside those pictures. I don't deserve this. I'm not like them at all.

It's okay, John. I insist. Take the books.

"Don't worry yourself, son," Somerville says. "I'll have Officer Rickers bring you something appropriate to wear. You can change in the command center on your way out."

My head pounds, slick with perspiration.

Where did you get the books, John? Don't lie to me! Nobody just gives *things like this! Not to kids like you.*

"But—"

"It's done, John." The warden prints my name in bold letters across the top of the release form, pressing hard enough to transfer the ink through to the pink and yellow copies below. He scrawls his signature at the bottom.

I stand slowly. My prison-issued jumpsuit weighs a pound for every day I've regretted taking those books. Warden Somerville flips up the top two sheets, checking to make sure the ink penetrated all the way through. It did. No taking it back. My name is there, in permanent letters.

I step out of the halo of his desk lamp and into Monetti's shadow. He opens the door, his face twitching.

I turn back to the warden. "Sir?"

I want to repay him, make his kindness a wash—turn his gift into a trade to satisfy the balance of whatever the universe or karma expects of me. A seed of regret burrows into my gut. I made a promise to Pink. Told her I'll see her tonight. But I take a last look at the girl in the photo. I imagine her spooning food onto a white china plate. My throat tightens around thoughts of empty thank-yous and emptier hands, around a gift that's too big to hold on to. I make the only choice I can. Screw Monetti. He doesn't think I deserve anyone's kindness anyway.

"The boys in B pod are brewing hooch," I say. "They're stealing fruit cocktail from the mess hall, and using plastic bags and sugar packets to get it started."

The warden's brow lifts to Monetti, inviting an explanation.

Monetti's reply is all smooth, cool steel. "The kid's lying. We tossed every cell in B pod last month and didn't find any—"

"You missed Elston and Miranda's cell," I say. I can almost hear Monetti crackle and freeze in the chilling silence that follows. It was a lazy mistake. Miranda's a quiet kid. Never gets in any trouble. Everyone knew the hooch would be safest in his footlocker because it was the cell most likely to get skipped. I didn't plan to roll Officer Monetti under the bus, but I'll be damned if I'll let him call me a liar in front of the only man in this place who treats me like I'm not one. The information is a token, and a small one at that, but it's all I have to give.

Monetti puts a hand on my shoulder, grinding his thumb into me where the warden can't see. I can feed them information all day long—I could tell them what I know about the knife—but Monetti won't care. It doesn't matter what I say, or what I can prove. In his mind, I'm not worth the breath I'd waste trying. I know, because I saw the same conviction in my father's eyes, right before he killed me.

ELEVEN

Monetti snaps the cuffs back on the minute we're out of Warden Somerville's office. Then he shoves me toward C pod. We both glance at the eye of the camera on the ceiling as we walk past it. Once our backs are to the lens, Monetti pulls a fresh stick of gum out of his pocket and folds it into his mouth, walking that slow saunter the camera ignores. The one that says, *We're cool, nothing to see here.* All the while, he's chewing the hell out of it, making the veins stand out in his neck. The kind of small details that get lost in the static of a closed-circuit black-and-white screen.

His phone chirps in his pocket, and he thumbs it on.

"Yeah," he answers sharply. A high, urgent voice wails like a siren through the connection.

Monetti cuts her off. "What the hell do you mean, he knows?" We're almost in sight of the sally port to C pod, and I start walking a little faster. Monetti grabs me by the scruff and holds me in place.

"How the hell did he find out?" A ripple of panic rolls through me. "I'll call you later," he says, but the shrill voice only grows louder. "Dammit, Lisa, I said I'll call you later!"

He closes the connection and slips the phone into his pocket.

My heart leaps when he grabs me by the elbow. He drags me alongside as his legs consume huge chunks of the hall. He shoots quick glances at the ceiling, finding the evenly spaced cameras, until we hit the blind turn—a four-foot section of tile and concrete the cameras can't see.

Monetti's forearm smacks me hard in the chest, knocking me breathless against the wall. He crushes his Maglite against my throat, prying my chin up until we're nose-to-nose. I cough and sputter. Monetti's knee is a hard threat against my groin.

His eyes flash white and blue. His breath is tobacco and spearmint and rage.

"Rickers kicked his girlfriend out on her ass and told her some asshole-for-hire in the Y's been paying someone to spy on her. What do you know, Smoke?" He sneers, articulating each word, his intonation hinting at a secret. *What do you know, Smoke?* Like he's heard people use it before. Like he knows the asshole-for-hire is me. "What did you tell him, you little shit?"

I can't answer, even if I want to. He presses the Maglite tighter while I struggle to suck air.

"I'm gonna drop this light, and you're gonna give me a name, Conlan." He waits just long enough to watch my eyes bulge and my face turn blue. A second before I think I might piss myself, he lowers the handle, but only by an inch. "Who's your source?"

My chest heaves and my eyes water. I can't talk past the pain in my throat. He swings the Maglite hard into my gut, doubling me over until I'm falling against him.

Monetti tips an ear toward the sound of approaching footsteps down the hall, and I hope like hell it's the warden. Monetti grabs a fistful of my collar and drags me upright. Then he leans into my ear. "You thought you'd bribe Rickers and score a night out? You're not the only one capable of dealing in secrets."

I'm coughing and gagging, bent over my own feet.

"You okay, kid?" Monetti asks loudly. He claps my back as two guards from A pod clear the corner. He nods to them, dismissing them with a casual wave of his fingers. "I told you, Conlan. It's dangerous to talk and walk at the same time. You should try keeping your mouth shut for a change. . . ." He slaps me hard between the shoulder blades, propelling another string of coughs. Then he bends close to my ear and whispers, "You might live longer."

Two lines of orange jumpsuits are making their way down the corridor toward us, their keen eyes darting back and forth between Monetti and me. He shoves me back under the camera's eye and walks me home.

I wake in a cold sweat two hours later, my pillow damp and my face crusted in drool. The buzzer sounds and I launch out of my bunk, nearly splitting my head on the metal frame. Orange bodies spill into the pod, a steady stream from the mess hall. Haggett peers cautiously into our cell, shuffling from foot to foot as the automated cell doors open in unison.

He keeps to the far wall, careful not to turn his back on me while he opens his footlocker and sets an unopened fruit cup inside. He looks guilty and shuts the door quick.

"You missed evening snack." His voice is unsteady. "I didn't know if I should . . . you know"—he gesticulates awkwardly with his hands—"wake you."

I stare at him, still foggy and swallowing dry fire. I can still feel the pressure of Monetti's Maglite against my throat. Talking'll hurt like hell, so I don't.

Haggett wags a finger at me, his voice rising and breaking on the high notes. "You told me I should only wake you if there's an emergency. I didn't think evening snack constituted a crisis or anything." He's wringing his hands and pacing. "But I could be wrong. They had those little Nilla Wafers. I don't know. I'm just the new guy. Maybe those little Nilla Wafers are like . . . I don't know . . . street gold or something. Can you buy shit in here with Nilla Wafers? Jeez." He sighs, raking a shaky hand over his head, feeling for hair that isn't there anymore. "It's not like you'd be able to eat cookies anyway." He makes a small motion toward his Adam's apple, and winces. He's right. The thought of eating anything solid is enough to close my throat. And judging by the way Haggett's staring at it, Monetti must have bruised me pretty good.

"Oh!" Haggett straightens up tall and reaches into his pocket. "I brought you this. I thought it might not hurt too bad going down." He holds out a plastic single-serve container of chocolate pudding. I hesitate, letting it rest on his open palm while I contemplate what it might cost me.

Haggett shrugs, looking deflated. A second before he slips it back in his pocket, I whisper past the burn in my throat, "Get rid of the fruit cocktail you just stashed in your footlocker. They'll be shaking down a few more cells, probably tonight, and you don't want to get caught with that shit."

Haggett looks incredulous, his eyes flicking from me to his locker. "A shakedown? For fruit cups? Are you feeling okay?"

"Trust me," I croak, snatching the pudding from his hand. "Now we're even."

Somerville probably won't shake down before midnight. He'll want to wait until after the night-shift guards have settled in, but early enough that they're still fresh on their game. I fed him a lead in B pod, hoping he'll skip ours, but leaving Haggett on watch is still risky as hell. Somerville could shake the whole place down to make the search seem less targeted—less like he got a tip. And since they only hit a few cells in C last night, there's no guarantee they won't come through for another pass.

I'm cutting it close. Staying put is the smart thing to do, but Pink and I have a deal. I told her I'll be at the club at ten, and that's exactly what I plan to do.

Haggett pulls his chair in close to my bunk, and we lean in to each other with our elbows on our knees. In less than a minute, the guards will call Lights Out. A minute after that, I'll be gone. I can make it to the club in less than an hour at a run.

"So let me get this straight," he whispers, rocking back and forth and holding on to his knees. "If they come searching cells, all I have to do is shake you real hard and holler in your ear? That's it?"

"Then get out of my way," I remind him. "Sometimes I wake up . . . disoriented." No point in telling him that the last time I came back to my body and someone had their hands on me, I killed him.

"What happens if you don't wake up?"

The question makes me pause. What happens to my body when my lifeline breaks for good? For that matter, what happens to the rest of me?

"Then I guess I've got bigger problems than a locker toss." I lie back on the pillow with my clothes on. I don't feel like getting caught in my boxers if they wake us up to toss our cell. Besides, Haggett's staring at me. Something tells me he won't sleep. He'll probably sit in that damn chair watching all night. And I just don't feel that comfortable with him yet.

I cross my arms over my chest and sink into the thin mattress, trying to ignore him.

"Do you sleep weird because of those plates in your head?" He's staring at my scar with a curious expression.

I roll my eyes at the underside of Haggett's mattress and shut them with a sigh.

"I was just asking because the guys in the chow hall were talking some shit about you dying and coming back to li—"

The lights extinguish, plunging the cell into darkness, silencing Haggett for the moment. I concentrate hard on my breathing, ignoring the tightness in my throat.

"Hey, Smoke?" he asks in a voice that's too fragile to ignore. "You're not going to like . . . die in your sleep or anything like that, are you?"

I think about that long enough that he probably thinks I'm already asleep. When I finally answer, his chair nearly comes off the floor.

"Hope not. Good night, Ben."

By the time he recovers and wishes me the same, I'm a smoky figment of myself. I hover close, watching him watch me. After a few minutes, he props his feet up on my bunk, and soon after that, his head lolls against his shoulder. Our breaths draw out, long and deep, chests rising and falling in a soft harmony of snores as Ben falls asleep on the job. Only then do I trust him enough to walk away.

TWELVE

I'm almost to the end of the pod. Bumper's tossing in his bunk, already half-asleep. Six's bunk is empty. He's probably still in the hole. Possession of a soup can is one thing. Possession of that black-handled knife will have Six in Segregation until he comes clean about where it came from. And Warden Somerville's not the only one itching to know.

Time is short and it's getting away from me, but the opportunity is too good to pass up. I melt through Six's cell door, not exactly sure what I'm looking for, or how to find it. I mean, it's not like I can toss his shit around and really search. Or can I?

Officer Rickers works nights. Maybe he could be persuaded to look for something during the next shakedown, but given all the searches already this week, that might not happen for a while. The phantom ache in my throat is a painful reminder that I probably shouldn't let anyone see me talking to Rickers anyway, and that won't be easy, considering the "big brother" arrangement the warden's got planned.

I nose around the cell, searching for any clue to the connection between Six and the black-handled knife. Six's footlocker is shut up tight, but Bumper's is open, its contents spilling out. All I spot inside are a couple back issues of *Car and Driver*, a wad of letters from home, a few remedial schoolbooks, and some fancy deodorant that's supposed to make women throw themselves at you. I drift down to the floor and look under the bed, but it's too dark to see anything. Then I stick my head between the bunks, twisting to look at the underside of Bumper's mattress.

A local phone number is etched into the frame. I read it aloud, repeating it until it's burned into my brain. Then I take a shortcut to the end of the pod through Rico's cell. All our cells look the same, all viewable through the doors that open onto the main corridor, so I close my eyes, imagine the cell, and slide through the concrete like a spoon through pudding.

I cross the entire cell in three quick strides, chanting the phone number under my breath to help me remember. I'm halfway through the opposite wall when I'm silenced by a muffled cry. I turn and find the wide whites of Rico's eyes blinking at me in the dark. He squeezes them shut, praying to himself, and throws his blanket over his head. I hold perfectly still, my spectral body half-frozen in concrete, while he recites something that sounds a lot like the Lord's Prayer in Spanish.

Oscar hollers from down the hall, "Shut up, Rico, you pussy. Jesus is trying to sleep." Laughter erupts in the neighboring cells, and Rico's celly leans over the edge of the bed and pitches a pillow at his head. I slip quietly through the wall and keep walking, nerves prickling. Even if no one here ever believes him, Rico knows my secret.

I'm too keyed up to head straight for the club. Between Monetti and Rico and Six's knife, it feels like the walls are closing in. So I do what I always do when I feel like I can't breathe in this place. I run.

I take off through the East Wing and don't stop until I'm halfway across town. I can't stop thinking about the knife in Six's cell. Or the phone number under Bumper's bunk. I can't help wondering where their trails connect.

In my first few weeks in the Y, I spent a lot of time exploring—eavesdropping on conversations, spying on the addresses of letters from home, figuring out where all the boys in C pod grew up and went to school, who their friends were outside—slipping out when I could grab nights alone and gathering up useful bits of information about their lives to keep in my pocket. Where some guys banked cigarettes and snack credits and favors, I stockpiled information—the strongest currency in the Y. And right now I feel bankrupt. I don't know exactly where Six lives, but Bumper's house had been easy to find, because of all the letters he's always writing to his mother back home. I'm not far from Bumper's house, so that's where I go.

The place looks the same as the last time I was here, only this time there's a big black pickup truck parked out front. And a girl—Bumper's little sister—crying silently and hugging her knees in her pajamas on the front porch. She jumps at the sound of glass shattering inside. A man is hollering in the house. I ghost to the living room window and peek through a broken slat in the blinds, just as he hits Bumper's mother in the face. She cowers on the floor, her lip bleeding, and the man turns and pours himself a drink.

I turn away. There's a phantom ache in my head. I can't do anything more for Bumper's mother than I was able to do for Simpson's. So I go.

I'm late. It's well after eleven o'clock when I sift through the brick wall of the club and ghost through the bar to the break room. The door is open an inch or two, and it feels like an invitation. I don't need one. I can still picture the room. Every detail is committed to memory. The hairline crack at the top of the mirror, covered by photos from magazines of Disney World and Las Vegas. How the third bulb from the left is burned out. The *Travel + Leisure* magazine folded open on her dressing table beside three tubes of lipstick and the bottle of blue nail polish lying sideways in the plastic tray.

Even so, I think about knocking. I pause and call her name instead. "Pink?"

"You're late," she says back. I sift into the room and find her scooping magazines off the sofa cushions. She's still in her work clothes. She tosses the pile of *Travel + Leisure* and *Budget Travel* magazines to the floor by her feet and drops onto the farthest corner of the sofa, pulling a ragged-looking throw pillow into her lap. She's fidgety, twisting a pink strand of hair around her index finger. I take a step toward the sofa, and she adjusts the pillow to cover more skin. Like maybe I'm making her uncomfortable, so I stop halfway through the room and look away.

She curls herself around the pillow and picks at a loose stitch. "It's not like I have cooties."

"No," I say too quickly. "No, it's nothing like that." I don't say that it's harder to talk to her like this, without bulletproof glass and her big, ugly coat between us. I came here with all these questions, and now I'm not really sure where to start. "It's just, I don't think I can sit down, is all."

I can't tell if she looks relieved or disappointed. "You can't stay?"

"No," I say, gesturing to the sofa. "I want to stay. For a little while, at least. I just haven't quite figured out the whole sitting-down thing."

She blinks a few times. Then she laughs, a loud, raucous, grown-up laugh that makes me feel like exactly what I am—a brain-damaged kid sneaking around in a ladies' break room in a nightclub.

“Wow, John Conlan. I guess there are a whole lot of things you haven’t figured out yet. Just because your ass isn’t really here doesn’t mean you can’t sit.” She slides her feet off the side of the couch. Then gives me a wary look before clearing a space on the saggy cushion beside her. I get the distinct impression I make her anxious, only I can’t figure out why. She was so self-assured the other night, even when that jerk, Panagakos, was all up in her grill. And here I am, freaking her out, nothing more than ashes and dust. I can’t even sit down beside her.

“Obviously, you know a lot more about this stuff than I do. That’s kind of why I’m here.”

She looks me up and down, scrunching her nose like she’s thinking. Her apron is slung over the lamp in the corner, dimming the room just enough for me to see my own silhouette, and I look down, too. I glow an eerie grayish white, my shape blurring, shifting and swirling where I move. I hold perfectly still, letting the smoke settle, allowing the finer details to clarify against the backdrop of the darkened room. The rise-and-fall shape of my knuckles, the outline of my legs. I wonder what my face must look like to her. If the hollow places where my eyes should be frighten her. Or if she’s more afraid of the real ones—the cynical, broken ones—she saw in the visitation room in the Y.

“You’ve got a pretty good grasp of projecting yourself. Your image is pretty clear.... I can see your prison jumpsuit, your sneakers, and the shape of your face. Your lips and chin... even your ears are pretty consistent.” She frowns and bites her lip, studying me. “Your scar is bigger than it ought to be, but there’s nothing I can do about that.”

I raise a hand to cover the dark void at my temple, but she isn’t looking at my scar anymore. She’s looking at the rest of me, like she’s trying to figure me out.

“Are there a lot of people like you?” My thoughts run to Rico. I wonder if there are other mediums in the Y. If they can recognize each other as easily as they recognize me.

"Doubt it. But it's not like we all run around wearing T-shirts that say 'I see dead people.' The live ones would think we're crazy, and the dead ones would never leave us alone."

Which means my secret's probably safe with Rico for now. If he tells anyone, he'll never live it down. And Dr. Manning would analyze him to death.

"Let's see if we can figure out what else you can do." Pink taps her chin thoughtfully. "Well, we know you've got the whole walking-through-walls thing down. And we know you can move pretty far.... What's the farthest you've been able to go?"

"Only as far as I can run in a night."

"Anywhere you want?"

"Only places I've been before... places I can picture in my head."

"What happens when you try to sit down?"

I hesitate to tell her. It's humiliating as hell. "I fall through the furniture and wind up on the floor."

She bites her lip, trying not to smile, and picks up the pillow, not so cautious of me anymore. "If I throw this at you, will you catch it?" She winds back, like she might actually try.

"I didn't come all this way so you could throw things at me!"

"Come on, John. You said it yourself. It's all in your head."

It's like she already threw that pillow, straight through my chest. "There's nothing wrong with my head!"

"Then catch it. It's easy."

"That pillow'll go through me just like everything else!"

"All you have to do is think about it."

"Thinking about it and touching it are two different things! I can't touch that pillow any more than I can touch you!" An uncomfortable silence fills the space between us. She lowers the pillow to her lap and looks at me deeply, like she can see every detail of me that I can't.

"Interesting . . ." she says quietly. Her eyebrows raise like she knows something I don't. She stands up, tossing the pillow aside.

"What's that supposed to mean?" I say, trying not to snap this time.

"You can move through the world, but you can't change it. And if you think you can't, you won't." Pink crosses the room, all business as she snaps a card facedown on her dressing table and anchors it with a bottle of nail polish remover. "That guy you wanted me to tail? The big, ugly one we saw in visitation with the messed-up eye? I followed him to his car when he left the Y and wrote down his tag number. The guy's name is Anthony Verone. His address and license plate number are on the back of the card."

"How the hell'd you get all that so fast?" Vehicle registrations in Colorado aren't easy to backtrack. She couldn't have gotten all this information so quickly on her own.

She jerks her chin toward the bar. "One of the regulars is in security. He's got a thing for my sister. I told him her car got dinged in the grocery store parking lot and I needed the guy's contact information. I gave him Anthony Verone's tag number and he pulled a few favors for me. What are you waiting for?" She gestures to the card. "Take it and go. That's what you really came for, isn't it?"

The card might as well be anchored in quicksand, facedown, the bottle perfectly covering Verone's address so I can't read it. I feel like I've just been schooled in the fine art of dealing information. "You know I can't."

"No, *I* know you can. *You* just haven't figured out how yet."

I drift to the dressing table and stare at the card, stalling. I know exactly what'll happen, but I reach for the card anyway. I try closing my fingers around it. When that doesn't work, I try scraping them across the surface. The card doesn't move, making me all the more frustrated to see what's on the other side. I wonder whose name is printed on the front. Who pulled a favor for an underage waitress in a nightclub, and what he expects in return.

"We had a deal," she says, smiling to herself because she knows she's got me. "I'll give you Verone when you answer my questions. And don't even think about backing out on our agreement. Verone's number and address are unlisted. I already checked." Pink crosses back to the sofa and drops onto it. She moves the pillow, suggesting I should do the same.

There's a challenge in it. A dare. But I don't take it.

I stay where I am beside the dressing table.

"What happened the night you died?" Pink leans forward, waiting for me to pay up. Her elbows are crossed on her knees, like she's ready to listen but not necessarily ready to believe.

I'm not ready to throw in all my chips, either. I settle for a cheap token and toss it out with about as much care. "My dad was messed up. He got mad. Busted my skull with a plumber's wrench." The words come out dispassionate and flat. Same as the million times I spoke them before my trial, infuriating the public defender who insisted he could save me if I would just crack myself open for the jury and bleed a few tears. That the judge might be lenient if he felt sorry for me. I never took the stand.

"We all know that part," Pink says, dismissing my story. "It made every news channel in Denver. I want to know what happened *after* you died."

One look at her face, and I know I can't renege on the deal.

The address I want is sitting on the tabletop, buried under a bottle of nail polish remover. The answer she wants is buried much deeper. A familiar numbness creeps through me, a thick, dampening fog. Remembering is like that moment when I first saw myself from *outside* myself. A dissociation from pain, from emotion. A self-preserving disconnection between body and soul. Talking about it feels an awful lot like dying. Like watching my blood run out of me until I'm so empty I don't feel anything at all.

Pink waits.

I don't know how long I've been lying on the kitchen floor.

I know I feel pain, but I'm aware of it in some distant, out-of-body way, the same way I know that I am wet and freezing. My father is yelling words I can't make out through the layers of noise. Ms. Cruz is screaming outside in the hall. She's leaning on the buzzer, loud and insistent, and rattling the doorknob. Then come the big, loud thunks, as if she's throwing herself at the door.

I open my eyes. All I see is red. Red sprays on the wall. A mangled red face wearing my clothes. Below me, the apartment is silent, except for the spatter of blood from the tip of a wrench and water dripping in the sink. My father is sitting in blood—my blood. I know the body on the floor beside him is me.

As I watch the scene unfold, trying to make sense of it, an odd sensation—a pull—drags me slowly toward the ceiling by my feet. Another anchors me to the kitchen, tethering me to the body on the floor by some connection I can't see. The connection strains as I float higher, to a series of small pops, like the snapping of threads.

A bubble of panic rises as I drift higher, farther from myself.

Sirens whine, growing louder.

Car doors slam in quick succession. Feet pound. Radios chirp and squawk in the parking lot outside.

Ms. Cruz is crying, "Hurry, please!"

The apartment door slams into the wall and my father doesn't look up when the police officers barge through. But he fights like hell when they drag him to his feet and struggle to cuff him. They're all too distracted to notice when Ms. Cruz slips inside. But I do. She backs herself silently into a corner as they take him away. She is crying, rocking, slipping down the wall, boxed in by their trail of red footprints. Her lips move. "I'm sorry," she says over and over again. I want to tell her the same. I never wanted her here. Never wanted her to see him. I reach out to touch her, to push her out the door, but she's farther away. I am slipping higher, inch by inch, farther from myself and closer to the ceiling.

The paramedics rush in. They're all over me in a rush to stop the bleeding, but I've already lost so much. Ms. Cruz pulls herself upright against the wall. My blood is creeping across the floor toward her, and the speed of it feels very wrong. It reaches my outstretched hand in seconds, consuming the book just beyond my pale fingers. What's happening to me?

Frantic voices talk over each other. Someone says they can't find a pulse. But that's bullshit. It has to be bullshit because my heart is racing and my lungs... God, my lungs are heaving and I'm shaking all over.

The kid on the floor is still. I panic. Scream out to them.

"I'm not dead! Listen to me!"

No one hears.

Pink's still waiting. I'm not really sure what she wants to hear. I look down at the floor. I don't want to see her staring at the hole in my head. She must be staring. Otherwise, I wouldn't be so damn aware of it, or so concerned with what she might be looking for inside it.

With an exasperated sigh, she stands up, snatches her apron off the lamp, and heads for the door. I have the same infuriating urge I had yesterday. To take her hand. To make her stop. To make her hear me.

"You don't want to talk? Fine," she says, grabbing the knob and swinging the door open. Something leaps inside my chest.

"It hurt . . ." I blurt out.

She pauses. She doesn't turn to look at me, but I know she's listening.

"At first. But then I didn't feel much. I passed out, I guess. Next thing I know, I was floating, out of my body. Like a balloon."

Pink pushes the door shut quietly. She leans against it, waiting for me to speak.

"I saw myself. Saw my dad. I heard the sirens coming. Then the police broke down the door and took him away."

She eases back into her place on the couch and looks at me. I've answered her question. I can stop talking if I want to—could twist all this around and make it her turn—but I don't. I've said enough to satisfy the deal but not to satisfy the urge to keep her here. Listening.

"The paramedics were all over me with tools and radios, saying they couldn't find any vital signs. So I panicked. I was kicking and screaming, but I just kept floating higher. It was like there was no gravity, nothing holding me down, but it was more. Like something was pulling me up by my feet."

I speak slowly, pausing long enough between breaths to study her reactions. Waiting for a narrowing of her eyes, a wrinkle of disbelief.

"The thing that was pulling you . . . What did it look like? What did you see?" she asks.

"Are you gonna give me that card if I tell you?"

She cocks an eyebrow, as if the answer is entirely dependent on me.

But the truth is, I couldn't see anything.

I thrash wildly, but I'm floating, the threads snapping and unwinding faster. Something's pulling me toward the ceiling. I blink hard against a white light. It's drawing me higher, and I claw at the air, terrified, as the paramedics count to three, then lift my body onto a backboard and press bandages to the flowing wound in my head.

Fabric tears, seams ripping as they cut off my shirt. They count together and thrust. One of them holds an oxygen mask to my face, but I'm slipping higher.

The paramedics put stickers on my chest. The defibrillator shocks me, and my body arches against the floor. I'm jerked down hard toward my body, and for a searing second I feel pain. But the threads feel like they're fraying again, and I know with a strange certainty that if I let myself go, there's no coming back. I lunge blindly for the fraying connection and drag myself down, hand over hand against the pull of the light, until I'm chest-to-chest with myself, staring into my own face. One side of my head is badly misshapen, the eye swollen shut. My hair and skin are saturated red.

"He's been gone almost five minutes." One paramedic breathes hard, sweat dripping down his face.

"Don't stop the compressions," says the other, still holding the oxygen to my face. "Come on, kid. It's not too late."

But I'm not so sure. The pull is relentless. It wants me to let go. And for a minute, I think maybe I want that, too. The closer I am to myself, the harder it is to hold on. It hurts to see myself this closely. What if I can't be fixed? I look to my battered face for an answer, but I can't even make out my own eyes. I don't know what I want beneath all these broken pieces. Or how much I'm willing to suffer for the consequences of what I'm about to do. All I know is I'd rather be trapped inside a broken body than risk being face-to-face with the unknown.

When the defibrillator fires again, my body lurches off the ground. I grab hold of the bloody boy on the floor, wrapping both arms firmly around his chest. My chest. I hold on tight, knowing my life depends on it. And I make my choice. I relieve the pressure on those last remaining threads, and I pull myself back home.

My mouth feels dry. I know it's only in my head, but the words still come out hoarse and brittle. "All I know is when the shock hit me, I grabbed myself and pulled. Everything hurt a lot after that. And sometimes I wish I hadn't." I've never told anyone this part before, and I'm not really sure why I'm telling Pink now. But as soon as I say it, something eases inside me.

Pink is quiet for a long time. Her eyes shine a little. "You were dead."

I shrug off a phantom throb in my head. "For six minutes. At least, that's what they tell me."

"But you held on. You came back. Why?"

It's a question I've asked myself over and over. But the answer makes me feel small and weak. I look away. "I don't know. Maybe I came back for Ms. Cruz."

"Doubt it," Pink says. "If that had been the reason, you would have stuck to her instead of climbing back into you. I see it all the time, people hanging on to loved ones too tightly. It just weighs them down. They get stuck here, and they can't let go. They can't move on to better things." Her eyes take on a faraway look, and she stares off into the pile of magazines.

"Better things?"

Her eyes lift to mine. "You know . . . heaven." She reminds me of Simpson, spilling over with hope I don't deserve. Waiting for me to eat it up and tell her everything she wants to hear. That I wasn't terrified of that light. That I wasn't petrified of what I couldn't see, waiting on the other side. That I didn't crawl back into myself because it's the only place I've ever been able to hide.

"Tell me the rest," Pink says before I can tell her she's wrong.

I think back to the weeks I spent at Mercy Hospital. I tell her the parts I remember. "I couldn't wake myself up, and the life support was still doing some of the work, but I was . . . aware. . . . I guess that's the best way to describe it. That's when I realized I could do this." I gesture to myself, not sure exactly how to put into words what I can do. "It was hard to control at first. Took a lot of practice, learning to move around like this. Every day, I'd try going a little farther. When I woke up a few weeks later, I thought that would be the end of it. But whenever I fell asleep, I'd travel. All I had to do was close my eyes and let go."

"Travel?" Her head tips curiously, as if she's never heard it described this way before.

"What would you call it?"

Pink scratches under her wig, thinking. "My grandmother told me stories. About people who had near-death experiences. People who'd seen the other side and come back. She said once someone's left their body, their mind sort of remembers how to do it. And if their mind is strong enough, they can propel their spirit—or consciousness or whatever you want to call it—between the astral planes at will. What you call traveling has a name. It's called astral projection."

She looks at me with some kind of twisted fascination, and I laugh derisively. "You make it sound like it's all scientific and important. Like I've got some superpower."

She throws herself back into the crook of the sofa and crosses her arms. The skeptical wrinkle I've been looking for is there now, and it's deep. "Yeah, because closing your eyes and going anywhere you can imagine isn't special at all. I can't think of a single person in the world who'd want to do that!"

"Look, I didn't get bit by a radioactive spider. And I don't own a damn cape. I wear a prison jumpsuit issued by the State of Colorado. I hate cats, so I'm not rescuing them out of any trees. And I sure as hell never saved anyone's life!"

"Back off," she says. "Nobody accused you of wearing tights."

"No, they accused me of killing someone!"

The lights on her dressing table flicker. Pink glances at them uneasily. I catch a glimpse of my reflection in her eyes and back away.

"You killed that boy," she says soberly. "But not her. Not Ms. Cruz. So why did the police think it was you?"

"Because I was in the wrong place at the wrong time." It's a line. A cop-out. The second the words leave my mouth, I know they're not enough to get rid of that damn crease between her brows.

"What happened to her?"

That's what I've spent the last four months trying to figure out. Four months searching for any connection between the man who killed Ms. Cruz and the boy I gutted, and coming up empty. After I was indicted,

I kept waiting for the police to find him. To find the truth. But no one was looking. Everyone was ready to put the knife away—to put me away—and close the case. I never thought I'd see it again, until Warden Somerville found it in Six's cell.

I haven't told the story in a long time. Whenever I start talking about it, all the circumstantial details build on one another, growing into a snowball of evidence that rolls straight for me. The more I try to explain it away, the guiltier I seem. But Pink's still listening, and the knife is back, and I keep talking, feeling like maybe something's changed.

"Ms. Cruz came to see me in the hospital every day after school," I tell her. "She'd saved these books she gave me from my dad's apartment and brought them with her. She read to me every day, waiting for me to wake up. After a few weeks, the doctors told me I was ready to go home. Only I didn't have one . . . a home. So Ms. Cruz started asking all these questions about custodial parenting and foster care. She told the hospital and the social workers she wanted to take me in. Like I was some kind of stray animal she could bring home and fix. But I was so messed up by then, and I didn't think there was anything left worth fixing."

There's a knock at the door, and Ms. Cruz marks her page before standing to answer it. She presses a finger to her lips, hushing the caseworker before the woman can step into my room.

"He's sleeping," Ms. Cruz says softly, ushering the woman out into the hall. I sift through the closed door after them. I've become good at this. I can pass through any wall, as long as I know what's on the other side. I've spent months slipping through doors behind nurses and lab techs, committing every inch of this place to memory.

By the time I catch up, they're deep in conversation. Ms. Cruz's posture is rigid, and she pushes her glasses firmly in place.

"Have you been able to locate his mother?"

"No. At this point, we're assuming she doesn't want to be found. In the absence of any next of kin, the hospital plans to release John into Social Services' custody tomorrow—"

"Tomorrow? Where will he go?"

I feel like someone's kicked the wind out of me, and I wonder if my body is still breathing. I circle them, anxious to hear the answer. My caseworker's messenger bag cuts deep into the shoulder pad of her suit jacket. My file is probably in there. Maybe even my mother's last known address. There has to be some mistake. If she knew, she would come. And everyone knows. It's been all over the news. She promised she would come back for me. So why isn't she here?

"The hospital won't allow him to stay any longer—"

"Is it the money? We can raise more money. The community has been very generous. I'm sure they'll give more if we—"

"The hospital has filed for Medicaid on John's behalf. It's not a matter of money. John is young and resilient. He's done very well in rehabilitation. The doctors feel he's ready to go home."

"John doesn't have *a home!"*

"We're working on placement options for him—"

"You're telling me they're kicking him out of here tomorrow, and you don't know where he's going?"

The caseworker blinks several times, as though to avoid looking Ms. Cruz in the eye. "I assure you he will have a foster placement ready before they discharge him." She makes a show of checking her phone. "Now, if you'll excuse me, I have to take this call. I'll be back tomorrow to sign him out."

Ms. Cruz and I watch her go.

They're kicking me out. Tomorrow.

Ms. Cruz charges after the woman, fighting her way down the bustling hall. I follow close at her heels.

"I'll do it!" she calls out, stopping my caseworker before she reaches the elevator. "I'll be his foster parent."

I freeze. My caseworker takes Ms. Cruz gently by the elbow and ushers her into a quiet corner. It's all I can do to collect my racing thoughts and follow.

"I understand you care about John very much, but do you really think that's such a good idea . . . under the circumstances?" She looks down her nose, as if appealing to Ms. Cruz to think hard about her offer.

Deep, angry lines cut into Ms. Cruz's brow, and I can almost hear the growl climbing its way out of her. I've never seen her like this before, and I'm not sure if I'm proud or ashamed to be the cause of it.

"If by circumstances you mean the crock of bogus accusations Mr. Conlan's defense attorney is throwing around about me in some last-ditch effort to distract the jury from the fact that his client beat his son to death, then you might want to consider hiring a lawyer of your own before slandering me again. Now, if you'll excuse me, I have to say goodbye to John and get my things. I'll be in your office in an hour to discuss his placement options."

I watch Ms. Cruz storm down the hall to my room. What did she mean about accusations? What could they be saying about her? None of this was her fault. All she did was give me a gift. A personal and deeply meaningful one. One I knew I shouldn't accept . . .

The truth sinks inside me like a stone.

I bolt down the corridor after her, sliding through the wall and snapping back into myself just as she opens the door. My eyes fly open and I sit up too fast.

"I can't go home with you." The words are out before I can take them back.

Ms. Cruz stops in the middle of the room. The color drains from her face and I know exactly what she's thinking as she slowly comes to stand by my bed. She's wondering how I could know. How I could possibly have overheard.

"The doctor told me they're discharging me tomorrow." The lies fly out as I rush to explain. "I know social services probably doesn't have a place for me. And I know you're a good person, and you'll want to do something nice, but you shouldn't. I don't want you to."

She's already done too much. Given me things I can never repay. And my father and his damn lawyer have thrown them all back in her face. Turned her gifts into something dirty for the sake of making him look like less of a monster by comparison. I should never have taken those books.

"Would it be such a bad idea?" she asks quietly, tipping her head to look me in the eyes. But my caseworker is right. It's a terrible idea.

"I won't go home with you." I turn to the window so she won't see what I really want. I feel it, etched all over my face. She'll see it, just like she saw how badly I wanted to keep those books, even as I tried to give them back.

"I want to do this, John." She touches my hand. "I can give you a home. Just until you turn eighteen. I'll sign papers and make it official."

I turn on her and snap, "Sign my name? Like you did with those books! I told you that was a mistake, and look what happened!"

Her wet eyes flicker over my scars and her lip trembles. I feel even uglier, hurting her like this. But there's no other way. She's stronger than she looks. Determined. So I have to be, too.

She steels herself with a deep breath, reminding me why I took those books in the first place. She won't take no for an answer. "John Conlan," she says, slinging her purse over her shoulder, "what your father did to you wasn't your fault. And it wasn't mine. You deserve a home just as much as you deserve those books."

She turns before I can utter another word. Before the welling tear behind her glasses can gather and fall. She swipes at it while she walks to the door. She doesn't give me another chance to argue. None of that bullshit I said matters. She sees right through it. Right through me. Without looking over her shoulder, she says, "I'll be back for you tomorrow." She leaves, and I'm left with the weight of all those books in my hands and the emptiness of a promise I've heard before.

"We argued," I explain, my throat thick. "The nurses in the hall in the hospital that day all heard us. Some of them testified. I told her I didn't want her as my foster mom. That I didn't need her charity. I left before sunrise the next morning. I never checked out. Just took a pillow and blanket and the clothes the social worker had brought me. I left the books on the nightstand, and I just walked out.

"I went to the high school and holed up in the old boiler room." My eyes skate to Pink's. I wonder if she knows kids hide there sometimes. If she's heard the rumors. "It's where I'd sleep when things were bad at home. Someone had left a blanket rolled up under some pipes, so I knew I wasn't there alone. But kids sleep there all the time, so I didn't think much of it. That's where I left myself. My muscles were tired from walking, so I laid down to give my body a break while the rest of me wandered around the halls for a while. It was Sunday. They were supposed to be empty. But Ms. Cruz must have come straight from the hospital, looking for me. She was calling my name. She knew I slept in the boiler room sometimes. She'd caught me coming out of there before. That was the direction she was headed when I found her. But she never made it that far."

I breathe past a lump in my throat. It's not really there, I remind myself. Just a ball of pent-up emotion that makes it hard for me to speak. "She was calling my name, looking for me . . . and then she stopped. Next thing I know, she was arguing with someone. When I found her, she was standing in the hall, shouting at the man, and this kid was watching. It was hard to see—the lights were out and the hall was dim. All I know is that he was tall and wearing a hood. He had a knife."

"What did you do?"

"The only thing I could. I left her. I ran back to get my body." My eyes burn and I wonder if deep inside the Y's concrete walls, the other part of me is crying. This is the first time I've told anyone this. These are the details I couldn't tell the police, or the lawyers, or the doctors in the Y—the gaping hole in my story, the missing details that condemned me. They would have found me guilty by insanity and sent me someplace else. But Pink's still listening, so I keep talking, tearing open old wounds and letting my confessions trickle out.

"I woke myself up and ran to help her. But I was clumsy and slow. I'd been in a hospital bed for so long, and I wasn't strong enough. I couldn't save her. The man with the hood stabbed her and ran. The kid—Cameron Walsh—he ran, too. I was too tired to chase them."

I'm too weary to run after them. My body's too heavy. I shut my eyes and shake off my skin, my limbs falling in a heap alongside Ms. Cruz's. I'm faster this way. I can find them.

I search the walls and doors for traces of blood, traces of the hooded man, but there's nothing. I circle the building, searching frantically for foot tracks in the dirt, but the grass is brittle and brown and bare. Nothing.

I turn back for the school, shock and disbelief giving way to rage. How could they kill her and just disappear?

But then I hear it. . . .

The high-pitched whine of the hinge on the back door. The one with the bad lock I'd used to get into the school earlier.

I look just in time to see the door snap shut. Someone's inside. Every terrible possibility flashes through my mind—custodian, vagrant . . . cop.

Whoever it is, they're about to walk down that hall and find me.

I race for the door, but something jerks me by the shoulder. I swirl around and stare at the empty space behind me.

Another hard jerk, but no one's there. I feel a tap-tap-tap *against my shoe.*

Then a whisper in my ear. Hey, are you dead?

Suddenly, I'm yanked off my feet, crashing through walls and doors. The wind howls against my ears. I'm being dragged through space, bricks, and sidewalks, and exit lights are blurring by. I'm falling toward myself, and I see him. The kid who was here earlier is kicking my shoe.

My body doesn't move. He waves a hand in front of Ms. Cruz's face, then eyes her open handbag. Its contents are scattered beside her. He sidesteps a dark puddle of blood, and bends to snatch something off the floor. He stuffs it into his pocket. It all happens in the span of a few seconds, but it feels like time stands still. As I hurtle toward my body, I see his red hair and the back of his T-shirt, kneeling over me. He's shaking my shoulder. Saying something.

"Hey, are you dead?"

I snap back into myself, hard. The impact hurts, and I cry out with the needlelike pain, every nerve awakening as my spirit slams home. And that's when I smell it. The gagging, coppery tang of blood is thick all over me, bringing everything back in a rush.

My eyes fly open. The kid's fingers are at my throat.

I suck in a fast breath, scrambling and sliding in the blood. My hand brushes something, and I grab it. The handle of the knife is wet and cold in my hands. I don't think. Just bring it up hard and fast, through his shirt and skin, until I feel it slide home. The boy's blue eyes bulge. I'm holding him up by the hilt of the knife, his full weight falling against me. His face is close enough to count the acne on his chin. Close enough to conjure his name out of an old memory of freshman gym class. Cameron. Cameron-something. A strange shadow passes behind Cameron's eyes, and the light in them dies out.

I shudder, shaking off the memory of Cameron's face, until I'm the only ghost left in the room. "That's where the police found me. No one believed me about the man in the hood. He must have been wearing gloves. The only prints on the knife were mine."

Pink doesn't say a word, and for a moment I feel that knife in my hand all over again. I can cut the tension in the room with it. I head for the door. "I told you, I'm no superhero."

"They said it was a crime of passion." Her voice catches in her throat.

I stop.

"They say you were involved with her, and that's why she gave you those books." Pink stands behind me. "Is it true? Were you in a relationship with her?"

I know what the lawyers said. What the jury believed. What the TV news people spread like a fungus, coating Ms. Cruz's good name in dark and slippery filth. They said we had a fight. That I killed her because I didn't want her to be my foster mother. That I'd wanted her to be more. That maybe she *was* more. They said I killed Cameron Walsh because he'd been living in the boiler room and probably heard the scuffle and got in the middle. Bullshit. All of it, bullshit.

"It wasn't like that," is all I have the energy to say. This whole thing was a bad trade. I'm tired. I don't have much time left. And she wasn't going to give me Verone anyway.

"I believe you," Pink says softly. "Don't leave."

I feel the tug of threads as she tries to take my arm but can't, like I'm being pulled in different directions. "I have to go."

When I get back to my pod, the corridors are quiet. Ben's still asleep in the chair. I settle into myself and lie there, waiting for sleep to take me, but my mind is somewhere else. Far enough away that when the sun rises in the morning, I feel like I've been running all night.

The next morning, when I wake up, Officer Rickers is already waiting for me. He looks as tired as I feel. I hurry into my jumpsuit and brush my teeth fast, hoping no one bothers to notice him standing there.

"Just go," whispers Ben. "I'll make your bunk for you. Don't worry. I won't tell."

I walk fast out of the pod, forcing Rickers to keep up. I head straight for the yard, knowing it's the only place that'll be empty this early. I hold back my flinch when the door buzzes open, and step into the cold air outside. It's freezing, and I wish I'd thought to bring my hat. I ought to find a place somewhere in the sun where I can get warm, but I stick to the shadows. I can't afford to let anyone see me alone, talking to a guard, when I'm supposed to be doing chores. I already have privileges the others don't have, and no yard fight will wash me clean of a reputation for being a snitch if I'm not careful.

"You should have tossed my cell the other night," I say when we're far away from the pod door. He's new. Maybe he doesn't know how these things work yet. "People are gonna start talking. They'll assume I was the one who ratted about that knife in Six's cell." I look over my shoulder to make sure no one's watching. "I don't know if this whole big brother thing is a good idea."

Rickers winces, looking crestfallen. His blue eyes are creased at the edges and ringed in shadows, and the end of his nose is ruddy with the cold. "I get it. And I'm sorry. I thought I was doing you a favor with the warden."

I don't want to be a smart-ass and say it, but these early-morning one-on-ones aren't doing me any favors. "Look, about what I told you the other day. Don't worry about it. Let's call off this whole mentor thing and call it even. I should have told you, Officer Monetti gets around. It's no secret." I know, because I've seen him a few times in the bar down the street from the Y. I can't remember him ever being there with the same girl twice.

"How'd you know, anyway?" There's a curious twinkle in his eyes, like he's studying me. "I mean, it must have cost you something, right? You had to pay somebody to check out my house. I can't just call it even."

Even if I used a phone, or arranged it during visitation like everybody else would, I wouldn't tell him. It would tip the scales on an already-precarious balance of power, and I don't want to give him that much.

"Don't worry about it," I say. "The best thing you can do for me is treat me like everybody else so nobody gets pissed off and tries to kill me."

Rickers smiles. "I get it. You kids are a lot like the ones I used to work with in probation—always ready to dive back into trouble just for the sake of keeping up appearances. Too afraid of what people might think if you say no. But I want you to know, you can be real with me, Smoke. If anyone gives you a hard time about this, I've got your back."

He pulls his hat low over his eyes and reaches out a gloved hand. "It's cold. We should get you back inside." I can't tell if we're breaking a deal or making up some new one. When we shake on it, I have a strong sense of déjà vu that leaves me uneasy inside. I look up into his eyes, the same clear blue eyes that watched me through the slat in the Segregation cell door, asking if I had everything I needed, both of us knowing the question had been all about him.

Rickers lets me lead the way inside. But this time, he gives me some room, hanging far enough back that I hope nobody notices.

After first chow, I head to the library to see Martín. The library cart squeals from somewhere in the stacks, and I find him, plucking books from the shelves and loading it up to make his rounds.

"Finished the ones I gave you already?" he asks without looking up.

"Not yet." I'm still not caught up and he knows it. I can feel his disappointment. I came in here for the first time when I got here four months ago. Martín was shelving books. He'd noticed the leather-bound collection in my cell and been eyeing them for weeks. He'd also noticed I don't read them. So when I started coming by the library, checking out books, he asked if I'd be willing to trade for them. Which got me thinking... I told him I wouldn't part with those books, but maybe we could work something else out. I started feeding him information about his family and checking in on his sisters. Mostly it involved hanging out in their family room while they all watched late-night TV. But sometimes I'd sit under the open windows of their bedrooms, listening to phone calls to their boyfriends in Spanish, trying to reconcile their tone of voice and their body language with what I could figure out from a few familiar words. I'd tell Martín how they're doing in class, who they're dating, and who's getting in trouble after school. In return, he spread the word. It started slowly at first, a few books at a time. But Martín has been in the Y a long time and his library cart is a passport into every pod. He knows a lot of people. It didn't take long for the boys in the Y to start calling me Smoke, and now I have so many orders backed up my threads'll probably snap for good before I ever get to them.

"I need to ask you something," I say quietly to Martín when I'm sure we're alone. "Have you ever heard of a guy named Anthony Verone?"

Martín nods. "He got out of here about a year ago. He did a few years in C pod. Aggravated assault."

"Any idea who he was hanging out with?"

Martín thinks for a moment, like he's retracing the steps of his library cart. "He shared a cell with Six for a while. Did his time, and transitioned into probation right before you got here. Monetti fought it tooth and nail—he hated the kid—tried like hell to get him flunked from the program, but the warden signed off on his release."

They were cellmates. That explains Verone's connection to Six. And obviously, they were still friends. But how did Verone get into visitation without anyone recognizing him? He must have bribed his way in the same way Pink did. The warden has been doing a lot of housecleaning the last few years. Maybe all the turnover in staff made it easier for him to get through.

All the better. If I were to sneak around Verone's place and follow him around for a while, I could probably turn up enough dirt on both of them to keep Six off my back. And if I don't come up with anything valuable enough, I can always rat them out to the warden. But then there'd be a big shake-up in the administration office. Somerville would crack down, people would get fired, and who knows if Pink would ever get to come back. I should have stayed at the club last night. I should have made Pink give me that damn business card. Instead, I walked out, and she's probably still pissed off at me.

"Got any travel books?" I ask.

Martín looks up at me. The top of his head barely reaches my shoulders, and yet his eyes seem old enough to have seen the whole world. "Where do you want to go?"

I think back to the break room. To the postcards on Pink's mirror. The glossy, full-color centerfold of the Great Wall of China on the coffee table. To the beaches on the covers of the travel magazines scattered on the floor. Martín stacks his arms full of books and sets them on a table beside a narrow window, just wide enough to frame a sliver of the Rockies beyond the yard wall. I spend the rest of the day reading about places I'll never see.

When I get to the club after Lights Out that night, I enter through the back wall in the alley. The blue-haired waitress is there, digging in her purse for something, and then she's gone, shutting the door behind her, oblivious to me.

Pink's coat hangs on the rack. She's sitting on the sofa with her legs curled under her, flipping pages of a magazine and pretending I'm not here. The card with Verone's name on it is in the same place she left it, the address still hidden. I wave a hand over it. Then the other. I poke it with a finger. Nothing happens.

I feel her watching me.

"I just came for the card. And then I'll be out of your hair."

She snaps her pages.

I pick at the edges of the card, but I can't get any traction. "Did you know there are one hundred and thirty-five rides and attractions in Disney World?"

She snaps another page.

"Or that the Vegas Strip is 4.2 miles long? Who would have thought you could fit sixty-two thousand hotel rooms in just over four miles?"

She heaves an exasperated sigh.

I drift to the sofa and read over her shoulder. "You know that thing people say about the Great Wall? How it's so big you can see it from the moon? That's not really tru—"

She slams the magazine on the table, crosses her arms, and stares at a wall across the room. "What do you want?"

"I want what you promised me."

"Fine, I get it. You gave me two questions. I owe you one back." She kicks off her shoes.

"One?"

"One plus the card makes us even."

"No," I say, calling her out on her bullshit. "You said you'd give me the card if I agreed to meet you. We were even the minute I walked through that door."

"If we were already even, then why'd you tell me all that stuff?" She peels off a sock and tosses it at me, just missing my head. I don't even know why I'm here. I should in my cell, sleeping. I was up all night after I got home from the club, too keyed up to sleep, tossing in my bunk, thinking about my conversation with Pink, waiting for the guards to wake us all up anyway. Somerville didn't shake the place down last night, but that doesn't mean he won't.

"You owe me two questions," I grumble, dodging the subject that's been bugging me all night.

She strips off her other sock, considering. "Fine, but you already asked one, so you only get one more."

"I never asked you anything."

"No." She points at the card. "But you were going to."

I want to throw something at her, too. But I can't. Which only proves that she's right.

"Do you want to know how to pick up the card or not?"

She's infuriating as hell, batting those bug-leg lashes at me and drumming her fingers like she's the one in a hurry.

"Fine."

"All right, let's start with something easy." She backs against the sofa and drops into it. Dust clouds lift from the fabric, and she pats the space next to her. It's late. Almost eleven. For all I know, Somerville's already tossing cells. And I have other questions—more important ones—like what Pink is doing waiting tables on school nights in a dive like this.

I turn my back to the sofa. Take a deep breath and let myself fall right through it, like a bag of sawdust, breaking into a swirling, cussing cloud across the splintered wood floor. I leap to my feet, brushing myself off and only making the cloud worse, while Pink laughs herself into hysterics and slides to the floor.

"See? I told you!" I say in vehement defense of my pride, as if I intended to humiliate myself just to show her I was right. "I told you I can't do it!"

She snorts, tears streaking her eye makeup.

"If you know so much, why the hell is it that the floor is always solid but everything else is just"—I wave my hands around the room—"I don't know . . . unreliable? Tables, chairs, walls—nothing wants to hold me up." I sit on the floor beside her, just to prove my point, and wait for her to choke back the last of her giggles. She muffles them with her hand, overly conscious of her wide-open smile. Her teeth aren't perfectly ordered and straight like the girl in Somerville's photos, but they come together when she smiles in a way that's sort of spontaneous and pretty. Her laughter is almost contagious, and I feel my cheeks warm in spite of myself.

The laughter distills into a strange sort of light-headedness and we just stare at each other until it passes. When her breathing quiets, she tips her head to me and breaks the awkward silence.

"Do you ever doubt the ground will be there?"

I'm not sure I understand.

She lays her hand palm down on the narrow stretch of knotted planks between us and looks into the dark holes of my empty eyes. She doesn't look afraid of them. She looks deeply, thoughtfully. Like she might actually see something inside them.

"It's always there because, in your mind, the ground is solid. You never question it. You know it's going to hold your weight. And it does . . . because you *think* it will." She pulls her wig off and drops it to the floor. The pink strands scatter on impact, then rise up in a static halo. She taps her temple. "The way you look when you project yourself, the places you can go, the things you haven't figured out how to do yet . . . it's all in your head."

She stands slowly, arching up in an easy stretch, her knuckles crackling softly.

"Then what are you doing here?" I catch myself asking aloud.

She trades her laughter for a bone-tired smile. "Not all of us can climb out of ourselves and run away, you know. I guess, in a way, I'm sort of trapped here, too."

I think about the travel magazines piled high on the floor, the postcards and stickers taped to her mirror. I wonder if she looks at them like I look at those pictures in Somerville's office, knowing it's as close as I'll ever get to the people and places inside. "What was the place you wrote about in Ms. Cruz's class? The place where you weren't supposed to be?" I feel like I'm sitting behind her, trying to read her journal over her shoulder, but she's hunched down over the words and I can't see.

She presses her lips tight. Ms. Cruz said she didn't have to share with anyone she didn't want to. And I don't know why I want her to give me this one piece of her so badly.

"It's late," she says. "My sister's a dancer at the club next door. She's the one who got me the job here. Her shift starts in an hour, and I need to get home to take care of my mom." She reaches down with an open hand, even though I wouldn't begin to know how to take it. "Come on, John Conlan. I think I'd like you to walk me home."

THIRTEEN

I wait for Pink in the alley behind the break room. A single streetlamp at the opening and one tiny bulb over the exit door dimly light the filth spilling out of the Dumpsters and the swirls of spray paint on the walls. I imagine the air probably smells like urine and desperation. I kick at an empty bottle. It doesn't move.

She's taking too long and I'm twitchy waiting. It's a long walk to my old neighborhood. Ben could pull me back any minute, and I don't like the idea of leaving her alone. I forgot all about the damn business card inside, and I hope Pink remembers to bring it. I berate myself for wasting my trade on a personal question, rather than something important, like showing me how to pick it up myself. Or how to take her hand.

And she never did answer my question, about why nothing ever holds me up. Or maybe she did, and I just wasn't satisfied with the answer.

Whatever. I'm doing a fine job of teaching myself. I concentrate on the brick wall at my back, psyching myself up to give it my best James Dean lean, when the door swings open, flooding the alley with light. Pink comes out wearing her ugly blue coat and a wool snow cap. Her brown hair curls out from underneath it and clings to the side of her face. She struggles with two oversize trash bags, strained to near bursting with bottles and cans, that make her wobble side to side.

I reach out to help, before I remember that I can't. Her lip curls sardonically around frosty puffs of breath, and I step aside, feeling foolish as she slings the bags into the Dumpster.

She slaps together her fingerless gloves, as if wiping her hands of the night, and tilts her face to the sky. Snowflakes fall in lazy drifts, freckling her cheeks. She smiles wide and lets her mouth fall open, catching them on her tongue. The huge sleeves of her coat are splayed out to her sides as she starts spinning in circles, her pink hat tipped back far enough to make her dizzy.

"Come on, John," she calls out to where I lurk in the shadows. "Check out the sky! It's beautiful! There must be a million stars up there!"

I can't help it. I look up, too. "It's cloudy. It's snowing." I can't see a damn thing.

"Doesn't mean the stars aren't there." She takes a deep breath through her nose. "I bet you could go anywhere. I've never seen the ocean. Have you ever been to the ocean?" She stops, snowflakes catching in her eyelashes and in her hair. Her smile is lighter without all that lipstick.

Light as the falling snow, and just as quick to dissolve when I come back with, "You used up your questions already."

"Well then, give me one more."

"No." No, I've never seen the ocean. No, I can't go anywhere. And no, I don't give anything for free. I jam my fists in my smoke pockets. "I don't have time. Come on, I'll walk you home." My eyes never leave the ground.

“Time?” Her voice bounces off the brick walls, assaulting me from both sides. “You’ve got nothing but time.”

I shake my head and keep right on walking. “You don’t understand—”

“Oh, I think I do.” Her tone is like a push between the shoulder blades. I turn around and she steps right up to my face. Close enough I can see the snowflakes on her cheeks and the freckle on her upper lip. “Like it or not, you’ve got your whole life ahead of you, so when are you going to start acting like it?”

“A life? You call this a life?” I gesture at a body that’s barely visible.

She walks right through me with a look of disgust. “I’ve talked to dead people who aren’t as hopeless as you,” she mutters.

I fight to piece myself together, despite the swirling wind. It turns over sheets of old newspaper and tosses empty cans, cutting through me like I’m not even here.

“So I guess you know a lot of people in my shoes, then, huh?”

I watch her walk away, replaying the conversation in my mind, trying to figure out where it went wrong, so I can figure out how to . . .

“Wait!” I call after her.

She didn’t say she’s talked to people who’d *died*, like me.

She said, *I’ve talked to dead people.*

I stiffen as the implication coalesces into something tangible, hope and possibility.

The dead can’t speak for themselves.

But what if they could?

“What do you mean, you’ve talked to them?” I call after her. She’s almost to the mouth of the alley, just a silhouette in a puffy-sleeved coat.

“Haven’t we already been over this?”

And then she just stops, midstride. A figure stands in the opening of the alley, blocking her exit.

"Hey!" I shout.

But Anthony Verone doesn't hear me. He can't hear me. He thinks she's alone.

Pink steps backward, cautious and slow, not bothering to look behind her. She has nowhere to go. The back door to the club only opens from the inside. Beyond that is a dead-end brick wall.

Verone advances slowly.

"John?" she whispers.

"I'm here," I say in a low voice beside her. It's my fault she followed him. My fault he's here. Whatever he does to her, it will be on my hands. "I'm right here."

Verone's gait is uneven, like his knee might be messed up, and as he nears, I can just make out the swelling in his left eye. A pair of brass knuckles glint on his right hand. Pink stifles a small, involuntary sound. Her eyes flick to the door. I know what she's thinking, but the music inside is too loud. She'd only have a few seconds to knock before he's right on top of her, and no one would hear.

Verone stops a few feet away, waiting.

She'll have to fight her way out.

The light by the back door flickers. Verone's eyes dart to it, one dark iris, one too swollen to see.

"Take him on your right. He can't see much out of his left. And he's got a limp. If you can get past him, you can probably outrun him," I say, keeping my voice low and even.

She balances her weight, feet shoulder-width apart.

Her breaths come in rapid, shallow puffs.

"Keep your eyes straight ahead. There's an empty bottle beside your right foot. When I say three, you're going to grab it by the neck and smash it hard as you can, against the right side of his face. Take out his good eye. Then haul ass out of here and don't look back." The pink ball on top of her cap wobbles with her tight nod, just enough to let me know she's ready.

I circle Verone, coming up behind him. He flexes his fingers around the brass.

It's all in your head.

I stretch out my index finger and push my mind into his right shoulder.

I miss once.

I focus my mind and try again.

Verone stiffens. He turns.

"Three!"

Pink dips, snatching the bottle and backhanding it in a wide arc, shattering it against the side of his head. Verone staggers and Pink dashes to the opening on his right.

I think she has a chance, but he snags her under her arm, jerking her off her feet.

"John!"

Blind and howling, Verone yanks her back, shaking broken glass from his head. He sways and buries his face in his free arm, but his other fist has her by her sleeve.

Two hands grab my shoulders. I spin around, my fists swinging through empty space. No one's there.

"John!" Pink flails under the flickering streetlight, throwing her weight and putting up a fight.

I run for her, but something's got me by the back of my shirt. It's pulling me back. "John, wake up!"

"Let me go!"

The lightbulb shatters, and the alley is dark.

I'm being jostled and pulled, and blood's roaring in my ears.

"John, wake up!"

I'm yanked hard off my feet. Streetlights blur. Wind's whipping all around me. A suffocating pressure knocks the breath out of me, and a thousand hot needles pierce my skin as I'm sucked back into my body.

Shaking, I grab Haggett by the wrists and launch myself at him, throwing him backward into the chair. Metal crashes as I tackle him to the floor, knocking over his footlocker and sending its contents flying. I slam my knee into his chest and bring my wobbly arm up to swing, skin and muscle settling into place as I wind it back into a fist.

Ben cowers and covers his face, babbling and shaking while I breathe hard and wait for the dizziness to pass. Every muscle aches. My eyes tear against the overbright light, and my skin's prickling like it's on fire. I'm assaulted by the smell of piss and Ben's stale breath. Stomach turning, I wait for the nausea to pass.

When the room stops spinning, I lower my fist and fall back against the bedframe. Ben peers at me with wide eyes through the cracks between his fingers. A wet stain blooms between his legs.

"What the hell was that all about?" he sputters.

The lights are flickering on all down the cellblock. A guard hollers, loud enough to drown out the echo of Pink's screams.

My throat's tight, and it burns when I swallow. I shut my eyes and press a hand to the cold tile. "Just a bad dream."

FOURTEEN

Ben stands at the door, watching the guards search cells down the pod. I sit on the edge of my bunk, edgy and impatient, watching the back of Ben's knees. The piss stain stops just north of them. His arms hang low, hands folded over his crotch, strategically dangling his beanie, so the guys in the cells across from ours won't see.

"When do you think they'll get to ours?" Ben asks over his shoulder.

It's the same question I've been asking myself. *How quickly can I get out of here and make it back to the alley? What will be left of Pink when I do?* On the other end of the pod, guards drop mattresses and slam footlockers in a steady rhythm, calling out when they find stuff we're not supposed to have. We could sleep while we wait for our cell to be called. But none of us ever do. We all waver on our feet, watching who gets searched, what gets found, and who gets passed over so we'll all have gossip to trade around the chow table by morning. A real young kid in one of the cells across from ours rubs his eyelids and yawns.

"Not much longer," I hope.

They're two cells down now. When the guards call out "pornographic magazines in the lower bunk mattress," the boys handcuffed in the hall set to arguing and pointing fingers at one another. I want to pass through the bars and pound the crap out of both of them. Only it's my own damn fault I was dragged out of the alley at the worst possible time. I was the one who suggested Rickers search my cell, too. I have no choice but to stay awake and wait, worrying about what might have already happened to Pink.

Antsy, I get up and stand beside Ben, angling my face to see as the guards move on to the cell beside ours. One thing's for certain. It was no coincidence that Anthony Verone showed up in that alley wearing a pair of brass knuckles. He came to kill her. Or send a message. Six could have set up the hit. He saw me with Pink during visitation. Is this retribution for the locker toss that cost him his knife? I scan the long hall of orange jumpsuits peering through cell doors, but I already know he's not here. If he were in the pod, I'd know. He'd take credit with one smug, well-timed look. And then I'd kill him. Supermax be damned, I'll rip the skin off his neck before he can promote himself to Seven, and take two broken bones for every one of Pink's in trade if I find out he was responsible for this.

Across the corridor, Bumper sits alone in his cell, leaning against the door, looking like he might fall asleep. He and Six are tight. But if he knew what was supposed to go down in that alley tonight, he'd be gloating, too. Six has been in the hole for a couple days now. Which means he's not talking to anybody, much less Anthony Verone. Which makes me wonder if maybe I'm wrong about this.

What if it wasn't Six who set this up? Maybe Anthony Verone is just some hired thug. Who would have hired him to hurt Pink? What about that guy Panagakos? The one who got rough with her in the club when she wouldn't take his free drugs in exchange for letting him put his paws all over her? Maybe. If he thinks she ratted him out to Holmes. A knot tightens in my belly. I was the one who told Holmes that Panagakos was giving freebies to the waitresses in the club. It would be my fault if he did.

I close my eyes and try not to imagine Pink lying there in the cold, or the way blood from a head injury spreads like a slow bloom. How quickly it cools. Or the color of a body when there's nothing left in it. The shakedown is taking too long. The steady rhythm of the search has gone quiet. The guards are whispering in the corridor to each other, their radios turned too low for me to hear.

I flinch at the slam of the next cell door, which means it must be our turn. I stand up fast, ready to get the search over with. It's just for show. It'll be over quickly. But Rickers and the others walk right past.

"Search is over. Get back to bed," Rickers calls down the pod, without so much as a passing glance at my cell.

Relief floods through me. I want to run through the concrete walls, but I wait, heart pounding, listening to the muttered swears that roll through C pod. The guards'll give us a minute before Lights Out, to pick up our stuff and take inventory of what's been taken from us.

Ben rights the toppled chair and sits down hard in it, covering his groin. His face is red, cheeks pinched with cold and embarrassment, like he's impatient for the lights to go out, too. I feed bad for making him piss himself. I can feel his narrowed eyes as I pick up one of my schoolbooks from the floor, dust it off, and lay it to rest on top of my footlocker where it belongs.

I sink into my bunk, waiting for the lights to go out. I pull my blanket over me and shift around uncomfortably. Every nerve is standing on end, shivering with fatigue and adrenaline. It's a struggle to stay in my body until I know it's safe to leave.

I try not to think about Pink.

I turn and look at Ben. A half dozen of his magazines still lay facedown where I knocked them to the floor, their pages torn and bent from our scuffle when he woke me up. Ben just stares at them, like they weren't that important anyway. For the first time, I find myself wondering if Ben ever had anything that meant more to him than those magazines.

"What were you stealing when you got busted?" I ask. Someone as honest as Ben would only break the rules for something he needed badly. Something worth risking his life over. And the defeated hunch of his shoulders makes me want to know what it was.

"I wasn't stealing anything." His face screws up as if he bit down on a bitter memory. "I was looking for someone."

"Did you find them?"

He wipes his nose on his sleeve and doesn't answer right away. Just folds his arms and leans away from me in his chair, like I'm trying to take something from him.

The squelch of walkie-talkies filters down the hall from where a group of guards remain clustered, talking in low tones. Too low. Too many guards for this time of night. The cells are quiet, all of us feeling stripped bare and waiting for the dark.

"No," Ben says, surprising me. He fidgets, glued by his wet underwear to the seat. His eyes are shiny, and I'm not sure if maybe he's been crying.

The lights snap off before I can look too closely. A slim ray of light from the corridor illuminates Ben's face. He massages his concave chest where I threw him into the chair. There's nothing to him. Just the husk of a boy, like maybe he died a long time ago. And something about that makes me both sad and hopeful that maybe no one can hurt him any worse than he is already.

One day I'll pay him back for making him piss himself. Maybe he'll tell me who he's looking for and I'll find them for him.

But not tonight. Only three hours until Lights On. Only three hours left to find Pink.

You've got nothing but time.

I shut my eyes and let go. I try not to worry about my threads breaking, or what will happen if she's wrong.

I pass through the wall, not bothering to wait for Ben to fall asleep. Rather than cut through cells, I stick to the corridors. The memory of Rico watching me makes me wonder if anyone else here can see me, too. C pod is dark and I sail right through, but there's a light on in one of the cells in B pod, and the corridor is clogged with uniforms. A line of guards stand at the opening of Simpson's cell. As I get close, Warden Somerville rounds the corner with two more guards, his dress shoes falling softly on the tile.

The fruit cocktail and sugar packets come from the mess hall, where Simpson works. Probably he's about to get his ass handed to him, plus a couple nights in the hole. But just then Simpson comes walking right out of his cell, right past the guards. Their hands are folded and their heads are down. They don't seem to notice or care.

I double-time it, closing the distance, not bothering to shout Simpson's name, because he won't hear me anyway. Where the hell is he going? If he's going to Segregation, an officer should be going with him. Why did the guards just let him walk away?

I pull up short in front of his cell and watch him fade into the shadows at the end of the hall. Simpson is barely there—a thin white figment like a cloud of smoke. He steps right through Warden Somerville's chest and disappears. I turn, throat thickening at what I know is waiting inside that cell door. Simpson hangs by his bedsheets from his bunk rail. His lips are blue. A note is folded neatly over his collar.

I back away, head shaking. This wasn't supposed to happen. It was an honest trade. I left nothing on the table for karma. I gave Simpson what he paid for. Guilt and regret press in all around me until I can't remember what it feels like to breathe. This can't be my fault. If he didn't already know his mother was dead, he would never have felt a need to ask. And I don't deal in bad information.

I run, breathless, faster than I've ever run before, unsure if I'm running toward something or running away. Flashes of memories chase me through the walls, through the mesh. I hurtle through the darkened yard, and it's like the ghosts of my past are grabbing at my ankles, the people I've lost coming back to haunt me—my mother's black-and-blue face, the copper-brown smears in Ms. Cruz's hair, Simpson's white skin and purple lips, and . . . no . . .

I run until I block out everything else. I run until all I see is Pink.

FIFTEEN

I tear out of the Y parking lot to the distant blare of sirens and head straight for the club. Headlights rush in both directions despite the late hour. Interstate 25 is an eight-lane gauntlet that grinds me to a halt. I stand a hair's breadth from the highway, toeing the white line. Tractor trailers whoosh by, and the rush of their wake throws me back and scatters my resolve. I've never crossed the line before. Have always chosen the safest route and run the extra few miles to the nearest off-ramp in either direction, running with the flow of traffic, then doubling back. But I can't afford that much time.

I suck a deep mental breath and hold it, wondering how many lives I have left to test, but feeling somehow like I deserve this—whatever hell I am about to walk into. I step over the line. Headlights race toward me, head level. Truck level. It's barreling down. Wheels humming loud, then louder. I turn in to the light, facing it straight on. I bring my hands to my face. My scream is swallowed by the grind of pistons and the rumble of air brakes as the force of ten tons of steel crashes through me. The world is reduced to the rush of wind that follows. It pulls the ground out from under me. I am everywhere and nowhere, twisting and swirling over the highway, tangled up in flurries of snow. I grasp at the scattered pieces of myself and pull them back together.

No pain, no blood. Just the flash of taillights as the trucker slows, then resumes speed. I barely have time to take stock of myself before another set of headlights is on me. I haul ass, running across the broken white lines, dodging at first, then resigning myself to the rush of lights and steeling myself before leaping in front of them. Each car that passes through me is like a fist to the face. A provocation. Frustration and fear give way to determination, and I dare all eight lanes to try to kill me.

When I'm on the other side, I push myself faster until the street-lights blur. I have never felt so alive. I've all but forgotten my threads.

I stand at the mouth of the alley, left breathless by the emptiness of it. Fresh snow blankets the pavement, inches deep, smooth and undisturbed. I pause at a mound beside the Dumpster. At the fresh red smears on the puffy blue fabric that shows through where the snow has drifted, revealing the empty sleeve of Pink's coat.

I turn back to the street, but there's no trail. Not even my own. If she managed to get away, she would have circled back to the club or tried to make it home.

Unless she didn't get away. What if she floated out of the alley, like Simpson. Like me. What if she left no footprints in the snow?

I throw myself through the rear door of the club and explode into the break room. Two waitresses are inside, taking off their wigs and heels. Neither of them are Pink. The clock on the dressing table says 4:00 AM. Closing time. Maybe she made it home.

I swear loudly, not caring if either of them can actually hear me, and I push myself through the wall into the hallway, poking my smoke head into every open door. The manager's office has to be here. Rosters, pay stubs, employment applications . . . something with Pink's address.

There.

At the end of the hall is a closed door with a sturdy-looking handle and a keypad. I step into it with the same reluctant determination I felt stepping into the first lane of an interstate highway, and bounce off it like a concrete median.

FUCK!

I pace the narrow width of the hall, chambering what little information I have like a weapon.

I don't know where Pink lives. Not exactly. And it would take too long going house to house, peeping in windows trying to find her.

But Pink knew where Verone lives. The card. She said his address and plate number are on the back.

I blow back into the break room, praying the card is still there. I find it, exactly where Pink left it last night, under the same bottle of polish remover. The girls are pulling on sweatshirts and slipping into their jeans, makeup already gone and hair tied back with rubber bands. I stand there waiting, hoping one of them will pick up the bottle of nail polish remover and reveal Verone's address. But they gather their coats and purses and head for the back door.

I lean over the table, sagging as the last of my hope slips out of me. The exposed edges of the card mock me, and I waste too much time trying to pick it up a dozen different ways. I earned that card, dammit! I answered all her questions. Just like I answered Simpson's. And now Simpson is dead. And Pink . . .

The door slams shut behind the last of the girls.

I want to punch someone or throw something. I want to put my fist through a wall. I swear, winding my arm back and swinging it hard across the table, loosing all my anger at Six and Verone and Simpson and myself on that damn bottle. It flies across the room and smacks into the wall.

My arm is still raised, and I'm panting, staring wide-eyed at the stream of toluene spreading across the floor.

It's all in your head.

The card is exposed on the table. I know where to find Anthony Verone.

Verone lives in a small bungalow in an old neighborhood on the west side of I-25. The roof sags, and the porch lights are busted out over a cracked front walk grown through with weeds. I can just make out the muffled laugh track of a television, and I drift around the side of the house, desperate for a glimpse inside. Every inch of glass has been carefully covered in blankets and sheets, and every door reinforced with shiny new dead bolts.

A crooked sign—BEWARE OF DOG—hangs on a shoddily constructed fence. I ignore it and walk right through. The postage-stamp lawn is patchy and overgrown under the snow, scattered with piles of frozen dog crap.

A rattle makes me pause—a *clink, clink, clink* like chain unwinding from a spool. It's coming from a doghouse at the far end of the yard. The Rottweiler's wet jowls appear first, followed by the rest of him. He growls, low and deep in his throat. When I inch backward, he bares his teeth. They glow bone white in the dark.

It's all in your head.

I hold perfectly still. Then take a slow step forward.

"Shhhh," I whisper, holding out my hand and crouching low as I slink toward him. His eyes narrow, but I keep coming. His nostrils flare as I come closer. He sniffs, alternating between growls and whines. He seems confused by my lack of scent. I wait for him to ease back onto his haunches, then I offer him my palm. He licks the drool from his lips and makes a soft, snuffling sound, lifting one leathery paw and trying to shake. "Good boy," I say gently. I reach to scratch his ear. He looks up and whines, expecting the touch of my hand, but it never comes.

"I'm looking for a girl. Maybe you've seen her?" I say, even though I know that hearing and understanding are very different things. He rests his chin on his forelegs.

Then he cocks his head and perks an ear toward the house, a second before Verone's back door opens.

Light spills into the yard. The dog springs, barking deep and loud. He launches through me like a bullet, jerking to a stop at the end of his chain.

"Call off your damn dog, Verone," a man shouts from the back porch.

"Fuck off." Verone slams the door, and the yard is dark again, except for the burning red cherry of the man's cigarette as he crosses the lawn to leave. Cussing, he fumbles with the gate. His gruff voice is familiar in a hazy, out-of-place sort of way. By the time I collect myself and get clear of the dog's chain, the man's already down the driveway, the interior lights of his car coming on and then off as he climbs inside. There's a low rumble as the engine turns over. I cut through the fence and head for the street, hoping to get a look through the windshield.

The headlights snap on, blinding me, and I throw an arm over my face. The stereo cuts on and the engine revs, and I leap out of the way just before he peels out.

The yellow Camaro passes under a streetlamp, the racing stripe on its tail like a thick black bow, practically gift-wrapping the driver's identity for me. The car's big chrome pipes howl down the street, and I blink against dust and rubber smoke, watching Officer Monetti drive away.

SIXTEEN

I stand staring at the empty stretch of road where Monetti's car just disappeared. The sun thaws the horizon from black to violet, melting away the stars one by one, leaving me no choice but to head home. I don't want Ben to have to haul me back the hard way. Even though my threads are pulling me in opposite directions, I abandon my search for Pink. For now.

I creep into my skin just as Ben leans cautiously over the edge of his bunk, peering at me in the dusky light. I blink, letting him know I am both awake and alive. But even though my body is accounted for, I'm not so sure about the rest of me. It's like I left part of me back at Verone's, and I can't snap it back to the here and now. What the hell was Monetti doing at Verone's house? Had *he* hired Verone to pay me back for ratting out his affair to Rickers? And most important, where the hell is Pink?

One thing's for sure, I can't wait for tonight to find out. But who would believe me if I told them what I know? Except maybe Rickers. He still owes me for that last trade—I haven't cashed out any favors yet, and if I have to choose between dinner at the warden's house and using up Rickers's goodwill making sure Pink is alive and safe, then it's settled.

Or at least it would be. If Rickers weren't working night shift.

Ben jumps down from his bed in his underwear. I don't blame him for not sleeping in the chair. Not after what I did to him last night. His jumpsuit is hanging over the end of his bunk to dry, and he steps into it, wearing a sour face. "Come on, man," he says, looking relieved that he doesn't have to wake me. "Time to get up."

We make up our bunks in silence and wait for the buzzer. The halls are already humming with rumors, everybody talking up Simpson's suicide like it's the only form of entertainment in the place. They probably wouldn't be so chatty if they knew he was still here.

We step into the pod. It smells faintly charred, like breakfast burning. I'm not hungry. All I can think about is finding Pink. I follow Ben to the mess hall, calculating my next opportunity to get out of my skin. It itches, hot and confining. I mindlessly scoop up a plastic tray and slide it along the chow line to the clatter of warming pans being dropped into place and the scrape of metal ladles against their shallow bottoms. The air is sticky, thick with hot grease smells and the humid exhales of the steam trays that separate us from a line of sleepy-eyed servers.

I slow, a shiver jogging up my spine and raising the hair on the back of my neck the nearer I get to the serving station. A new kid stands in Simpson's old spot, struggling to keep up with the line. I pause, waiting for him to spoon hash onto the trays in front of mine. He looks all wrong. Out of place. I can't help thinking Simpson should be here instead. As I watch, the new kid's face pales. He rests his ladle on the metal lip of the warmer, and a visible shudder passes through him. His face scrunches up and I think maybe he's going to be sick, until two black holes crest and emerge from behind his eyes, rolling out from his brow like a swirl of dense fog. It swallows up the kid's features and twists into a smoky human face that hovers, momentarily disembodied, like two people trying to occupy the same space. I glance anxiously up the line, but no one seems to notice. No one else can see. It's like I'm looking in a mirror, seeing my astral self emerge out of the boy's orange jumpsuit. But it's not me. I'm here. In line. Clutching my tray with cold white knuckles. And he is there, on the other side, holding the illusion of a ladle in the smoky curl of his hand.

The hazy apparition searches the faces in line, making me cold all over. Even though he has no eyes, I feel them when they find me. He freezes, his shape coalescing in the stillness, the same way I've seen my own do a million times before. The name on his pale white jumpsuit says SIMPSON.

Someone nudges me from behind, and I move forward, slowly, hardly feeling my feet. Simpson waits for me to come up the line, until we are eye-to-eye, his black holes endless and wide. When he speaks, his mouth stretches open like a slow yawn, slightly out of time with the words.

"Did you find my mother?"

I look down at my tray, darting quick glances at the other servers. At the other boys in line. They don't react. Don't hear it. It's a whisper inside my head. Only for me.

Cold sweat beads over my temple and I walk on, trying to keep my tray from shaking.

"Please?" he pleads, standing on his toes to see me, until he's keening loud enough to rattle my soul. "Please!"

I set my tray down next to Ben's and sink to the bench, shutting my eyes and trying to ignore Simpson's wails. I swipe my forehead with my sleeve, wicking away the guilt, but the sour smell of it lingers on me. It isn't my fault Simpson's mom couldn't live without him. It isn't my fault he couldn't live with that truth. We had a deal. A fair trade. I don't owe him anything. If I pretend he isn't here, he'll eventually move on. Won't he?

"You look like hell," Ben says.

"Just tired." I shovel my hash around my plate but can't force it past the tightness in my throat. I push my tray across the table and tell Ben I'm not hungry. Watch him scarf down both his breakfast and mine. I check the wall clock no less than a dozen times, my legs restless under the table. Simpson finally quiets, but the sooner I get out of the mess hall and find Pink, the better I'll feel.

"Where are you headed after breakfast?" Ben asks through a mouthful of toast.

It's Monday morning. I'll be in classes all morning. Four hours of algebra and English and SAT prep, all of it wasted and pointless. I raise my chin, checking out Six's table. His seat is still empty. It's a risk, leaving my body during the day, with guards and convicts coming and going through the pods. One of my biggest threats is still locked away in Segregation, but that doesn't make it any safer. If I'm smart, I'll wait for Lights Out, and give myself eight uninterrupted hours to find her. But I can't wait that long. Every minute of not knowing is like threads ripping, letting my mind wander to dangerous places: the alley, the club, Verone's living room. I'm already so out of my mind I can't stay in my body one more minute.

"I'm not feeling well. I'm going back to bed," I say. "You?"

"Wish I could skip. I've got orientation for the next two weeks. I don't know why they don't just call it gym class. I've never run so many laps in my life."

We dump our trash and head back to our pod. The guards watch us through the control room windows when we split off at the corridor. I rap on the glass, pointing to my scars. Then I mouth to Officer Brooks that I have a headache and point to my cell. If it were Officer Monetti, he'd tell me to get over it and drag me to class. But Officer Brooks is sympathetic and waves me through. They all know about my plates, and my headaches are nothing unusual, so I hope no one bothers to check in on me.

I don't waste time taking off my shoes. I dive into my bunk and close my eyes, never so desperate to get away from myself. I'm releasing my muscles and willing myself to sleep in a hasty malpractice of my usual ritual, when Officer Brooks startles me awake.

"Conlan, you up for a visitor?"

My eyes snap open. Every muscle tenses. "Who?"

"Control room says your cousin is here. Some kind of family emergency. That's all I know."

I stand up too fast, barely managing to shrug back in my skin. Officer Brooks lets me lead the way to visitation without cuffs or shackles, and my feet are light and too quick, forcing him to keep up. As soon as I clear the door to the visitation room, I arch up on my toes, searching for Pink's curls over the partitions. My pulse quickens when I don't see them at all. I almost walk right past her. She's sitting in front of an empty window, curled in on herself, hair tucked up tight into a Denver Broncos ball cap with the bill pulled low over her eyes.

I sit down slowly, taking her in, assessing the damage. She hugs her sweatshirt tight to herself, every inch of skin covered. Her throat's wrapped in a high turtleneck, and her hands are tucked inside her shirt cuffs. My eyes climb up her sleeves and sweatshirt, over her set jaw and the press of thin lips, and come to rest on her cheekbone. The skin is scraped raw, her eye tinged purple.

"You're okay," I breathe, forgetting to pick up the receiver.

Our eyes lock through the glass as we both reach for the line.

"You tell me what that was about, John Conlan," she hisses into the phone. "I followed that guy for you, and then he tried to kill me. What the hell did you get me involved in?"

I shut my eyes. She deserves an answer. I just don't have one. When I open them, she still looks pissed at me.

"How did you get away?" I ask.

"Unzipped my coat. I slipped out of it and took off running."

Quick thinking. Pink's smart. Capable of taking care of herself. I've seen her lug burdens twice her size, and hurl them into the air like they were nothing. She doesn't need my help. The cold look on her face confirms she doesn't want it, either. But the load I've dumped in her hands is far too heavy, and I hate myself for not being able to reach through the glass and take it back. Somehow this is my fault. I just haven't figured out how. I'm certain either Six or Officer Monetti hired Anthony Verone to hurt Pink . . . to get to me.

"He hurt you?" I gesture to my own cheek, mirroring her as she gingerly touches the wound.

"I fell. Slipped in the snow when I came around the corner." She blushes and covers the scab with her hand, but she's got no reason to be embarrassed. She's a fighter. She might be banged up and bruised, but she's here. Alive. And that's what matters.

"What about you?" Her eyes drop to the purpling bruises at my throat.

I shrug. "No big deal." No sense worrying her about what's going on in here. Monetti knows where to find me. So does Six. Either one of them could kill me on a whim. The more important question is, can they find her?

"You shouldn't be here. How did you get in?"

"I told the lady at the desk it was a family emergency, and I slipped her a fifty." She winces, the cost of admission to see me here is probably as much as she made waiting tables last night. "At first she said no, that I'd have to come back on the weekend during visiting hours, but when she noticed my bruises, she told me to wait here and she would have someone go get you."

"Where did you go last night? I came back as soon as I could, but you were gone." I hope like hell she went back to the club or picked up a cab and rode around town. Went anywhere but . . .

"Home."

My grip tightens on the receiver. It's easy to pick up a warm trail in the snow. "Did anyone follow you?"

"No, I lost Verone in the alley. I looped the block once and doubled back to be sure."

I let out the breath I'm holding. I'm trying to think of a way to keep her safe without scaring her. To warn her without saying too much. "You shouldn't walk home alone for a while. And you shouldn't come back here."

"Are you going to tell me what this is all about?"

Before I can answer, Pink spins in her chair and lowers the phone to look behind her. My side of the glass is silent. The screams are coming through the receiver in my hand. I leap up to see over Pink's head, at the chaos erupting through the window on the other side of the room. In the hall, a woman's crying. Shouting at a guard. She pushes her way past him and runs toward us, bursting through the door into the visitation room before he can grab her.

"Where is he? Where is my son?" She falls on knees so thin they don't look strong enough to hold her. She pounds the floor with bony fists, snot and tears streaming down her face. Two officers rush in behind her. "I demand to see the warden! I want to see my son! I know he's here!"

"Mrs. Simpson"—the guard reaches down to her, like she's a lost child—"you can't be here. You need to come with me."

"No!" she shouts, shoving his hand away. "The shelter told me he was here! I need to see him! Where is he?" The frail woman pushes to her feet and charges toward the partitions. The guards gently pry her back by the elbows, their hands cautious as if she might break. She struggles out of their grasp and surges toward us, pushing Pink out of her seat. "Where is my son? I want to see Matthew!"

I stand, tripping over my stool. The cold truth races through me like liquid metal, my hands heavy with the weight of it. I drop the receiver. It swings by the cord.

I saw Matthew Simpson's mother, dead in her bathtub, rotting in apartment 3B. But she was not this woman. Not this woman who's looking at me with Simpson's eyes.

Her mouth moves. "Please help me find my son." Her small voice sways like a pendulum through the phone by my feet.

I swallow, shaking as the guards peel her from the window and draw her away. Pink reclaims her seat, pale and confused. Slowly, she puts the receiver to her ear, waiting for me to do the same. I kneel and pick it up, still feeling partly outside my own body.

Simpson's mother came back. She came back. This isn't supposed to happen.

Suddenly all these ghosts in my head . . . my ghosts—Ms. Cruz, Cameron, Simpson, my mother—they're creeping into my mind, haunting me. My chest is tight with the memory of their faces.

Numb, I reach for the receiver.

Pink's trying to get my attention, knocking on the glass and calling my name. Her voice sounds distant and urgent, like her screams in the alley last night.

I lift the receiver slowly and do the only thing I can to keep from hurting her again. I give her the same line I give the ghosts inside my head to keep her from becoming one of them. "Go away," I tell her before I disconnect. "I don't want to see you anymore."

SEVENTEEN

On the way back to C pod, I stop outside the library door and knock on the frame to get Martín's attention. He glances up from the card catalog, darting a quick look between me and Officer Brooks.

"I need a book," I say.

Brooks checks his watch. "Make it quick."

I follow Martín between the stacks. He asks in a hushed voice, "Everything okay, man?" There's a crease around his eye I've never seen before.

"I haven't had time to check on your sisters. I'm sorry." I choke back the guilt, clearing my throat of things I can't control. I have to focus on what I need and what it will cost me. "I need one of those Sherlock Holmes books. You got any of those saved up for me?"

Martín studies me, like he's not sure he wants to deal. I don't blame him. I'm behind on my side of our bargain. He's eye level with the bruises on my neck, and his gaze lingers on them long enough to ask the question for him.

"Monetti," I say quietly, careful not to let Brooks hear me.

Martín hands me a short stack of books from his cart, already marked with my name on the hold slip.

I thumb through them, tossing aside two. The last one catches my eye, and that's the one I take. I sign the card in the back and watch as Martín stamps the return date. He hands it over but doesn't immediately let go. "Hope this gets you what you need."

"Don't worry. I'll have someone check on your sisters this week. I promise." I tuck the job under my arm. On my way out, I jerk my chin at the growing pile of books on his cart marked *HOLD FOR SMOKE*. "Send all the others back for me. After this, I'm done."

He raises an eyebrow. "You sure about that?" Not judging. Just making sure I've thought it through.

I have.

I carry the small paperback in one hand, detesting the feel of its slick cover and its marked and folded pages. I'm done. Done dealing information. Done trading in lives. One last deal, and then the universe and I can call it even. Karma's teaching me a lesson. The universe wanted me dead, but I didn't stay that way. So it took Ms. Cruz in trade. Then I took Cameron Walsh's life, so Karma took mine . . . again . . . and put me here. My life is gone, taken. I have nothing left to give—no way to balance my bad trade. I cheated Simpson. And now the universe wants something from me.

But it can't have Pink. Not if I can tip the scale some other way.

I tuck the book inside my jumpsuit and head back to my cell to wait.

When classes let out, I head straight to the yard. It's a mess of orange knots amid piles of melting snow. I find Holmes playing hoops with his buddies and see Ben standing among them, watching the game, safe within their circle. This will work, I tell myself. It has to.

I wait for Holmes's eyes to swing to mine, then I pull him off the court with a look.

"I can get you the list you want by tomorrow. Wednesday at the latest," I tell him when we're alone.

"Libro told me you were on vacation. What changed your mind?"

"I need something. . . ." I begin. But there's no time for nickel-and-dime bullshit. "I need an advance."

Holmes licks his lips and looks pointedly at the bruises on my neck. A knowing smile creeps over them. "That's unfortunate. I don't do advances, Smoke."

I look around the yard, trying not to come off as desperate as I feel. Every shadow seems to stretch in my direction, reminding me how little time I have to make this right. "The way I figure it, you owe me."

Holmes folds his arms over his jumpsuit, a gesture that probably appears relaxed to the guards but looks like a wall going up to me. "Yeah? How the hell you figure I owe you?"

I weigh my words carefully, reminding myself we are not "friends." "There's a waitress at that club you had me look into. She's run into some trouble since you came down on Panagakos for those freebies I told you about." I don't come out and say Panagakos is involved, because I don't think he is, or that Pink was the one to roll Panagakos under the bus, because she wasn't. Instead, I let Holmes infer what he will, hoping his rigid sense of loyalty will sway him to keep an informant safe. "You have people outside who can keep an eye on her. They can protect her. That's all I want in exchange for the list."

Holmes shakes his head and reclines against the wall, one leg propped behind him until we're eye level. I can picture him on the outside, leaning on the hood of some expensive car. His brother has money. Contacts. People who owe him favors. Enough pull to pay for the pricey attorney who'll probably keep him here, shielded under a mountain of legal documents and red tape until his twenty-first birthday. "That's a ballsy request on a day like today, Smoke. People are second-guessing the reliability of your source after what happened to Simpson. How do I know you'll make good?"

The memory of Simpson's mother clawing at the glass gnaws at me, tearing away the thick skin of the person I was before. But I can't let it show. Can't let him see that I'm second-guessing myself, too.

"You don't."

Holmes surveys the yard, wincing against the late-afternoon sun. He pushes off the wall and straightens up slowly, his decision made. He looks down at me, a palpable shift in the balance of power when he finally speaks. "You have twenty-four hours, Smoke. Don't fuck this up."

When afternoon recreation is over, Officer Rickers is waiting in the pod. He's freshly showered, his blond hair combed neatly back and his ruddy cheeks clean-shaven. He's early. His shift doesn't start for a few hours yet, and I hope like hell he's not here for a brotherly visit with me. Instead, he collects the members of our Monday afternoon counseling group and escorts us to Dr. Manning's room, his aftershave trailing behind him. I don't ask him what he's doing here so early, or where Officer Brooks has gone. I don't want to seem too friendly in front of the others. But I'm curious.

When we get to the counseling room, I take my seat in the circle, pulling the chair backward a few inches from the tight ring Dr. Manning always sets us in. Everyone else does the same, twisting it out of its suggested shape and leaving Dr. Manning alone in the middle.

A few eyebrows lift around the circle. Officer Brooks always waits outside, watching us through the window. But Rickers follows us into the room. We're all looking at him as if there's a new guy in the group, and our inquisitive stares draw Dr. Manning's attention.

"Charlie, what a pleasant surprise." Dr. Manning turns in her chair and flushes pink. She smooths her hair and stands to greet him. "It's good to see you."

Rickers's cheeks seem a little pinker as well. They exchange a clumsy handshake that lingers a moment too long. "It's good to see you, too."

"It's been a long time. I don't think I've seen you since we worked those probation cases. I was wondering what happened to you. How've you been?"

"I've been good."

"How are things with . . . ?"

"Lisa? That didn't end up working out." Rickers scratches the back of his neck. His voice takes on a shy, self-effacing quality that matches his smile. "But it's fine. I've been working here in the Y for a while. Night shift. Guess that's why we haven't run into each other. We should get together and catch up sometime."

Bumper lets out a wolf whistle. Dr. Manning clears her throat loudly.

"Where's Officer Brooks?"

Rickers tries to look polite while Oscar makes suggestive tongue-faces in the air. Skivvy wraps his arms around his own shoulders, like he's making out with himself. "Officer Brooks had a thing to go to at his kid's school . . . talent show or something. And I figured I could use the overtime."

Dr. Manning shoots us a look. Oscar and Skivvy freeze.

There's an awkward silence, and we all look on with raised eyebrows. Everyone except Rico, who stares at the floor.

"Well, I have to . . . you know . . ." She gestures to us without looking.

"Sure, no problem," he says, walking backward toward the door. "I'll be . . . you know . . . right outside. If you need me," he adds hastily. Oscar and Skivvy start massaging their own nipples and mouth *if you neeeed me* to each other across the misshapen circle. Rickers doesn't look amused.

Oscar, Skivvy, and Bumper cover their mouths, struggling to suppress their laughter as Dr. Manning turns back toward the group. She takes a minute to compose herself, pulling on her therapy face while she scrutinizes us.

"Fun and games are over, gentlemen. Time to get to work."

Skivvy and Oscar are still choking back the last of their dying giggles, and she's looking impatient. The door shuts quietly behind Officer Rickers. The next thing out of Dr. Manning's mouth sucks all the air from the room.

"By now, I'm sure you've all heard that Matthew Simpson took his life last night."

We're silent. No one moves. Not even Skivvy.

Dr. Manning's face is puckered with judgment, as if the tragedy was the theft—the *taking* of a life. Looking around the hard faces in the circle, it's clear we've all come to a different conclusion. Simpson didn't take his life. There wasn't anything left to take. He just made the choice to end it.

Rico crosses himself, his chin tucked tight to his chest.

"The holidays can be a difficult time—"

"This didn't have shit to do with the holidays." Skivvy's face twitches as he looks around the group for confirmation. "I heard it had something to do with his mom."

"I heard she died," says Oscar.

Bumper curls in on himself, quiet.

Oscar shakes his head, absently stroking the scars on his forearm. "I lost my mom when I was twelve, man. That's some rough shit to get over." But I'm not sure he ever did. Oscar's in C pod because he burned his house down when he was fifteen, while his stepfather was still sleeping inside it. The guys in the pod say that when Oscar got here, he was angry enough to burn down the whole damn world. I wonder sometimes, watching him kid around in group, where he hides all that rage . . . if it's still smoldering away inside him. I wonder if someone were to break down his door and breathe life into those memories, if the backdraft would kill everyone around him.

"I don't remember much about my mom," says Skivvy, rubbing the tattoo above his eye like maybe he's trying. "She's been in jail since I was five. I live with my grandmother, and she's as old as the dirt. She's got a pacemaker and wears diapers and shit, so it probably wouldn't surprise me if she went to the old-folks' home in the sky, you know? But if my mom was still around, and she died, I'd probably freak out, too." Skivvy shrugs and twitches a couple of times. "My grandma says my mom's out now, but she ain't allowed to come visit. So I guess I don't get to see her no more."

Manning leans back in her chair, lips parted and eyes darting between Oscar and Skivvy as they bat memories back and forth about their mothers. When they fall quiet, Manning turns her attention to Bumper and me.

"Today's group has taken an interesting turn. One, it seems, you all can relate to. Your groupmates have shared some deeply personal thoughts. I'm sure they'd be open to having you join the discussion."

Bumper folds his arms tight to his chest.

Dr. Manning taps a pencil against her notepad and bites her lip. "I'm going to try something new," she says, inching forward in her chair. "Since this group has been so reluctant to share, and today I feel like we stand a chance at making real progress, I'm going to give you all a little push. An incentive—"

"Incentive?" Skivvy squints, blinking forcefully. "Like a reward?"

"Yes, Steve, exactly like a reward." Dr. Manning turns her attention to the rest of us. "Oscar and Steve already earned theirs. They'll each get a pass on work detail this afternoon for their willingness to contribute to group."

Skivvy and Oscar bump knuckles and exchange crooked smiles.

"I'd like to give the same opportunity to Ricardo, John, and Berto." Skivvy's leg bobs, ticking away the seconds while Dr. Manning waits for us to weigh the risk against the reward. Work detail—what Warden Somerville calls "afternoon chores"—is a hodgepodge of custodial tasks, everything from cleaning showers to mulching the yard to scrubbing floors.

Rico touches the cross at his throat. "See, I heard something different about what happened to Simpson. I heard the devil made him do it."

"What's that supposed to mean?" Oscar looks at Rico like he's crazy, but Rico's looking at me.

"The devil does things like that. He'll come to you while you're sleeping and whisper lies in your ear."

Skivvy cups a hand around his mouth and whispers to Dr. Manning, "I think you need to up his medication."

"Whatever, man," Rico says. "Believe whatever you want. But

Simpson left a note saying he felt guilty for what happened to his mother. Someone told Simpson his mother was dead and that was a lie. I heard the guards talking. They're saying Simpson's mom was here in the Y this morning raising all kinds of hell, looking for him. Someone was dealing some bad information. And that's why he's dead." Rico glares at me, fear and accusations etched deep on his face.

I feel exposed under his stare. It guts me. Rico saw me walk through his cell walls. Saw me head in Simpson's direction right before they found him dead. He thinks I'm some harbinger of death, come to take Simpson's soul. Sad part is, I don't disagree. I screwed up, and now Simpson's ghost is stuck here indefinitely, trapped in some kind of purgatory because of me.

"Tell us how this makes you feel, Ricardo. How does what happened to Matthew make you reflect on your relationship with your own mother?"

"You want to know about *my* mother? My mother is in heaven, *que descanse en paz*. The devil can't touch me."

But Rico doesn't know what I know. That just because your mother's gone—because you've already died that slow death once—doesn't mean you're safe. You can be killed over and over again. Once for every person outside these walls you care about. The devil can wear your own father's face, a hood, a badge, a set of brass knuckles . . .

"John? Berto? Anything to add?"

Bumper and I lock eyes across the circle.

My mom left me alone with my father when I was eight. She promised she'd come back for me, but I haven't seen her since. Not even when the news broke that he'd been arrested for killing me. She didn't come back the first time I died. Didn't burst into the courtroom and fall to her knees. Didn't collapse in tears for me when my second life was over.

Maybe she was so far away by then she didn't know. Hadn't heard. I could share that, and earn points with Dr. Manning. No harm in anyone knowing there's no one left outside to hold over my head. Maybe Bumper will do the same and leak a secret. One I don't already have.

But one look at Bumper tells me his shell isn't cracking—there's no reward big enough to break his resolve or make him bleed for this group.

I cross my arms, mirroring the look on his face while I consider my next move. "I'll take the mop."

EIGHTEEN

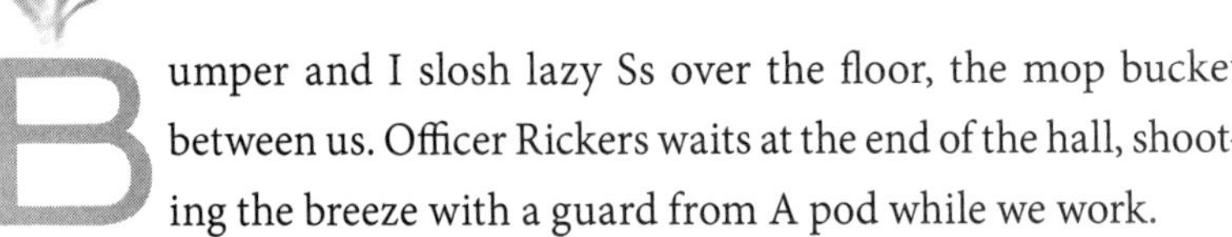

Bumper and I slosh lazy Ss over the floor, the mop bucket between us. Officer Rickers waits at the end of the hall, shooting the breeze with a guard from A pod while we work.

I anchor the head of my mop in the bucket.

"Where'd Six get the knife?" I say low enough that Rickers won't hear.

Bumper slaps his mop against the tile, spraying water on my legs. "I don't know what you're talking about, man."

"You know exactly what I'm talking about."

He mops faster. "You don't know shit. Shut up and keep up, Smoke. I ain't missing chow because of you."

"Maybe you're right." I pull my mop from the bucket. "I mean, how the hell would I know anything about the asshole your mom's dating. The one who busted her lip last week."

Bumper's mop stops moving. A cloud of gray water seeps from its ends. "What'd you say?"

"You heard me."

"You're lying. You don't know nothin'." He sops up the puddle and pushes it away.

"I know where she lives. I know he spends your mom's paychecks on Jim Beam and slots. I know your momma tries not to cry and wake your little sister when he hits her." I wait till Bumper's knuckles are good and white around his mop before cinching the truth tighter. "I know the license plate, make, and model of the car he parks in her driveway. . . ."

The suggestion trails like an invitation while Bumper mops the same circle of tile over and over again.

I shrug and start scrubbing. "But, hey, what the hell do I know?"

"You tell anyone, and I'll kick your ass so bad you'll be in the infirmary till your twenty-first birthday." He mops the same spot, hard and fast. "Six got the knife about a month ago."

"From who?"

"Don't know. All I know is he got it from someone inside."

"Inside?"

"That's what I said."

"Who sold it to him?"

"He wouldn't say." Bumper casts a cautious glance over his shoulder, but Rickers is busy checking his phone. "He was afraid to tell anyone."

Inside could be anyone: cafeteria workers, supply truckers, custodians, mechanics, therapists, guards, lawyers, nurses, administration . . . The Y employs hundreds. But who among them has access to the evidence from my trial? Who could break chain of custody without getting caught, and what did Six give them in return?

"What'd he trade for it?" I ask, struggling to stitch together threads that don't seem to connect at all.

Bumper jerks his mop handle toward his chest, looking offended. "What the hell do I look like, a priest? Six don't confess his shit to me." He slams the end of his mop into the bucket, but keeps the bucket where it is, teetering halfway through a job we should have finished by now.

Rickers calls our names and taps his watch. I don't have much time left, so I toss Bumper a bone.

"The guy's name is Ray, and he drives a black Dodge Ram." Or at least he did Saturday when I last ghosted around Bumper's neighborhood. "You get the rest when you tell me how the deal went down." I put my hands on my hips and lazily stretch my shoulders, making a show of it for Rickers.

Bumper wipes the wiry black hairs on his lip. We've only mopped about twenty feet of tile, but he's sweating. Six scares him, same as he scares everyone else. He has a long reach, a broad and tangled web of gangbangers outside the walls of the Y, just like his friend Anthony Verone. If Six catches Bumper trading information, he'll kill him in his sleep. Or worse, pay someone like Verone to take it out on Bumper's family. Bumper bites his lip, weighing his options, probably trying to decide who's the bigger threat: his mother's drunk boyfriend or his own cellmate.

Rickers slips his phone in his pocket and gives us a long look. We're out of time, so I give Bumper a push.

"We're done here." I stick my mop in the bucket and push it closer to Rickers.

Bumper blocks the bucket with his foot. He talks fast, before he can change his own mind. "We were working the laundry about a month ago. All I know is Six went to the guards' locker room to get the towels. He came back wheeling a bin full of dirties. The knife was in it. I saw him pull it out and hide it in his jumper. I asked him where he got it. He said it was none of my fucking business. That was it."

"Was it already marked when you saw it?"

Bumper pales. "How'd you know that?"

Exactly as I suspected, the knife had been marked for Six. Six didn't find it by accident. He was the intended recipient of a carefully arranged trade, executed by someone inside the Y. But I still don't know what he paid for it.

A bead of sweat trails down Bumper's chops. His eyes are black with fear and regret. The nauseated look on his face tells me I have everything he can give me, so I make good on our agreement. He nods tightly, committing Ray's name and license plate number to memory, and we resume our work in silence. Our business is done. A fair trade. Neither of us will speak of it again.

NINETEEN

The pod falls quiet after our final head count. No one talking. No one throwing insults or pillows while we wait for Lights Out. All of us too conscious of the fact that tonight's count was one man short. I collapse onto my bed. Ben climbs into his bunk above me. I don't bother to ask him to sit in the chair and watch me tonight. He's tired. The whole place is tired. Between the cell searches and Simpson's suicide, all the fight's been sucked right out of us, and I can't see anyone bothering us tonight.

When the lights snap off, I listen to Ben's soft breaths. I wait until they draw out, slow and deep. I want to sleep, too. To wake up tomorrow and pretend today never happened. But I've got one last trip to make. One last deal to do. I close my eyes and let go of my body. I make a quick pass through the control room and listen to the guards, but they're talking football and vacation. Doesn't sound like they've got any surprises planned for tonight, and I walk out of the pod, to the East Wing.

The desk in visitation is dark, barely illuminated by the soft glow of a computer monitor and a closed-circuit screen that mirrors the empty room. I drift through the metal detectors, where visitors are scanned and patted down, then past the lockers used to hold handbags, wallets, and keys, and anything else the guards don't permit beyond the red line painted across the floor—the one Simpson's mother ran right over. I pass through the desk. The clipboards are stripped of yesterday's visitor logs and a new kid will sleep in Simpson's bunk tomorrow, as if Simpson was never here.

I study the black-and-white image on the closed-circuit screen. The camera has a clear shot of the desk—the chair pushed up to it, and the back of the computer monitor where I'm standing. It feels strange to look at the picture and see only an empty room. To see this place without me in it. I think about my last conversation with Pink, when she'd tried to explain why I couldn't sit down. How it was all in my head. I try easing onto the rolling office chair, but I can't manage to turn it toward me, or hold it in place. Instead, it swivels away. After three tries, I give up and just step through it.

I stare at the computer. At the mouse and the keyboard.

I can do this. Just the tap of a finger. No different from tapping Verone's shoulder in the alley the night before. I look back and forth between the phone and the computer. The phone seems easiest, so I lean over the keypad, concentrating hard on the "speaker" button.

I focus my mind and poke it with my index finger, once. Twice. But no click. No connection. What if last night was a fluke? What if I can't do it again?

But I don't have any choice. I think of Six and the knife. I think of Monetti, chewing his gum while he strangles me. I think of his loud yellow car, peeling down Anthony Verone's street. I think of what Verone did to Pink.

I roll my shoulders, cracking my mental knuckles like I do before a fight.

It's all in your head.

I focus my thoughts and try again. I'm startled when a dial tone echoes through the room.

I press nine and get an outside line. Then slowly, one digit at a time, I punch the other ten numbers I saw under Six's bunk.

The line rings. Once, twice, five times before rolling to voice mail. A computerized, anonymous voice asks me to leave a message, and I disconnect.

Strike one for the night.

Exhausted, I stare at the Microsoft logo bouncing over the computer screen. Somewhere inside it is the information Holmes needs. The list he's expecting by tomorrow. I nudge the mouse with my mind, and I'm surprised when the screen flickers awake. The cursor blinks at me. I don't know this program, but there's a tab marked VISITOR RECORDS. I bend low over the keyboard, struggling to make out the down arrow in the dim light. I poke where I think it should be. The screen goes black again, and the Microsoft logo bounces in slow motion, mocking me as the damn thing goes to sleep.

I throw my hands up, taking it out on the swivel chair. The damn thing wouldn't hold still a minute ago and now it won't get out of my way. I kick the wheels hard, anger surging into my leg like a bolt of electricity. The chair shoots across the floor, knocks over a trash can, and crashes into the wall. When it comes to rest, the seat is still spinning on its base. The security monitor flickers. I whip around to check it. It's blurry with static. The chair spins empty on the screen. A heavy silence follows, and I wait for an alarm or buzzer. For someone to come rushing in. All I hear is the hum of the hard drive and the tick of the wall clock as the hour hand snaps to eleven.

My foot prickles, more alive than the rest of me. It glows, brighter than usual. I bring my hand up and study my fingers. They glow brighter, too.

I jump at a high-pitched whine in the far corner of the room, and a second camera turns toward the commotion. Toward me. I check the monitor, but I'm nothing more than a circle of refracted light on the screen. The camera eye rolls from side to side, doubling back and zeroing in on the spinning chair.

Shit!

I turn back to the keyboard and focus. Fear and frustration are building inside me, and for the first time, it all feels like something I can use. I pull the charge like a hot wire through my body. Static crackles the air, and I think about it flowing through my fingers. The key snaps down, and the screen comes alive.

I work fast, one stroke at a time, reaching deep for that hot line of concentrated emotion, that energy that connects my fingers to the keys. I click on VISITOR HISTORY. Inmate's last name or identification number. I type *Garrison*. First name, *Tyler*. I click on VISITOR RECORDS for the last sixty days.

The hard drive churns, pulling up the list I promised to deliver to Holmes. A record of all of Six's visitors for the last two months. The same names surface over and over. Anthony Verone comes up each week. I commit two other, unfamiliar names to memory, and one caseworker, before scrolling down to a name that jars me. My lawyer was here... on October 21. Checked in at 13:21 and checked out at 13:26.

I haven't heard from or seen my public defender since my sentencing. But he was here last month and spent five minutes with Six. He's a public defender—theoretically, he could represent Six, too. But five minutes? That's not near enough time to confer about a criminal charge or review court documents. Five minutes is just enough time to pass along information . . . or maybe arrange a trade.

Inside the visitation room, the door to the pods opens, spilling light into the room. The silhouette of a guard appears through the window. He peers into the shadows.

"Anyone here?" It's Rickers. I recognize his voice, even muffled by the glass wall that separates us. He flips on the lights and inspects the room, his Maglite blunt side up in his fist. Then he unlocks the secure door to the check-in area, where I'm standing, where the camera just caught the disturbance I stirred.

Rickers ambles in and gives the desk a quick once-over, taking notice of the misplaced chair, now motionless by the wall. I step out of his way as he grumbles to himself about people picking up after themselves and forgetting to notify the control room when they plan to work late. Slipping his Mag in his belt loop, he rights the trash can and wheels the chair back in place.

He turns to go, then pauses, a strange expression on his face. Rickers furrows his brow at the computer. He glances quickly around the room. "Anyone here?" he calls out again.

The room is quiet. My hands are still glowing, and I don't dare breathe.

Rickers turns his attention to the computer, studying the open file on the screen. Then, with a quick shrug of his shoulders, he snaps off the monitor, flips the light switch, and leaves the room.

It doesn't matter. I've already discovered more than what I was looking for.

TWENTY

Holmes's list is burning a hole in my pocket, a handful of loose change that I can't spend. I don't have any way to get the names to him tonight. The best I can do is head back to my cell and write them down on a scrap of paper, so I don't forget. But I won't forget. There's too much crossover between the list of people Holmes is watching and the ones who are watching me. All these names—Six, Verone, Monetti . . . hell, even my public defender—seem to come at me from all sides until the walls start closing in, blurring the gray line between the people you should never trust and the ones you mistakenly assume you should.

Holmes promised me an advance. He gave me until tomorrow to get him this list and said in return he'd have one of his friends watching Pink tonight. But a slithering unease makes me wonder if he'll live up to his word.

Which is why I'm standing under a streetlight outside the alley behind Pink's club at the end of her shift, hoping it's bright enough to conceal me. She might not see me if I stay in the center of its beam. I don't want to talk. Don't want to complicate her life any more than I already have. I just want to make sure Holmes followed through on our deal. That she's safe.

The snow's melted in the alley, small piles of it lingering where the sun doesn't reach. Her coat isn't lying beside the Dumpster anymore, and I hope that means she found it. That she's here.

The neon lights in front of the club snap off as the last of the die-hards are pushed out the door. A few minutes later, two waitresses emerge from the alley. Pink isn't one of them.

A young man wearing headphones in his ears waits by the front door. I only recognize him by the black crow tattooed on his neck. It matches the one on Holmes's, marking him as one of Holmes's gang. Part of me is relieved he's here. The other part of me thinks he shouldn't be. Because she shouldn't be. Because the club closed thirty minutes ago. Where the hell is she?

I push through the wall, apprehensive as I materialize in the dim room. I told her I didn't want to see her anymore. And here I am, making a liar out of myself. But the break room is empty. Pink's coat isn't in here, either, and the lockers all hang open and empty.

I leave through the front door. Holmes's man is still here, which means he must think she's here, too. But there are only two ways out, and he would have seen her leave. Unless . . . I look down the sidewalk. The club beside Pink's is still open. The neon lights beside the door flash TOPLESS GIRLS.

My sister's a dancer at the club next door.

Maybe Pink didn't go very far. I told her not to walk home alone for a while. Maybe she actually listened.

I wait for the door to the club to open. A woman leaves and I slip in after her. The room is dimly lit, and an easel is posted inside. OPEN AUDITIONS 4 AM–10 AM. Chairs are stacked upside down on the tabletops, and the main stage is dark. At the back of the room, a handful of girls in yoga pants and sweatshirts wait in line beside a cordoned-off room.

I slip through a velvet rope into a half-lit room behind a curtain. A girl stands on a small, private stage. There's no audience. Just a middle-age man in a velour armchair with his head in his hand, looking bored while he scrolls through his phone messages. He doesn't seem to notice when the music starts and the girl begins to move, swirling around the pole in a pair of purple sequined Converse. I step closer, hoping like hell I'm wrong. The girl's head dips backward, nearly touching the floor. She freezes, missing a beat when our eyes catch. Pink pales, humiliation and aggravation at war on her face. Some tightly coiled part of me relaxes, if only because I know she's here and she's safe. But every inch of me tenses again when she pretends to ignore me—pretends to ignore the fact that her hands and knees are shaking—and falls back into a carefully rehearsed routine.

I walk to the edge of the stage, forgetting everything I said earlier about not wanting to see her anymore. "What are you doing?"

She grits her teeth and stares past me. Keeps dancing. It's like that first night we met all over again. Same belligerent look on her face. Same frosty determination not to see me. I leap onto the platform, throwing her off beat. Then plant myself between her and the one-man audience on the floor.

"This isn't you," I say. This isn't the girl who stretches out her T-shirts to cover her ass and hides her legs under throw pillows. Her movements are rigid and awkward. And she looks like she wants to be sick.

She spins away using the pole as a means to ricochet in the other direction. But I'm faster and I slice right through it, reappearing a breath away from her face. She startles and trips. Cusses under her breath. A red flush races up her chest.

"You don't have to do this."

The man glances up in time to see her misstep and recover.

He shakes his head. "Stop the music."

Pink turns her back on me. Her hands grip the pole as she struggles to find her rhythm again.

"I said, stop the music." The man crosses the room and snaps off her portable stereo.

Pink looks past me, her face all bunched up and indignant. "I know. I made a mistake. I can do better." Her red mouth presses to a thin line, and she plants her hands on her small hips. Her curls are tied back in a frizzy, loose knot, and her curves are bound flat in bicycle shorts and a sports bra. She looks like a pissed-off little girl who got caught wearing her mother's makeup and high heels, and part of me wants to rip her off that stage and carry her out under my arm. But the other part doesn't want her to see the look on my face. I remember what shame and pity look like. Like the guilty verdict of a unanimous jury. Like the slow fall of Ms. Cruz's lips when she first realized it was me on the back of that truck picking up her trash every morning. She never had to tell me *You're better than this*. Her face said it for her. The way mine says it now.

I jump down from the stage and storm through the curtain, unsure if I'm more disappointed in Pink or myself.

"Look," I hear him say through the curtain while I pace on the other side. "Your sister's my best dancer. I did her a favor letting you wait tables—"

"A favor?" Pink raises her voice. "But I'm—"

"Does she even know you're here?" he asks. Pink doesn't answer, and I'm guessing her sister wouldn't approve, which doesn't make me feel any worse about screwing up her audition.

"That cop friend of yours has been coming around a lot."

"He's not a cop! He does security or something. And he's not my friend. He only hangs around because he wants to go out with my sister."

"Well, he's asking questions."

"So?"

"So, you're underage, kid!" It's more than an observation; it's a threat. And it renders her speechless, forcing me to peek around the curtain to make sure she's still there. "Look, you're my best waitress. You come in when you're supposed to, you work hard, and the customers like you. As long as no one finds out you're underage, you'll keep doing what you're doing. But you're not a dancer, kid." He gives her a minute to absorb the compliment-laced rejection.

"I can learn."

I hear his long sigh through the curtain, the deep pull of breath through his nose. He lowers his voice and speaks slowly, as if buffering his temper. "Candy, sweetheart. Don't make me say it."

"Say it," she says, trembling with frustration.

"You're a sweet kid. I've seen you balance a dozen beers with one hand while playing hopscotch over drunks on the floor, but you've got no rhythm. You've got no ass, your tits are too small, and you can't work the pole. You're a worker's compensation claim waiting to happen. Look at your shoes, for Christ's sake! You're just a kid."

"I need the money." Her voice strains, holding on until the last syllable to break.

"I know what you're trying to do. I want to help you, but I can't put you onstage, kid. I'm sorry."

The man dips under the rope and walks through me, as easily as he just cut every thread of confidence in her. He disappears into his office, leaving her alone to pull herself together, not realizing the damage he's done. He's probably assuming she'll bounce back, but I don't make those kinds of assumptions anymore. Everyone has a last thread—Simpson, my mom—and when it's cut, there is no bouncing back. Pink's sneakers shuffle slowly down the steps, and I hope she has something left to hold on to as I slip unnoticed through the wall.

Pink comes out wearing her ugly coat with her backpack slung over her shoulder. A light rain begins to fall, and I crouch under the brightest streetlight I can find, willing myself invisible. The logical part of me hopes she doesn't see me. She was safe before we met. Before she knew I existed. My head keeps telling me she'll be safer if we never see each other again. I wait for her to pass me. And when she does, every other part of me wishes she hadn't.

I follow, careful to stay a block behind both her and Holmes's man, but it doesn't really matter. She walks with both eyes glued to the pavement, her rain-soaked coat looking like it weighs five hundred pounds, dripping a trail behind her.

I expect her to turn down any one of a handful of side streets. Instead, she follows the railroad tracks, taking the long way around to our neighborhood, traipsing through puddles of mud in the dark. Slow freight cars rattle toward her and whistle past, and she looks after them with a sad sort of longing before turning away and cutting through my old neighborhood. Silently, she weaves through the parking lots of my old apartment complex, barely bothering to look up, and emerges in front of a row of tiny ramshackle houses. She climbs one of the rickety front porches and pauses at the door. The rain beads down her face. I can't tell if she's crying.

"You followed me this far," she says quietly to her feet. It takes me a moment to realize I've been walking beside her for at least a block. Maybe more. "I guess you'll come in whether I want you to or not."

"No." I check over my shoulder and peer through the dark. Holmes's man leans against a tree in a run-down playground one block over. "Not if you don't want me to."

She slides her key in the hole and turns the lock.

"I'm sorry," I say.

She pushes the door open and disappears inside. She doesn't leave it cracked.

I leave Pink's house and head south, feeling lonelier than I've felt in a long time. I replay the night over and over in my mind, and when I next look up, I'm standing in front of Martín's family's front door. I tell myself I'm here because I'm overdue on our arrangement. That I'm here to make good on our deal. But if that were true, I wouldn't be standing on his front porch at four in the morning, while all his sisters are asleep. Truth is, I'm not really sure why I'm here. I only know I'm sick of feeling like I'm letting people down. At least now, when I see Martín tomorrow, I can tell him I checked up on his sisters, and at least from out here, it looks like they're all right.

The house is quiet, and I'm getting ready to head home, when headlights cut across Martín's front yard. A white work van turns into his gravel driveway and pulls in close to the side of his house. Close enough that the driver can't see that he's been followed. A car idles a block down the street, and kills its lights.

The driver gets out of the van and opens the back doors. He's young. Not old enough to be Martín's father, and Martín only has sisters. His cousin, maybe? Lights flick on inside Martín's house, and one of his sisters unlocks the side door. I watch as the driver unloads a weary mother holding an infant and two sleepy young girls from the van and ushers them all inside, where Martín's mother waits to greet them. The driver pulls a handle inside the door, releasing a false bottom under the floor of the van bed. He checks it for the last of their belongings, retrieving a duffel and a small plush bear, then puts the cover carefully back in place. A light in a basement flicks on, and through the window, I see mattresses, spread with blankets across the floor. The little girls collapse against their mother, and fall asleep.

Down the street, the dark car is still idling. It gives me the creeps. Feeling a strange protective pang for Martín and his family, I ghost toward it. The car has all the telltale signs of an unmarked police car, so I duck down and push my face through the glass. The driver—some kind of law enforcement officer judging by his holster and his radios—talks into a cell phone.

"No, it's better if we wait," he says. "Let them develop a pattern. We can document all the trips he takes in and out to build a stronger case... Use it as leverage. He's using a small van... few enough axles to make it across the border easily with the right bribe. All we need is the name of the border agent who's letting him in."

I pull my head from the car. I'm not the only one watching Martín's family, and the knowledge might as well be a lead brick in my pocket. I don't know how to deal in this kind of information. The kind that leaves you feeling helpless because you can't change anything for the people you care about anyway. I don't want to make the same mistake I did with Simpson. Don't want to risk losing Martín. So I lock his secrets away in my pocket and head home to my cell.

He asked me to check in on his sisters, and I did. And tomorrow, I'll tell him the truth . . . that his sisters are just fine.

TWENTY-ONE

We're dismissed from classes early on Thursday. Once four o'clock rolls around, the Y is down to a skeleton crew of guards, just enough to keep us all in line while the rest of the employees head out for Thanksgiving dinner with their families.

Rickers finds me lying in my bunk, listening to Ben turn the pages of his car magazine. "Ready to go?" he asks.

It's hard to breathe. The air is different in the pod. Lighter. Thinner. It carries the smell of reconstituted potatoes and gravy, and the expectant chatter of seventy-two hungry guts. Mine isn't one of them.

I'm not ready. Not ready at all. I'd rather eat a dry pile of prison-turkey from a plastic tray and be left alone to fall asleep. I'd rather sneak off after Lights Out and find Pink, even if I'm just following her around town all night because she won't speak to me.

I stand up slowly, nervous for a million reasons I can't put into words. I've traveled outside the walls dozens of times in the last four months. Hell, I've been all over the city, but my body never left this place. The living, breathing parts of me have always been here. Safe, inside two feet of concrete and rolls of wire, with a roof over my head, three square meals a day, and bulletproof glass all around me.

"I'm ready." I look at my locker and my books. I look at Ben.

"You don't need to bring anything. I've got some things waiting for you outside." Rickers puts his hand on my shoulder and gives it a squeeze, like maybe he knows this won't be easy. I nod to Ben and follow Rickers through the pod. He's wearing a French blue button-down with a tie, and his shoulder holster is empty of its sidearm. His cuffs, radio, and pepper spray are clipped to the belt holding up a pair of crisp dress slacks, and his hair is fresh-trimmed and neatly combed to one side. I've never seen him out of his Kevlar, and suddenly I can understand how he and Monetti could share a girlfriend. He's not as tall as Monetti, a little older and softer, both around the middle and the cut of his jaw. He's not billboard-handsome like Monetti. But out of his uniform, Rickers looks warm and approachable. The comfortable kind of handsome that seems to draw you closer, rather than making you feel left out.

Skivvy whistles as we pass his cell, rousing his bunkmate's attention. Oscar grins and hangs his cigarette burn-spotted arms through the openings in the bars. He calls out, "Damn, Rickers! Lookin' fine! Got a hot date with the doctor?" The entire pod bursts out with laughter.

"Cool it, Oscar," Rickers chastises over the catcalls and commentary that follow. "And try not to burn the place down while I'm gone."

"Didn't Dr. Manning tell you? I'm reformed. No more fires for me, man." He holds up a two-finger pledge.

Officer Rickers shakes his head and mutters, "I'll believe that when the world runs out of matches."

The control room buzzes us through the sally port. Once we're out of the pod, Rickers hands me a paper bag with a change of clothes in it. I find the sliver of wall where the cameras can't see—where Monetti nearly strangled me to death—and begin to disrobe. Rickers averts his eyes, giving me a minute to slip on the khaki pants and pull the white button-down on over my undershirt. I button it slowly. Rolled inside one dress shoe is a silk tie. I unwind it carefully and lay the slippery material across my palms. Then clear my throat quietly.

Rickers turns. He seems to understand without me having to say it. "Need a hand with that?"

He takes the tie without waiting for an answer and winds it around my collar, sizing it up against my shirt before swinging it around in a quick, practiced motion. Then he cinches the knot at my throat. It squeezes out a memory of my father, tightening my tie on the morning of my grandfather's funeral when I was six. I swallow, feeling the silk knot constrict around the bruises Monetti gave me, and I'm grateful it's not him standing in front of me.

Another set of gates separates us from the exit. Rickers presents the duty guards my temporary release papers and signs me into his custody. One guard gestures me toward the metal detector.

I turn to Rickers, knowing exactly what will happen if I try to walk through the machine. "Why do I have to be scanned?"

"It's a condition of your release. To make sure you haven't brought anything into the warden's house you shouldn't have." There's a brief hiccup while I try to explain to the duty guards why I can't walk through the full-body scanner. After careful inspection of my papers, and the scars on my head, they concede to use the wand instead. Then I'm patted down before they declare me harmless to the world and Warden Somerville's family for the next four hours.

Rickers holds the front door open. I tremble at the sound of the buzzer and the ice-cold wind on my face.

"Don't just stand there, kid. Turkey's getting cold."

We follow the sidewalk to the perimeter gate, where an officer is waiting to let us out. The metal gates draw apart—a ten-foot opening that feels like a bottomless black hole, one I could lose myself in before I ever hit the bottom. The earth tips toward it until my insides feel like they're falling.

I have to remind myself to breathe. Somehow, it's the same air I breathe in the yard, but it smells different. It's as cold as the Rockies and as wide as the plains and blows hard enough to unravel me. I look down at my feet. Still solid. On the ground. Still there.

It's all in your head.

I shut my eyes and let Rickers push me through the gate.

Rickers's car is an older-model dark blue Crown Vic. He opens the passenger door for me. An old CB radio is mounted to the dash. Rickers reaches into his glove box, withdraws his handgun, and clips it into his holster. Prison guards aren't allowed to carry guns inside the gate unless they're working the towers, and I'm not used to sitting so close to one. I fidget, feeling like I'm in the wrong seat of a police car.

Last time I was in a car like this, I sat in the back.

"Are you a cop?" I ask him.

"Used to be."

His answer is too short. It dangles, like it's waiting for something in trade.

"Why'd you quit being a cop? I thought cops made good money."

Rickers laughs and shakes his head as we pull out of the Y. "There's more than one way to make a living, kid. And for the record, I didn't quit. Just made a career change."

I watch him sideways, waiting for the rest of the story. Talking takes my mind off the drive. Rickers stops for a red light and stares out the windshield. He drums his fingers lightly on the steering wheel.

"Lisa didn't like living with a beat cop. Said she was always worrying. She made me choose between her and the force. So I took a job in Corrections as a probation officer for a while. You talk about shitty salaries... And it wasn't any safer. I got assaulted by a kid on the job once. Lisa was done after that." He shakes his head at the memory. "Then I heard about the opening in the Y. The hours suck, but it pays a little better. Lisa was okay with it because she thought it was safer than being out on the street. The rest is history." He shrugs.

So he chose her. They made a deal. And after all that, she chose Monetti.

I wonder if he regrets that decision now. I wonder if Lisa regrets it, too.

"Maybe it's not serious between him and Lisa. Maybe she'll come around." I can't tell if this is any consolation. Or if it's only rubbing salt in a wound.

"Or maybe things like this just happen for a reason. Sometimes it's better just to let it go and move on. Maybe something better will come along."

"Like Dr. Manning?"

Rickers gives me a side-eye, like maybe I've crossed a line. "Maybe so," he says, turning back to the road.

"Would you go back to being a cop?" I don't know why I feel the need to grill him. Probably because the farther we get from the Y, the more vulnerable I feel. It feels like I'm scraping stray bullets off the floor and stuffing them in my pockets.

"I don't know." He reaches to adjust the thermostat, then cups a hand over the vent to make sure it's working. "I kind of like working in the Y. I ran a juvenile surveillance unit for a while." He shakes his head at the memory. "I saw the same kids screw up every day. It was like watching life kick them down a flight of stairs. Nothing you can do but hope they don't break their neck on the way down. But see, all you kids in the Y already hit the bottom. As long as you're inside, you can't go anywhere but up, right?"

We ride most of the way in silence. I think about Monetti. I imagine him holding me by the neck against the bottom of that flight of stairs. All the burning questions I have for Rickers—*Why are you doing this? Why are you being so kind to me, and what do you want in return?*—taste ungrateful and insolent on the tip of my tongue.

We make a turn into a neighborhood that doesn't look anything like mine. A neighborhood where tax dollars are well spent. The roads are smooth with wide sidewalks. The houses are fixed up, and the yards are tidy. The cars don't have boots, and no one looks over their shoulder when they walk down the street. I don't belong here.

"How come they're letting you do this?"

Rickers taps the butt of his gun in his holster. "I guess they figure I'm qualified to escort you to and from the warden's house." He's only thinking of logistics, the rules the deputy director set in place. But that's not what I'm asking. Anxiety creeps over me as the car slows. It's too late to renegotiate whatever deal I made when I stepped out of those gates and sat down in this car. I just want to know what's expected of me. What it will cost.

"But why me? Why'd you tell Somerville you want to be my mentor?"

Rickers chews on this for a while. "I guess I feel like I owe you."

I don't realize my muscles are tense until the moment they release.

I slouch against the car door, letting my head rest on the glass. He owes me. It's the right answer. The answer I needed to hear. I'm not a charity case. This isn't a gift. He's settling a score, which means after tonight we're even and he—and the universe—won't expect anything more from me.

TWENTY-TWO

We park in front of a small, well-maintained bungalow on a neatly manicured street. A warm glow radiates from the windows, and a cranberry wreath smiles at me from the front door. The porch is offset from the other houses, shaded by a fat blue spruce on one side and a cluster of aspen on the other. Their leaves crunch under my feet as we climb the porch steps. I smooth my shirt for the third time and run a hand over the hair covering my scar. I wonder what to say when . . .

The door opens.

Her eyes are gray.

She smiles at Officer Rickers and extends her hand to him. Then, more cautiously, to me. I look to Rickers for consent before reaching out slowly, the way I've imagined touching those pictures.

"Welcome. You must be John. I'm Vivian." She doesn't let go right away, and she blushes when I catch her staring at my scars. She backs away and motions us into a warm room that smells like woodsmoke and pie and books.

"Come inside. You must be freezing. Why on earth aren't you wearing a coat?"

I know she's making small talk, trying to mask the fact that I make her uncomfortable.

"They didn't give me one," I say too fast without thinking. She makes me uncomfortable, too. *Vivian.* It's a sophisticated name. A grown-up name that carries weight and probably comes with expectations. I had assumed when Warden Somerville was talking about Vivian, he'd been speaking of his wife. I look casually past Vivian, into the rooms I can see, counting place settings at the dining room table and sneaking glances at the photos on the credenza in the hall... in loving memory. A tall, delicate-looking urn is centered on the mantel over the fireplace.

Vivian's face flushes and a lock of strawberry hair slips over her shoulder to hide it. I feel my face go hot, too, but no one seems to notice. Rickers is too busy looking at the chair by the fireplace, where Monetti sits, drinking a beer. Monetti raises the bottle to his shit-eating grin. He takes a long pull before getting up and crossing the room.

The two men look at each other with frosty expressions. Vivian and I pale.

"I guess Dad forgot to mention James was going to be here," she says, putting herself squarely between them. "Dad?" she calls loudly. "John and Officer Rickers are here."

The kitchen door opens, and Warden Somerville emerges wearing an apron and singed oven mitts. The smell of turkey and stuffing chases him into the room, and his face lights up in a wide smile. It's a smile I've never seen him wear inside the Y, and it perfectly matches the ones in the pictures.

"You're here just in time, gentlemen." He pulls off his mitts and shakes each of their hands. My own hands feel awkward, like they're shackled to my sides. I stand a respectful distance back, with Monetti and Rickers flanking me. "Vivian and I are very glad to have you in our home, John." He reaches out and shakes my hand, too. "What can I get you to drink, son?"

My mouth is dry. "Water would be fine, sir."

Vivian disappears into the kitchen and returns with a tall glass. She hands it to me without touching me, without looking in my eyes. I thank her and suck the whole thing down, and then apologize when she politely insists on getting me another.

"Why don't you all sit down and make yourselves at home. Vivian and I are just putting the finishing touches on the meal."

Monetti slumps into his chair by the fire, and Rickers and I ease cautiously onto the sofa across from him.

"What the hell are you doing here?" Rickers asks under his breath. He snaps open the top of his pop can and glares at Monetti. I disappear into the cushion.

"I happened to mention to the warden that I didn't have any plans for Thanksgiving again this year. So he extended me an invitation. Same as he did last year, and the year before that." Monetti looks entirely too comfortable, proprietary even, slouching in the warden's armchair, drinking his beer.

"That's too bad."

Monetti tips the bottle to his lips and considers that with a wry smile. "The way I see it, this worked out better for both of us. Lisa didn't do her best work in the kitchen, if you know what I mean."

The Coke can in Rickers's hand crackles, and his face turns red to match.

"Hey," Monetti says coolly. "Water under the bridge, right? Besides"—Monetti points his bottle at me—"I figure you could use the extra set of hands to keep the kid in line."

Monetti looks at the fire. Rickers glares at the metal poker beside it. "The kid's not the one I worry about stabbing me in the back."

Warden Somerville bursts through the kitchen door carrying a platter of steaming turkey. Vivian follows with a casserole dish. Monetti jumps to his feet and heads for the table, and Rickers and I do the only thing we can. Follow him and keep our mouths shut.

Vivian ushers us to a rectangular table, extended to encroach into the small living room, and covered with a fancy white tablecloth. The table shimmers, neatly set with silver and glass. Warden Somerville takes the seat at the head of the table closest to the kitchen, and Vivian directs us all to our seats—Rickers beside her father, then me next to Rickers at the end of the table. She sets her own glass in front of the place setting directly in front of mine, and I wonder if anyone else notices her shy smile.

The warden gestures to the empty chair at the end of the table. "What happened, James? I thought you were hoping to bring a date."

Rickers pales.

Monetti shrugs. "She works nights. Couldn't make it."

The tension at our end of the table releases like a breath. Lisa didn't work nights. That was the problem. Which means either Monetti was two-timing with someone else all along—which wouldn't surprise me—or he's already moved on to someone new.

"Working on Thanksgiving? That's a shame."

"Yeah, but the bars are still open, and it pays the bills."

"In other words, she turned you down again, huh?" Vivian teases.

Monetti chokes on his beer. "No, she's just busy."

Monetti leaves himself wide open for a comeback. But Rickers is quiet. I hope that's because he's moved on, too.

The warden laughs. "Oh, I'm sure she'll come around, James. You're nothing if not persistent."

Vivian excuses herself and disappears through the kitchen door. While she's gone, Monetti casually moves her glass to the remaining space next to her father and sets down his beer with a heavy thunk, easing into the seat in front of me. A moment later, Vivian emerges, carrying a bowl of hot mashed potatoes and a gravy boat with a delicately curled handle. She sets them down and takes up the seat next to her father, giving no notice to the fact that her place has been rearranged. Maybe I imagined the smile.

The warden pulls a deep, satisfied breath through his nose as he looks across the table. A golden turkey drips between a steel carving knife and a two-pronged fork long enough to disembowel a man. I fidget, unsure what to do with my hands. Do I keep them in my lap, away from the utensils, or on the table, where the guards can see them? I settle for my lap, taking inventory of the place setting that sits where a plastic tray should be: a wineglass filled with water, two metal forks with actual tines, two spoons that reflect the entire distorted room in their surface, and a knife.

"Vivian Lee, you've outdone yourself," the warden says proudly. Everyone is looking at the food—except Monetti and me. "Let's all join hands and give thanks."

Vivian reaches for her father's hand and turns her other palm up so Monetti can take it. He stretches his other across the table for mine, smirking the entire time. All eyes are on me as I rest a reluctant hand in each of my guards'. We all lower our heads as the warden says grace. I look up in time to see Monetti palm the knife from my place setting and pull it across the tablecloth, out of reach.

"Dear Lord, we thank you for this meal and for your many blessings. We thank you for the company of friends and loved ones, both those who are here with us tonight and those who live forever in our hearts. Amen." The warden looks up, and there's a shine in his eyes. Vivian gives his hand a squeeze. "Let's eat."

We all take turns passing our plates to Warden Somerville, who carves up thick slices of turkey before passing the plates to Vivian. She spoons out mountains of stuffing and potatoes, then drizzles hot gravy over the top before passing them around. I think maybe she's poured a little extra gravy on mine, and I feel anxious, wondering what it means. But it doesn't matter. Monetti takes one look at my plate and takes it for himself, passing me his instead.

We are all quiet for a while. I eat slowly, careful not to scrape the china while I saw my turkey with the side of my fork. It's probably delicious, but my stomach is full of knots, ready to toss the food back up. It knows as well as I do that I don't deserve it. I chew, forcing it down, all the while feeling like a thief. But I make myself finish the whole plate before setting my fork down where everyone can see it and folding my hands in my lap.

Warden Somerville looks at each of us, lingering over the last bits of food on his plate. "I'm going to an interesting conference next week," he says, breaking the uncomfortably long silence. "Heading to Texas to a state school for youthful offenders. They've had good success with that resocialization program we talked about." He looks at Rickers. "You should take a few days and come with me, Charlie. With your background in juvenile probation programs, you could really contribute something to the conversation. Plus, they've got a mentor program running. Might give you some ideas. I'd love to see us head in that direction in the Y."

Monetti grunts. "Resocialization suggests these kids were ever properly socialized to begin with."

Warden Somerville forks the last of his turkey into his mouth and talks around it. "They must be doing something right. For the last three years, they're reporting recidivism rates as low as ten percent. In our best years, the Y reported sixty percent. I, for one, would like to get in there and see how they're doing it. I think programs like theirs—intensive therapy, mentorship, and strong academics—those kinds of changes could give some of our kids a second chance at life."

Monetti's getting loud. There's a touch of slur on his tongue. "Some of them already had their second chance. Just look at Conlan." Suddenly, all eyes are on me and no one's eating anymore. "Hell, the doctors brought him back from the dead, and he walked out of the hospital and murdered his teacher. Second chance, third chance, fourth chance... We keep treating these thugs like kids and pitching them back out on the street and then taking them back in, and before you know it, we're cooking them Thanksgiving dinner."

The warden sets down his wineglass, sloshing the contents. His voice rises, too. "Maybe because we're thinking of them as thugs. Whatever mistakes these kids made, they're still just kids." He blows out a long breath, and the frown lines lie back into his face. "James, you and I have worked together a long time. I know how you feel. And I understand why. I do. But you need to let it go, son."

The warden looks at me apologetically and pushes back his chair. "I hope everyone saved room for dessert," he says, masking his disappointment with a sad smile and disappearing into the kitchen.

Vivian's water glass is halfway to her lips, poised midair. Her stare burns a hole in my scars. Her expression is one of twisted fascination, like I'm some hideous bug trapped under a glass. When she sets it down, her hand is trembling slightly.

"I didn't kill her," I say, more to Vivian than anyone else, though I'm not sure why. Maybe just to deflect that look on her face.

Monetti snorts.

"Then who did?" Vivian asks quietly, looking to each of us for an answer and locking eyes with Rickers when the rest of us look away.

"Maybe this isn't the best time—"

"Go ahead, Charlie," Monetti says, laying the sarcasm on thick. "Tell her a story."

Rickers shifts uneasily in his chair. "John believes that he saw two other assailants at the scene. The boy he sta—one of the victims," he corrects himself, probably trying to spare me any more scrutiny than I've already endured, "and a man in a hood. No one ever identified him."

"That's because he doesn't exist," Monetti grumbles.

"I believe that the hooded man is a projection . . . a product of John's intense emotional distress resulting from the events."

"What kind of emotional distress?" The prosecutor plants both hands on the witness box and leans against it.

Dr. Manning pauses, like she's dissecting her explanation before speaking, trying to find the right words. "John was party to a highly traumatic and violent incident. When we met, he expressed a great deal of guilt and responsibility over what happened, specifically for the crime against his teacher—"

"Guilt?" The prosecutor wastes no time mincing words. He throws

this one like a blade, hard and fast, straight into the jury box. "He expressed guilt?"

"Objection!"

"Overruled." The judge leans forward in his chair.

A hint of a smile teases the corner of the prosecutor's lip. "It's no matter, Your Honor. The court may strike that last question from the record."

But they can't take it back, and he knows it.

He wipes away his smirk and gestures for her to finish. "My apologies, Dr. Manning."

Dr. Manning clears her throat and continues cautiously. "John expressed significant emotional distress over her death, coupled with a sense of responsibility for the outcome of the events that day, namely the fact that she was there looking for him. It is my belief that John created a coping mechanism in the form of a projection. That his mind fabricated someone else—a nameless, faceless aggressor—to take blame, as a way of cushioning his psyche. To make his feelings about the incident more manageable to bear."

"So it is your professional opinion that this hooded man is a figment of John's imagination?"

"Yes," she says cautiously, "Although you must realize that, to John's mind, this projection is very real. John truly believes a hooded man was responsible for the murders."

"And, to quote your written evaluation, you say"—he looks down his nose at the legal pad he's now holding—"'the imaginary hooded man represents an outward projection of the defendant's inner sense of guilt and responsibility.'"

She grips the stand with more force than she puts behind her words. "But that doesn't necessarily mean—"

"No further questions for the witness, Your Honor."

Vivian's looking back and forth between Rickers and Monetti, her mouth parted with an unasked question. Rickers mutters, "Cut the kid a break, Monetti."

"Like the judge did?"

Rickers cringes. "Don't do this—"

"You know as well as I do, Conlan got off easy being sent to the Y." Monetti shoots me a cruel smile. "Oh, right. I forgot. In Conlan's *mind*, he's actually innocent. Therefore, we should all feel sorry for him. Well, if he's that crazy, maybe he should've been sent someplace else."

"So what if it's all in his head? Who the hell are you to decide where he belongs? You're no doctor."

Monetti tosses his napkin on the table and reaches for the last of his beer. "Shrinks. They're the worst cons in the joint. I can't believe you actually went out with Manning. The woman's a quack."

"It wasn't a date," Rickers says, shrinking into his chair. "We were just catching up over a few drinks."

"Yeah? She looked pretty tired this morning—"

"Stuff it, Monetti."

"Stuff you."

The warden emerges from the kitchen carrying a pie in each hand.

"Gentlemen! If I have to ask you to take it outside, I'll lock both of you out there without dessert."

It's like I'm sitting here, but none of them see me. Just like before. Sitting with my head down behind the defense's table, someone else telling a different version of my story. The public watching it all go down in newspapers and TV, laying bets on the verdict. Everybody passing down judgment, like I'm not even in the room.

My public defender sits across the table from me. He smells like coffee and sweat and impatience. "They found your prints all over that knife and the victim's handbag. You were found at the murder scene, with two bodies, in an otherwise empty building, with their blood all over you. And you argued with one of the victims in front of multiple witnesses the day before she was stabbed to death. I don't care who you think you saw. That jury is going to convict you of two counts of murder!"

"I won't plead guilty." I push the plea bargain papers back across the table. "I had every reason to defend myself. He put his hand on my throat. He stole her money. He watched the hooded man kill her—"

"Enough with the hooded man, John! We can't build a case around a suspect who doesn't exist! It's all in your head! And talking about it isn't helping your cause! The court psychologist is going to tell everyone on that jury that you're imagining him because you feel responsible."

"That doesn't mean I'm guilty!"

My lawyer throws his pen down on his notepad and scrubs his face with his hands. "Look. My job is to defend you. If you go in there insisting you're innocent, they'll charge you as an adult. That's hard time in Supermax. Our best shot is to cut a deal. You plead guilty on both counts in exchange for a reduced sentence. We'll get you a couple of years in the Y, and if you play your cards right, you'll be free when you turn twenty-one. Take the deal."

He doesn't know what it means to defend someone. He is not strong. He is not determined. He is nothing like Ms. Cruz. And she would not take no for an answer.

But Ms. Cruz isn't here.

It wasn't your fault, John.

But no matter how many times I play it over in my mind, it feels like it was.

I stand up. Monetti's hand reflexively moves to his waist. It's hard to breathe. The room feels like a baton at my throat. "I'd like to use the restroom."

The silence is thick around the table. Monetti stands and drops his napkin on his chair. "I'll go with him."

Warden Somerville gestures for Monetti to take a seat. "I'm sure John's quite capable on his own."

"I'll show him to the bathroom." Vivian pushes out her chair.

Monetti stands between us. "Don't be too long." The warning is clearly directed to me.

I circumnavigate Monetti, feeling his eyes trail after me, and follow Vivian down a short hallway to the bathroom door. She flips on the light.

Two toothbrushes, a scented candle and a book of matches, a can of aerosol hair spray, a shaving kit, a toilet plunger with a long wooden handle . . .

"Is it true? What James said about you?" she whispers in a rush.

"I didn't kill my teacher." I reach to pull the door shut between us, aggravated that I feel a need to defend myself to her.

"No, the other part," she says. "Did you really die? And come back?" She's standing close. Close enough I can feel her breath when she whispers. Her hand covers mine where she holds the door open. Her pulse is racing. Or maybe it's mine. I haven't stood this close to anyone . . . haven't touched anyone like this in a very long time.

I nod, my thoughts lost somewhere in the gray of her eyes. They're welling up with emotion, but I can't tell if it's hope or sadness. I stare, but she's not staring back. Her gaze is superficial, focused on my scars.

I pull my hand gently from hers. This question . . . this moment . . . her hand on mine. It has nothing to do with me. Her question might as well be penciled in one of Martín's books. A deal. A trade. "What do you want from me?"

"Is it true what they say? About the light?"

She's asking me for something I don't want to give her—something personal that I've only ever shared with Pink.

A tear spills over, and she brushes it away. "It's okay, you don't have to answer that."

But it feels like I do, if only to balance the heaviness of the meal. If I give her this, we'll be even. "Six minutes. It was only six minutes."

"Did it hurt?" Her eyes are fixed on my scar.

She's afraid of the answer. I can see that much. The same way Simpson was when he asked me if his mother was okay. He knew the answer. Knew it before he asked and before I said it. But I'd said the wrong thing.

"It didn't hurt."

She presses her lips to my cheek. They linger there, a soft touch that tilts the ground under my feet and asks nothing in return. Then she's gone.

I lock myself in the bathroom and lean against the sink, staring at my face in the mirror—at the puckered dark scar, pocked with stitch marks that Vivian couldn't look away from. The skin is still warm where she kissed it, leaving me full of emotions I can't place and hungry for things I can't have. This dinner, this kiss, this fucking mirror . . . none of it feels like a gift anymore. It's just one more punishment. Just me, sitting in the warden's office, looking at a pretty picture and wishing I could be on the other side of the glass.

I wretch up dinner and wash out my mouth without looking in the mirror again. I pick up the matchbook. It would be easy to smuggle one into the Y, but that would be a shitty way to pay back the warden's kindness . . . his charity. Because that's really all it was, wasn't it?

Bang, bang, bang!

Monetti growls, "What the hell's taking so long, Conlan?"

I think about the knife he palmed from me at dinner. How he made me eat like a convict at the warden's table. I slip two paper matches into the waistband of my Jockeys as a fuck-you to Monetti before I open the door. He didn't trust me anyway.

Rickers puts himself to work washing dishes while Vivian clears the leftovers from the table. Monetti's taking up real estate on the couch in the living room, starting in on another beer and watching me like a hawk. We all jump at a yelp from the kitchen. Rickers comes out wearing a towel around his hand. There's blood on his sleeve.

"What happened?" Vivian rushes to inspect the wound.

"No big deal. Just slipped and cut myself."

She peels back the towel, and Rickers sucks in a sharp breath through his teeth. "It looks pretty deep. You might need stitches."

Rickers dismisses her suggestion and wraps the towel back over his hand. He winces. "It can wait until after my shift."

Monetti leans in and looks at the wound, pressing a heavy hand to my shoulder. "You should go to the emergency room. I can take Conlan back to the Y."

"No," Rickers and the warden say in unison.

The warden points at Monetti's beer. "Don't think I haven't been counting those. You'll stay here and sober up before you go anywhere. You can help Vivian with the dishes. I'll take John home."

The warden might as well have signed orders in triplicate. It's settled. Vivian packs Rickers a slice of pie to go and shoos him to his car to get his hand fixed. I listen quietly, nibbling the edges of my dessert so I don't look ungrateful, as the others talk over coffee. Monetti's cheeks are flushed from too many beers, and he's smiling more than I've ever seen him. They talk about Thanksgivings past, when Mrs. Somerville—Gloria—was still here. Before the cancer took her. Then the warden shares stories from before that, the early days back in North Carolina when he was teaching Corrections at the technical community college where Monetti went to school. Their relationship goes back much farther than the Y. Much farther than I realized. And I tuck this information away like another matchstick. We are all quiet, lost in our own reflections when the warden's cell phone rings.

There's been an incident in the Y. Time to go. Vivian looks disappointed but not surprised. I look back once, at the mountain of dishes on the table and the table linens we dirtied, at her mother's urn on the mantel, and I fight the twinge of guilt I feel for every fight I've picked that might have kept the warden from making it home for dinner.

From the front seat of the warden's car, I see Monetti standing behind Vivian in the open door. His hand rests on her shoulder, and I have the nagging feeling that we shouldn't be leaving her alone.

TWENTY-THREE

The warden signs me in, and I thank him for dinner. He leaves me in the custody of a guard and is about to walk to his office to deal with whatever adolescent stunt landed him back at work on his night off when he turns to me. He hesitates a moment, then says, "I'm sorry for Officer Monetti's behavior at dinner."

Now that we're in the Y, we're back to titles and last names. It's oddly comforting. I didn't particularly want to be on a first-name basis with Monetti.

"You know, you kids aren't the only ones with files around here. We all have one. We all have a past... tough times we've had to get through. Believe it or not, Officer Monetti's had it pretty rough. When he was a kid, his family was a victim of a home invasion. Some gang initiation that went too far. The perpetrators were all minors. Most of them walked or were out on the street in a matter of months. He's never come out and told me exactly what happened, and it's not my place to ask, but whatever he lived through that night changed him. Made him who he is. He's tough and resilient. He worked hard in school, never expected anything to be handed to him. It's one of the reasons I liked him as a student, and one of the reasons I hired him to come work with me here. He's got a rigid sense of right and wrong. He's slow to trust, and when he does, that trust is earned. When I got here four years ago, corruption ran deep. I needed a hound. Someone who wasn't afraid to ruffle some feathers. Officer Monetti's methods might be a little rough around the edges, but they're effective. And in the long run, this place will be better off for it." The warden taps a thoughtful finger to his lip, like he's trying to think of a way to make me understand. To soften the hardness I feel for Monetti, the anger that's probably written all over my face.

"This place isn't full of bad people. Just people who have lived through bad things. We've all got scars, John, no matter what side of the bars we're on. But we're the product of our choices as much as our circumstances. And as long as we're breathing, we've all got choices left to make."

He pats me on the shoulder and leaves me to them. My choices that somehow never really feel like choices at all.

I submit to the duty guard, raising my arms when he instructs, allowing him to search me. The paper matches are too small to be felt during the frisk and go undetected by the scanning wand. Another officer meets me on the other side with my jumpsuit and tennis shoes. He takes my dress clothes as I shed them and puts them in a bag, and I slide into my prison jumpsuit like it's a pair of well-worn pajamas, all the tension of the evening evaporating out of me and leaving me raw and weary.

It's already dark in the pod.

Bumper and Six lean against the bars of their cell, sneering at me and gobbling like turkeys. By morning, the entire pod will be talking about my night out. Speculating on what I had to do to earn it.

If they think I'm blowing the guards, no big deal. They'll just cackle about it for a few weeks till it's old news. But if they figure out I've been selling their secrets—that I was the one responsible for the last two shakedowns—I'll be dead by lunch.

And that choice belongs to Monetti.

The guard opens my cell, and Ben stirs. I slip off my shoes and fall into my bunk. Something crinkles between my head and the pillow. It's an envelope—the flimsy white ones issued to us by the Y for writing letters home. I've never used one.

I hold it under a thin beam of light from the corridor. My name and cell number are printed in the space for the return address. But the handwriting isn't mine, and the recipient's address is left blank.

It's one of the oldest scams in the place, taught from celly to celly. This method of communicating privately between pods is unreliable and risky at best, which is why I've never used it to take jobs or pass information. The con puts the name of the inmate he wants to pass information to as the sender, leaving the recipient blank. The guard who collects the mail is supposed to check each envelope, but guards get lazy or distracted like anyone else, and sometimes, an inside letter slips by. Unable to forward it to anyone, the mail room sends it back to the sender, who is actually the intended recipient anyway. At this point, if the guards are on their game, the letter is searched and confiscated. On rare occasions, it slides by unnoticed and makes it to its destination intact, like the sealed envelope in my hand.

I press it between my fingers, searching for anything I wouldn't want to get caught with. But it's no thicker than paper. I tear it quietly, careful not to wake Ben, ease out the contents, and unfold a single sheet of Y-issued notepaper. A noose is crudely drawn in pencil. I count six hash marks underneath, plus one extra, presumably for me. I crumple it and toss it on the floor, wondering if Monetti had something to do with making sure it made it to my pillow.

I like the warden. Like Officer Brooks says, he's a fair man. A kind man. I admire that he wants to see the best in people, but I can't understand this blind spot he has for Monetti. The way he defends Monetti's character—his "rigid sense of right and wrong"—when all the evidence points to the contrary. If anything, the warden is too trusting. Just because Monetti was his student doesn't make them family. It shouldn't entitle Monetti to a place in the warden's house. And the warden is too blinded by his own compassion to understand that he's wrong. He's wrong about Monetti, and if he's not careful, he's going to get hurt.

Disturbing thoughts creep through my head. Monetti is probably still pounding beers in the warden's kitchen, and Vivian is there with him. Alone.

I shut my eyes, and before I can talk myself out of it, I'm halfway to the warden's house.

Monetti's car is still parked outside, and I push myself through the front windows just as he's drawing the blinds closed. I flip him the bird, raising my finger close to his face, making him frown against the chill. A stupid, childish thing to do, but for some reason, it makes me feel better.

I head to the kitchen and find Vivian standing at the sink, her hands submerged in a mountain of suds. Monetti comes in. He leans against the counter and sucks down a big glass of water.

"You need me to dry?" He stands close beside her and picks up a towel. She inches away.

"No, thanks. I've got this. You don't have to stay." The pans clatter, and she scrubs hard enough to scatter bubbles and spray. "I stay alone all the time."

"Yeah, well, you shouldn't, Viv. It's not safe."

"Yeah, well, you shouldn't be rude to my dad's dinner guests. Why were you so rough on him?"

"Who, Conlan?" Monetti asks, looking all kinds of indignant. "That kid's a bad seed. They should have let him die."

"No one deserves that."

"You're more like your old man every year, you know that?"

She shoves a wet casserole dish in Monetti's gut. "That's not such a bad thing."

"I guess not," he says, leaning back against the counter to dry the dish. He bumps her clumsily with his elbow, eyes heavy-lidded with beer. "Just don't go making a charity case out of that kid, like your dad. If you want a pet, get a dog." My hands tingle with the urge to shove him, and all I can think of is breaking his—

The lights unexpectedly flicker, and we all look to the ceiling. Vivian slips, dropping a pan into the basin of suds, hurling a wave of water on Monetti's shirt. He brushes it off while she mutters what only sound like half-sincere apologies.

The lights flicker again. I remember the bursting bulb in the alley. The flicker of lights in Pink's dressing room. The static in the security cameras. It occurs to me that I might be causing this, though I haven't the faintest idea how or why.

Monetti pauses to look at the light fixture. "You need me to change a bulb for you?" He pinches free the top button of his shirt.

"No." She turns away, holding one hand over her eyes. "And if you insist on changing anything, you can do it in the bathroom. Wait here. I'll get you a clean shirt."

I walk with her to her father's bedroom, and the flickering lights follow me down the hall.

She opens her father's closet, muttering quietly to herself, and pulls out a shirt. I listen, ears piqued, as she directs Monetti to the bathroom. I should stick close and keep an eye on him, but I stay where I am, transfixed by the phone on her father's nightstand. It's old, the kind with big buttons. One of them reads SPEAKER.

The water is running again in the kitchen. I check to make sure Monetti is still in the bathroom. Then I lean over the phone. I concentrate on the speaker button, pointing at it as much with my mind as my finger. The dial tone roars.

Shit!

I focus hard on the volume button, silencing the drone. The house seems to hold its breath. I hold mine, too. The water turns off in the kitchen, and I'm half expecting Vivian to come bursting into the room. I wait through a silent pause and only start breathing again when she turns the faucet back on.

One at a time, I punch in the numbers I found stuck to the underside of Six's bunk, one ear toward the bathroom, listening for a ringtone. If Monetti and Six are working together, maybe the phone number is his. But the call rolls straight to voice mail.

"We're sorry, the party at the number you're trying to reach is not available. Please leave a message."

"James?" I don't have time to disconnect before Vivian is through the door. She takes a puzzled look around the room, then at the phone. She picks up the receiver.

"Hello, is anyone there?" She listens for a moment before hanging it up. Then turns and knocks on the bathroom door across the hall.

"James, were you using the phone?"

Monetti opens the door, bare-chested and holding his wet shirt in his hands. He's tanned, broad at the shoulders and narrow in the waist, and Vivian takes a small step back and blushes.

"No. Why?" Monetti reaches into his back pocket and fishes out his cell phone, drawing my attention to a long pink scar across his chest.

Vivian must have noticed, it too. "Ouch." She winces, averting her eyes. "What happened to you?" She doesn't stare at his flaws the way she stared at mine. She scratches her head and looks everywhere else. It's like she's got the same blind spot her father has, and I hate Monetti even more for it. It takes him a minute to figure out what she's talking about.

"It's nothing." He rushes to pull on her father's clean shirt. "Just an accident. Did you need something?" he asks, changing the subject.

"No, it's weird. I must be losing my mind. I just thought I heard voices in the house."

Monetti sobers, listening. He moves quickly, room to room, checking the windows and door locks. I'm standing too close, and he barrels through me. The chill makes him pause, the dark hair on his arms and neck standing on end. He shakes me off and crosses the hall to tinker with the thermostat. "It's drafty in here. Is the heat on the same circuit as the kitchen lights?"

Vivian answers with a noncommittal shrug.

Monetti looks at his watch. Bites his lip. "Look, there's somewhere I need to be. But I can stay if you want me to."

"No." She waves him off. "You go ahead. I'll be fine. Dad should be on his way soon."

He kisses the top of her head as she shuffles him out the front door, like he's done it a million times before. Like he doesn't even think about it. Like it doesn't mean anything. And I add this to the long list of reasons why I hate him.

"You really should call an electrician," he shouts through the door as Vivian snaps the dead bolt. She leans back against the door with a tired sigh, a softer, smaller echo of her father after a long day in the Y. Then she reaches out and traces a photo on the wall.

"I wish you could have been here tonight," she whispers to it. "I almost got your stuffing just right."

Monetti's engine growls and peels away from the curb. I should leave, too. Now that he's gone, I've got no good reason to stay. But instead, I come closer, too close, to get a better look at the picture. A small girl with strawberry hair sits between a younger version of the warden and a pretty woman with freckled cheeks and an infinite smile.

Vivian wraps her arms around herself and shivers. She kicks off her shoes, and pads into the kitchen. I follow, careful to give her more space. While she fills a pot of water and sets it on the stove and pulls a mug and a tea bag from the cabinet, I make a list of all the reasons why I should go. All the reasons why it's wrong to be here. But there's still this lingering feeling of debt, this weird, unfinished business of the questions she asked and the kiss she gave me. Maybe Monetti can walk out and not think about it. But I'm nothing like Monetti, no matter what Warden Somerville says.

She leans against the range, watching the water boil. Steam billows over her face, clouding her reflection in the smooth surface of the microwave above it. I take a cautious step toward her, then around her, and yet when I look at our reflection in the glass, I can't see myself in it. It wasn't me she wanted to talk to when she walked me to the bathroom. No more than Simpson wanted to communicate with me when he asked me to look in on his mother. What she wants from me is the comfort I failed to give Simpson. The reassurance I can't even give myself. That we are not alone.

I draw my finger down the condensation on the glass, up and then over, until letters appear, dripping down the face of the microwave.

I'M HERE.

Vivian pales. She clutches the counter and sways on her feet.

"Mom?" she whispers.

I back slowly away, giving her time to realize the cold spot is gone so she won't stay here all night, burning pans and waiting for messages from the dead. She switches off the burner and drops into a chair at the breakfast table, staring at the microwave.

This is the trade she wanted, an answer to the question she was too afraid to ask before she kissed me. And now we're even. I can go.

TWENTY-FOUR

The next morning is a holiday from classes, but that doesn't excuse us from chores. Ben and I are pushing brooms over the sidewalks in the yard. The air's crisp and clear, and the sun's hot on our backs. We work slowly, savoring the daylight.

"Tell me again. Only this time, tell me all about the gravy and potatoes. Were they lumpy, like homemade? What about the stuffing? I bet that was homemade, too, huh?"

It's the fourth time Ben asks. *Was it hot? What did it smell like? Did I need to undo my buttons afterward?* I indulge him because it makes him happy, and because someone else's memory might be the closest thing Ben's had to a real Thanksgiving. Up until last night, it would have been mine, too.

So I tell him one more time about the drop biscuits and how the butter leaked down into the crannies. When we hit the end of the sidewalk, we change direction and talk about dessert. I don't mind sharing a meal with Ben. But the kiss I keep to myself.

"Who else knows about last night?" I ask during a break between courses. Ben's quiet, still digesting the details.

"Probably everyone. No secrets here."

"How'd they find out?"

"Monetti was mouthing off about it to Brooks. He told everyone you're bending over for Rickers. The dude's a prick." Ben looks over his shoulder to make sure nobody heard.

Actually, Monetti could have said a lot worse, but Ben scares easy and I don't want to give him indigestion.

"Tell me again about the whipped cream—"

"Conlan!"

I turn to see Officer Brooks waving at me from the fire door.

I drop the broom and double-time it across the yard.

"You've got a visitor."

My heart skips a beat. I pull off my beanie and use it to wipe the perspiration out of my eyes. Sweat stains bloom in the creases of my jumpsuit, and when I swipe my sleeve across my face, it comes away as filthy as the rest of me. I thought I made it clear to Pink she shouldn't come here anymore. I want to tell her so myself, to see her face one more time. But it isn't safe. She's better off forgetting all about me. Especially now, in light of what Ben just told me.

"Can't you tell her I'm busy?"

Brooks scratches his head. "I don't know. Viv seemed pretty insistent—"

"Vivian's here? Why?"

"Apparently she's here to see you. And she's got a Thanksgiving leftover sandwich with my name on it if I bring you down to visitation. So let's go, kid. I only get thirty minutes for lunch."

I slap my beanie back on with an exasperated sigh and follow Brooks to visitation, where Vivian is busy passing out sandwiches to all the guards. When she sees me, she leaves the platter on the check-in counter, drawing all their attention to the far side of the room. I sink into a chair and pick up the receiver.

"What are you doing here?" I bark, looking around to see who might be taking notes.

"We didn't get much of a chance to talk last night. I thought maybe—"

"No, you didn't think. You shouldn't be here."

"I want to help you find the hooded man."

Of all the reasons I expect her to cough up, this isn't one of them.

"I spent the morning reading everything I could find about your trial—"

I shake my head, incredulous. "What are you talking about, Vivian?"

"I can't get over all the holes in the case. The whole thing is like some gross miscarriage of justice. There was too much reasonable doubt for a jury to convict. Clearly the jury was tired and the public defender was lazy, and the foreman had a big mouth. But that's the only part that makes sense. The rest doesn't seem fair. The motive the prosecutors came up with was weak, for one. You had no criminal record. No history of violence. Then there was the whole thing about the positions of the bodies. When they found you, your back was to the wall and the position of the entrance wound . . ."

She's talking so fast she's making me dizzy. Regurgitating old arguments that no one bothered to care about before. Why would anyone care now?

". . . It all points to self-defense. If you can find out who the hooded man is, and prove he was in the school the night Ms. Cruz was killed, then you can fight for a mistrial."

"And do what?" What the hell does she want from me?

Vivian looks at me like I'm the crazy one. "Get out of here."

I laugh, until I realize that she's completely serious. There's so much hope in her eyes she can't see clearly. It's so easy for her to imagine passing through those gates. Her own future is wide open and safe. Warm clothes and roasted turkeys and brass locks on her doors. Getting straight As in college, writing highbrowed thesis papers about people like me.

"Where would I go? Look at me, Vivian! I didn't finish school. I've got no job, no money, no family. This is where I belong."

"You mean to tell me you've never wondered who that man was? Never wanted him brought to justice?"

"There is no justice! He's out there! I'm in here!"

"That doesn't mean it shouldn't be the other way around!"

We stare at each other, both of us breathing hard from the strength of our spent conviction. I scrub a hand over my face. Of course I want to put a name to the man who murdered Ms. Cruz. I'd kill him if I could, without hesitation or regret. But switch places with him? Leave the Y? She doesn't know what she's saying. How could she? Her entire life is outside those gates.

"Why are you doing this? You don't even know me."

She stumbles on her reply. "Because . . . because I believe you."

"You shouldn't. Everyone who believes in me gets hurt."

"I'll take my chances."

"That's stupid."

"No, it's right!" Her eyes light from within, all twinkling determination. But I can't afford faith in false promises. And I know she's leaving something out.

"What do you get out of being right?"

She looks stricken. "Who says I want anything? Why can't I just see someone who needs help and want to do the right thing?"

Because then karma will take her away. Because then I'll have Vivian's blood on my hands, too.

"It doesn't work that way. I won't be your charity case."

"Then what do I do?"

She isn't giving up. Her hands are bunched in tight little fists. This is about more than doing right. She wants something. Something selfish. Something only I can give her. Otherwise she wouldn't be fighting this hard.

"Ask me," I say, knowing I'm right. "Ask me for something in return."

She narrows her eyes at me as if she's insulted. She looks at my scar. Her lip's quivering. She takes a deep, trembling breath. "I want to know what it's like. On the other side. I want to know if my mother's all right. If I can talk to her. You're the only person I know who can answer that."

I should have seen this coming. It's all my fault. I wrote the message on her microwave, and now Vivian's on some quest to find her dead mother because I let her believe she's still here. I dig my fingers into my scar. I must be fucking brain-damaged.

"You should go." I stand up to leave. Vivian flies to her feet and presses a hand against the glass.

"Please!"

Behind her, Pink emerges through the door and stops short in the middle of the room. She looks at Vivian and me. She presses her thin lips together and walks out. I reach out and call her name, but she doesn't hear me through the window. She's already out the door. My hand is up against the glass, mirroring Vivian's, frozen in place by the shock on her face as she looks over my shoulder.

“What the hell is going on here?” Warden Somerville says behind me.

I pull my hand away from his daughter’s, realizing how this must look to him.

He snatches the receiver from me. “Vivian Lee. In my office. Now.” I jump when he slams the phone into the cradle.

“Officer Brooks, take Mr. Conlan back to finish his chores. He’ll have no more visitors until I get to the bottom of this.”

I know that’ll be a while. I survived my kick down the stairs, and I know firsthand that the bottom is a long way down.

TWENTY-FIVE

It's after Lights Out, and I'm camped out under the streetlight in front of the alley, taking stock of my thinning threads. It's too late to fix them. All I can do is try to make the ones I have left count. They hurt a little every time they break—an anxious discomfort like pins and needles. I tell myself this must be the reason for the ache in my gut. It began the minute I saw Pink's face through the visitation window. Right before she walked out. When she left, I felt like something inside me was ripping.

Pink throws open the break room door and tosses her garbage bags. I'd planned to step out of the light. To talk to her. To explain that I didn't ask Vivian to come. That Vivian's unexpected visit had nothing to do with why I told Pink I didn't want to see her anymore. But the words don't feel like enough, and there's nothing else I can give her. So I conceal myself in a circle of light, wishing myself invisible.

A man with a black crow tattoo on his neck is parked along the sidewalk. When Pink emerges from the alley, Holmes's man pulls into traffic, heading west toward her neighborhood. But that's not where Pink's headed. She's going east, which feels altogether wrong. I watch Holmes's man brake at the next intersection. He's probably going to make a U-turn and come up behind her. He'll hang a few car lengths back, close enough to see her, but far enough that she won't notice. That's what I would do. But traffic is thick and she's walking fast, turning down a darkened street, and I can't stomach the idea of leaving her alone. So I follow.

She walks a few blocks before Holmes's man rolls up, blending in with the rest of the moving traffic. But she must see him. She cuts across a four-lane street, nearly stopping my heart as she darts between cars to ditch him.

She starts zigzagging up and down side streets. North and then east, and then north again. Then darts down 17th Avenue, checking over her shoulder for Holmes's man before she walks off the sidewalk into the park.

When I finally catch up, there's no sign of her, but a long stretch of chain link still shivers where she must have ducked under it. I find the opening in the fence where she slipped through. It's been cut—a long time ago by the look of the rusted edges—and laid in place just enough so no one will notice. I peer in, but the fence is lined with a dense, dark hedge, and I can't see through it.

I kick the metal, my foot breaking apart as I watch the taillights of Holmes's man's car do a slow pass around the park and drive away.

Twenty miles of city streets and a twenty-foot-high prison wall? No problem. And here I am, locked out by a damn boxwood.

If you think you can't, you won't.

I think about what might be on the other side of that fence. I try to picture something. Anything. But nothing comes. The only thing I know for sure is that on the other side is her. Her frizzy brown curls and her big, fat coat and the color of her skin when she's mad. The way her chin turns up when she's feeling defiant, revealing the single brown freckle at the crest of her upper lip. I shut my eyes and I step through the fence, emerging far on the other side of the hedge.

"I thought you said you didn't want to see me anymore."

Pink's voice comes from behind, startling me. She deliberately crashes into my shoulder and keeps walking, leaving me standing in a grove of trees, a pale white shadow against the dark.

I gather up the parts of me she just displaced, still feeling a little off-balance.

"I just needed to make sure you were safe."

"Safe from who?" she asks, but this isn't a question I'm ready to answer. I'm still not quite sure myself.

I follow her through a manicured maze of paths. They cut through trees and tall grasses that bend in the breeze. Small thatched-roof shelters appear out of the shadows, their doors and windows barred shut. I pause at a placard with a picture of an ape on it.

"Where are we?" But I don't need to ask. There's chain link and Plexiglas everywhere I look, and small signs reminding us not to feed the animals. "What the hell are we doing here? It's closed."

"Didn't stop you from coming through the gate, did it?" She's still walking, puffing hard and fast, and I have to chase her to keep up. She won't even look at me, and when she does, it reminds me of the first time she saw me in the club. How pissed off she was by my very existence. She looks as angry and confused now as she was when I told her I didn't want to see her again. As offended as the moment she saw me looking at Vivian through that same window.

"Who is she?" she asks, as if she's reading my mind. She climbs over a waist-high fence with complete disregard for the DO NOT ENTER signs and drops to the ground.

I heave a sigh. I want to dissolve and materialize two days ago, or two months ago. Before things stopped making sense. "The warden's daughter."

Pink snorts into her hand and falls back against a tree trunk. Just like Martín would probably do. Only his face wouldn't move and he wouldn't make a sound. Woman problems, he'd say.

"So is it *her*, or just the *idea* of her?"

I don't want to talk about Vivian. It had never been *Vivian's* hand I wanted to hold. "It isn't her at all."

Pink's eyes are glassy and distant as she picks at a blade of grass. She's still not looking at me, but if she didn't want to talk, she'd be sitting on the slatted park bench ten feet away. Sitting on the ground feels like an olive branch, or maybe an invitation, so I sink down beside her.

"What are you doing here?" It's the same question I asked her that night we talked in the break room. I'd only had two questions to trade, and this one had felt like a waste. But somewhere between then and now, I stopped counting. "Shouldn't you be at home?"

"Some nights it's hard to breathe at home." A sad smile crosses her face. "I've been breaking in through that hole in the fence since I was thirteen. In here, I can be anywhere. Like right now . . . tonight . . . we're sitting in the Congo Basin, an entire ocean away." She tips her head to look through the naked branches and smiles at a violet sky dotted with stars, and I'm struck by the memory of her, sitting in front of me in English class. I wonder if this place, the zoo at night—an imaginary passport to the rest of the world—was the place where she wasn't supposed to be.

I look up and try to imagine what it'd be like to be somewhere else. Somewhere other than this city. But I can't picture anything beyond the hard wall of the Rockies or the infinite expanse of the dead-brown plains. When I think of leaving home, of escaping somewhere, I think of the boiler room floor. I imagine Pink curled up there beside me.

"If things are so hard at home, why not leave?"

"I'm stuck. I can't leave. Not now." She shakes her head. "But if I could do what *you do* . . . if I could do more than just imagine it . . . that'd be something special."

I wonder if that's the reason she fought so hard to get a job dancing in that men's club. If that's what she'd needed the money for. To get away. Out of this city. To see the world.

"There's nothing special about what I do." Nothing glamorous about sneaking into clubs and condemned apartments. Nothing heroic about ghosting around, watching people do horrible things. I want to tell her the same about stripping. That it's just a job, not who she is. That she's beautiful, just like she is now, sitting on the ground with no makeup on in her big, ugly coat.

"No, you're right. It's not the traveling that makes you special." She's not looking at the sky anymore. She's looking at me. At my face. I stare at her cock-eyed, trying to figure out if this is just another sarcastic undercut, but she's looking in my eyes, not at my scars. Her expression is soft and serious, her face so very close to mine, when she whispers, "What's special about you is . . . all the other stuff."

The question is hot on my tongue. It's burning my lips. "What other stuff?" I want more than anything to lean in and taste her answer even though it feels like it will cost me more than I can afford. I close my eyes, remembering the feel of a kiss, and the softness of a hand holding mine, and wishing this was something I could give her.

A lightbulb somewhere close flickers and pops, startling both of us.

She blinks and lowers her eyes to the ground. Flustered, she stammers, "I mean, technically, every one of us can travel outside our body.

You know when you're sleeping, and you have that dream where you're falling? My grandmother always said that's just us, falling back into ourselves. We all drift a little outside ourselves when we dream." She pauses. Looks back at me. "The rest of us just can't go as far."

But it sounds like she's saying more. That this . . . us . . . is just a dream. That's all it could be. If I had leaned in and closed that gap between us, it wouldn't have mattered. I couldn't have touched her anyway. All I would manage to do is push her away. And I'm surprised by how angry this makes me, all these things I want that I can never have, and these gifts I never asked for that I don't deserve.

"Why me?" It's the question I asked Ms. Cruz when she gave me those books. The same question I asked when I woke up alive in that hospital bed.

"Why any of us?" Pink answers with a sad smile.

"But why is it different for me?"

"It's different for you because you've died already," she says gently. "Maybe once that connection between body and soul's been damaged, it's easier to walk away and leave part of yourself behind."

"So you're saying I'm broken."

"All of us are broken, John. I just think that once you've lost everything, maybe there's nothing left to hold you back."

The room is shrinking. The walls close in around me, reality racing in from all sides.

I'm awake. This is real. I am not inside my body.

The screen beside the bed is bright with green and yellow numbers.

Pulse rate. Oxygen levels. Something is taped to the finger of the boy's hand. My hand.

I'm not dead. I'm alive. So what's happening to me?

I drift backward, into the far corner of the hospital room, those small popping sensations coming faster with each step. A pull, a force like gravity, ties me to the bed, but the farther I walk away, the thinner and more tenuous it feels. Like a tow cable fraying. I stand in the corner and hold perfectly still. A flutter of panic rises inside me. What happens if it breaks?

I shut my eyes and concentrate on the sound of Ms. Cruz's voice. I grab the invisible cord and pull myself toward the bed. The connection has an elastic quality to it and feels almost like a living thing, flexing and retracting, holding the pieces of me together. I test it gently and realize I am aware of every single strand, every individual fiber, including the broken ones. I feel them drift, disconnected from the rest of me like spider silk in the wind. Irreparable. Gone.

I stand beside the bed, face-to-face with myself. Close enough to count the bruises. My stomach turns. The left side of my head has been shaved. Gauze-lint catches on the stubble around the wounds and clings to the trail of course-cut stitches. Black monofilament darts in and out of the swollen purple and yellowing skin like shoestrings, and there are thick silver staples above my ear. I swallow back the sick and bitter taste on my tongue, trying to recognize myself in a face that looks more like the busted aluminum cans my dad kicks around the living room.

My grip is tentative around the connection to that messed-up kid. I don't want to look at him anymore. Remembering hurts worse than the stitches and scars. It hurts worse than being inside that body, and I inch farther from the bed, but the pain follows me. Because this is the inside kind of pain, the kind that stays with you even after the rest of you has been sewn up. I feel the pop and sting of a fraying thread. I think about running, even if it means the whole damn thing might snap.

I turn away from myself just as Ms. Cruz reaches out and brushes the boy's remaining hair back from his forehead—my forehead—even though the blond bangs are still gently brushed aside from the last time she did it. Her expression is tender—the way I imagine a mother's should be—and her touch is probably featherlight, just enough to let me know she is here. She opens a book and begins reading aloud. When I close my eyes, I can almost smell the tang of book leather that always seems to waft from her clothes like perfume. And I think twice about running. Because this is something I would miss.

The day nurse pokes her head in the door. "Visiting hours are over."

My threads feel brittle and thin. Like a rubber band that's been stretched too far. Too many times.

"I want you to promise me you'll be careful."

"What do you mean?" Pink asks.

"It means I might not always be around to keep an eye on you."

She bites her lip and smiles. "Come back tomorrow night. I promise not to walk so fast." She elbows me playfully where my ribs should be, and it feels good, to joke with her like this. To just be here with her, talking, even if I can't give her anything else. I would come be with her every night if I could, but I can't make her that promise.

"What happens when I can't come back?"

She turns to me with that same haunted look I saw in her eyes the first night we met, when she thought I might be someone she'd known once, and lost. "What do you mean?"

"Remember when you said all I have is time? This thing I can do . . ." I shake my head, unsure how to tell her. "I can't do it forever. I don't know how many more trips I can manage before I can't make it back."

She stiffens, a horrible realization passing behind her eyes. "The connection . . . the one you told me about . . ."

Neither one of us can finish that thought, like if we say it out loud, I might disappear.

"You knew," she says, her breath hitching. She pushes off the ground and backs away. "You knew, and you tried to tell me. That day in visitation when you told me you didn't want to see me anymore. That's what you were trying to say. That it's too dangerous."

Too dangerous for her. Not for me. Either way, it doesn't matter anymore. The stakes are too high, for both of us.

"You can't leave the Y. . . ." Her eyes are dull and her voice sounds distant, like a glass wall just snapped in place between us. When she says good-bye, I feel the slam of a cell door deep inside me. "You shouldn't have come. You were right, John. We can't see each other anymore."

TWENTY-SIX

Ben and I hit the showers on Saturday morning without a word. I slip off my shoes, shrug out of my dirty jumpsuit, and turn on the spray without feeling any of it. I don't wait for it to heat up, just step under the stream and shut my eyes. The cold water washes away the burn from my sleepless eyes and jolts me back to myself. I haven't been able to stop thinking about last night and what it all means. What it will mean to go to bed here each night and never leave. What it means to never see her again. Even if Vivian's right—even if I could find the hooded man and get out of here on a mistrial—where would I go? All I want to do is sleep. I'm so tired I can't even think about the possibility of not waking up.

I let the wall hold me, listening to the steady patter of the spray, fighting to stay awake as the water begins to warm. The locker room is silent. Quiet enough that I could almost fall asleep.

Too quiet.

My eyes fly open just as a hand closes over the back of my neck and shoves me down hard. My cheek smashes against the tile floor, pain exploding under my scars.

Someone's laughing.

I struggle wildly as my wrists are pinned behind my back. My

I'm about to shake my head again. But I think better of it and choke out a hoarse, "Yes, sir."

Six's face twists with disgust. "Why does he get to go to the nurse? I'm the one who's bleeding!"

Monetti strikes before any of us can breathe. He grabs Six by the back of the head, rolls him over, and presses the butt end of his Maglite into the groove below his back. He growls low in his ear, "You fuck up one more time and I'll tear you up so bad the nurse won't know what to do with you. Am I clear?"

Six doesn't say a word. Sometimes keeping your mouth shut is the only right answer. He glares at me out of the eye that isn't smashed to the floor. Monetti releases him with a shove, drags him to his feet, and practically drop-kicks him out of the locker room, taking his friend with him.

When the storm is over, Ben and I are the only ones left standing. He hands me my jumpsuit and turns off the water.

"Why'd you do that?" I ask him. "Six could have killed you."

Ben shrugs, still looking a little shaken. "Nah, I don't think Holmes would've let that happen." He casts a quick glance down the row of showers; Holmes's celly slings a towel over his shoulder and walks away. We hadn't been alone after all. "You all right?"

I step into my pant legs, my knees still watery. "Yeah, I owe you. Your timing is good." He swells at the compliment, standing taller than I've ever seen him. I scrub the towel over my head, looking him over, trying to figure out where the hell he stowed the blade. "Cool trick. Show me sometime?"

"I can make you one if you want. I made one for Holmes, too. He offered me a job hooking him up with shanks, but I just didn't feel right about it. Never know whose hands they might fall into. I told him I needed to think it over." He gives me a lopsided smile, looking a little sheepish. He isn't like any other con I've ever met, and I wonder if he's also here by some "gross miscarriage of justice." An impatient jury who just wanted to get home. Some cop's or lawyer's mistake.

"You coming to chow?" he asks.

I pitch the towel in the dirties bin, thinking about the black knife. It came in through a laundry bin one month ago, around the same time my lawyer visited Six. Now someone wants me dead. And someone's already tried to kill Pink—the only person outside the Y anyone's ever seen me talk to before yesterday. Someone's trying to silence me. But why? What does it have to do with that knife? As far as I know, only one other person in the world knows that knife was never mine.

And I never saw his face.

My pulse quickens, all the loose puzzle pieces coming together to form a picture.

If you can find out who the hooded man is, and prove he was in the school the night Ms. Cruz was killed, then you can fight for a mistrial.

But *he's* out there. And *I'm* in here.

That doesn't mean it shouldn't be the other way around. . . .

"Go on without me," I tell Ben. "I'm not feeling so hot. I'm gonna take Monetti up on his offer and go see the nurse. Maybe he'll let me crash for a while." Group doesn't start until after lunch. If I leave now, I'll have at least four hours before they kick me out of the infirmary. "I'll be back by chow."

Hopefully with answers, and hopefully alive.

TWENTY-SEVEN

I'm standing outside Pink's house, staring up at the windows, wondering which one's hers. She's probably sleeping, but I only have a few hours. I start hollering her name loud enough to wake the dead, looking for some sign of recognition. A cat blinks down at me from an upstairs window with mild disinterest, and a large dog tied to a signpost in the neighbor's yard barks loud enough to drown me out.

"Come on, Pink! Please! I need to talk to you!"

"John?" asks a quiet voice behind me. I spin and see Pink, frozen and ghost-white about twenty yards behind me. A backpack is slung over her shoulder, and she grips it tight. "What are you doing here?"

Relieved, I take a quick step toward her, and she mirrors it with a quick step back. Her face has a haunted expression, and it takes me a minute to realize what she's so afraid of. I lower my voice. "I'm okay."

She cocks her head and doesn't come any closer.

"I'm alive, I mean. Can we please talk? I only have three hours left before I need to get back to the Y."

The color rushes back to her face. She opens her mouth to holler at me, then looks at the neighbor peering through his window and thinks better of it. Instead, she opens her front door and holds it wide enough to let me see inside, so I can follow her in.

"Jesus, John," she whispers, clutching her chest. "You scared me half to death. I thought . . ." She lets the rest trail off. "I thought maybe you'd never made it home from the zoo, that's all." She hangs her coat on a peg and pulls a paper bag from her backpack. "Come upstairs. There's something I need to do, and then you can tell me what the hell you're doing here."

I follow Pink up a narrow flight of stairs that creak under her feet. When we reach the top, she opens the paper bag. There's a pharmacy logo on it. She turns it upside down, and the contents rattle into the palm of her hand. Carefully, she checks the labels on the bottles, then quietly pushes open the bedroom door.

I wait in the hall, feeling like an intruder, but the place is too small not to see inside the room. The blinds are closed, and a woman lies sleeping. She's barely a lump under the blankets. Her hair is thin, mostly gone in places, and her lips and eyes are sunken, as though the skin is pasted to the bone. Prescription bottles cover the surface of the night table, neatly ordered in rows. A young woman, maybe three or four years older than Pink, stirs on a mattress on the floor. But as Pink straightens the blankets first around her mother and then her sister, something in her face seems to narrow the gap in age between them. In this room, Pink is older than I've ever seen her.

A clipboard hangs from a nail by the window. Pink pulls it to her silently, examining the handwritten notes. She returns it to its hook, and with one last look at them both, she pulls the door closed.

I follow her downstairs to the living room. She falls onto a worn-out sofa and props her feet on the armrest. I sit beside her on the floor.

"I'm sorry," I say. It's the same thing I said to Simpson about his own mother, and I could kick myself. "I mean, I'm sorry I blew your audition." I'm not sure how else to apologize for that night, and I'm not sure I really want to. Her mom's medication is probably expensive as hell, but so is the price of taking that stage. And yet, watching her brush the hair back from her mother's face, I know it's a price she'd pay. That she would give anything—trade anything—to fix her.

"It wouldn't have mattered. You heard what he said." She hugs her knees to her chest and curls into the cushions. "Whatever. In six months, I'll be done with school and I can take a day job."

What we both know and don't say is that her mother probably won't be around that long.

"I just want her to pass peacefully. You know?"

But I don't. I only know what happens when a person dies violently—what they see and what they feel when it isn't their time to go. When Vivian asked about the other side, I had no answers. I have no idea how someone gets there. Or if there's even an other side at all.

"What happens then?" I ask.

Pink sniffs and wipes her eyes. She sits up and shakes off her exhaustion. "I'm not sure. All I know is they're not stuck here. If they go peacefully, they don't fight the light. They accept it and pass through it. The ones who fight it get stuck somewhere in the middle, like you. They get confused, or freak out, or feel like they have a score to settle. Sometimes they cling too hard to a loved one and can't let go. Then they're trapped in that place until they resolve whatever it is that weighs down their soul." Her gaze drifts to the closed bedroom door. She pitches her voice to a whisper, as if she's afraid to say the words. "I'm afraid I'll open my eyes one day and Mom'll still be here. That she'll cling to us and won't let herself go. I'm afraid she'll get trapped here. That if she doesn't move on . . . neither will we."

I think about Simpson, stuck in the Y, haunting the lunch line for the rest of eternity. I picture Pink getting old under that same tree at the zoo. I wonder, when my last thread breaks, who I would cling to.

"How do they... you know... let go?"

"I don't know. How does anyone ever let go of someone they care about?" Her eyes bore directly into mine. It feels strange, knowing that to anyone else, I'm invisible. Just a cold spot in the room. Even in my skin, to most people I'm nothing more than my scars. But Pink seems to see through me. To see more than anyone else since Ms. Cruz. And the thought of letting go of this—of her—leaves me with a phantom ache in my chest.

She takes a deep breath and wipes away a tear. "It's different for everyone, I guess. My grandmother said sometimes they just need someone to tell them it's okay to move on. Other times it's more involved. Maybe they need to pass on information about how they died, or protect a loved one they couldn't leave behind. I've only met a few. They always seem sort of lost. Sometimes a little crazy. It can be hard to talk them over. My grandmother was better at it than I am."

"Talk them over? You mean they can actually hear you?" I remember Simpson screaming at me from the lunch line. Getting louder and louder when I didn't listen. What if I had? What if I'd talked to him? "What do you say?"

"It's kind of like being a crisis operator on one of those hotlines. I ask them how they died and let them ramble awhile. Then try to figure out what's keeping them here. If it's something simple, I try to persuade them to let it go and move on. Once they make the decision to go, the light comes back for them, and I never see them again. But the angry ones..." She shakes her head and shivers, hugging her knees. "Not much I can do with those. They hang on too long and get crazy—all poltergeisty and mean. My sister and I used to work at a nicer club in LoDo. It was cleaner and the customers tipped better. One night, a group of guys came in celebrating a bachelor party. By the end of the night, they were all messed up. One of them got hold of some bad drugs and died of a heart attack in the bathroom. He was young, and I guess he was pretty mad about that. Anyway, he got all shady and started haunting the place. Once he figured out I could see him, he started tossing drinks off my tray and trashing the break room during my shifts. I tried talking to him, but he was too angry to pass on. It was him or me, so I quit."

I remember the first time Pink saw me in the club. How pissed off she was. She probably thought I was no different from the ghost who'd been haunting her. I can't blame her. Here I am, not much more than a ghost myself, showing up uninvited and pushing my way into her life, because she's the only one who hears me.

She must see it on my face, that I want something from her I don't deserve and don't know how to ask for. She slides down the side of the couch and settles beside me on the floor. She leans into my field of vision. That small space between her face and mine feels like the gap she left open in her dressing room door.

"Why'd you come?" she asks. "I thought we agreed it's too dangerous. You shouldn't be here, but you are. I want to know why."

I look everywhere—at the cheaply framed posters of exotic beaches on the wall, a crumpled pharmacy receipt on the floor, the worn issues of *National Geographic* open and dog-eared on the table—anywhere but her face, knowing I can't give her a single thing she wants in return.

"I need your help," I say, choking on the words. "I need to talk to someone. Someone who can't hear me."

"Okay," she says, but there's an underlying hesitation. Maybe because the last time I asked her for a favor, she almost got killed. "Who?"

"Her name is Vivian. Vivian Somerville."

She nods slowly. Her forehead creases, like she's confused. "Is she a relative or something?"

"She's Warden Somerville's daughter."

Pink throws her arm out, shutting me up before I have a chance to explain. "Let me get this straight. You want me to talk to the girl I saw you with in visitation? I thought you said there was nothing going on between you two."

"It's nothing like that."

"Then tell me, John. What is it like?" Her laughter boxes me in like an accusation.

"Not like what you think. She thinks I'm innocent. She wants to help me prove it. But her father won't let her see me."

"And this surprises you? Do you seriously think he's going to let his daughter spend her Saturdays hanging out with a convicted murderer? He's probably scared to death she'll fall for you. She's got a big future ahead of her, and being in love with someone who can't ever leave will only hold her down." Pink flushes and turns away.

I've told myself this a million times—that I'm not good enough for anybody—but the affirmation hurts more coming from Pink's lips. "She's not in love with me. And I'm not looking to hold anybody down. I'm not a murderer. It was self-defense—"

"Yeah, we've established that. You don't need to prove yourself to me. But how does Little Miss Public Defender plan to prove it?"

"She wants to help me find the man in the hood, the one who killed Ms. Cruz."

Pink's snicker dissolves and her face falls slack. "Is that even possible?"

"I don't know. But it might not matter, because I think the man in the hood is coming for me. Someone stole evidence from my trial. A knife. That knife found its way into the Y. Whoever stole it hired an inmate to put a hit on me. I think the man in the hood is trying to make sure the investigation is never reopened. I'm the only living witness to what really happened that night. If I'm dead, any chance of him being implicated dies with me. He's trying to get rid of me, and everyone I've been talking to. Like you."

The color drains from her cheeks. "Verone?"

"I think he was a hired hit man. But he's not the man in the hood. Verone would have been in jail when Ms. Cruz was killed."

"So if he's not the man in the hood, who is?"

The details of that night have always been sketchy. Investigators asked all kinds of questions. What was the man wearing? What did he look like? Did he have any jewelry or tattoos. But when I tried to focus on him, all I could remember was the hood, like my mind had erased all the details, as if he never really existed at all. And that's exactly what the police and the prosecutors believed.

"I don't know. I never got a clear look at his face. And no other witnesses came forward. The only person who got a good look at him was Ms. Cruz."

Our eyes hold.

"How much time do we have?" she asks, launching off the couch and pulling on her coat.

"Enough."

TWENTY-EIGHT

I'm awake and dressed in the clothes the caseworker left for me yesterday. I stuff my hospital blanket inside my pillowcase with my toothbrush and soap, and give my room one last look around for anything I can claim as my own. One hand holds my pillowcase open, the other hovers over the books. I have every right to take them. They're mine. The name inside the covers says so. But just because someone signs their name to something doesn't mean it truly belongs to them. And taking the books doesn't feel right.

So I don't.

I sling the pillowcase over my shoulder and slip into the hall. I've already mapped out my route through lesser-used hallways and stairwells, and I walk out of Mercy Hospital through the rear service doors.

I won't be here if Ms. Cruz doesn't bother to come back for me. I don't want to know if she never comes back for me at all.

I head for the only safe place I can think of. It's late August and classes will be back in session in a couple of weeks, but for now, the high school is empty. I don't bother checking the front doors. I head straight to a side entrance with a faulty lock that releases easily when I slide a smashed-up pop can between the latch and the frame.

I'm greeted by a wall of stagnant air. The smell of old sweat and textbooks is as familiar as breathing, and I move with a clear sense of direction through the dark corridors to the water fountain. I lean into the slow dribble, trying not to touch my lips to the spigot. It's warm and metallic and tastes like the school smells. I take a long pull, come up for air, and go at it again. It's not served up cold in a Styrofoam cup with a bendy straw, but it doesn't cost anything, so it tastes just fine going down.

I wipe my mouth on my sleeve and look down the hall at the long, silent rows of banged-up lockers, interspersed by locked classroom doors. Nothing's changed. It's an old high school in a crappy neighborhood that hasn't gotten around to being renovated yet. No security cameras to worry about. Nothing here worth stealing. The only thing new is the graffiti, and even that's not worth breaking in to see, but the classroom doors are locked for the summer anyway.

Pink rounds the corner by the water fountain before she realizes I'm no longer behind her. I'm frozen, feet glued to the blue-and-white tile. The ghosts of this place—the smells and sounds, the memories of what happened here—are all telling me to get out. School's closed for Thanksgiving break, and the emptiness of these halls is painfully familiar.

"Come on. What are you waiting for? This is the place, isn't it?"

The brick walls stretch and narrow around me, closing over escape routes and sources of air. I step back, my smoke chest pounding. I can't catch my breath. It's all in my head, but so real I can taste the burn in my throat. Can feel the race of blood to my core and the chill it leaves in each of my fingers.

"I can't," I croak, certain I'm going to be sick, or worse. Something terrible will happen if I walk down that hall. Dr. Manning calls it post-traumatic stress. Says it'll take time and distance to heal. That this is my body's way of coping. But my body isn't here. It's minutes and miles away, so why do I feel like every piece of me is dying? Like something inside me is breaking.

I hold tight to my threads, ready to pull myself home. "I can't do this."

"You have to do this. I'm coming with you."

"What if she's here?" I'm paralyzed by the horrible possibility that Mrs. Cruz has been trapped here all this time. What if she's around this corner, waiting, two black holes of pity and regret?

"That's what I'm counting on. Come on." Pink reaches out a merciless hand. I'm hanging on to my sanity, to her, to my threads, by my fingertips. "You can do this."

I push her hand away, ignoring the hurt on her face. "I know."

I steady myself and take the empty halls in long, brash strides, afraid I'll chicken out if I don't. I tune out the buzzing in my head. Ignore the red glowing exit signs that taunt me. I move past Pink, ahead of her, so she won't see me flinch as I round every corner.

I push open the old boiler room door, ready to slam it behind me and hide inside. Pink stands in the doorway, watching me. The room is empty. No gym mats. No blankets. Nothing but memories.

I push open the door and step inside the old boiler room, into a cave of dust and forgotten rusty pipes. I pull the chain on the lightbulb over my head and blink into the shadowy corners, making sure I'm alone. I'm not the only one who knows about this place. Not the only one who's needed

it. So I'm not surprised to see a rucksack and a blanket, rolled tight and tucked under a set of pipes.

I set my pillowcase down on the far side of the room, giving the other kid some space. I've been gone a long time, and he might not know me. Unlikely, given my story and the TV crews who followed my father's trial all summer. But best not to get too close, just in case.

I spread my blanket over the cold concrete and ease myself down. I strip off the sneakers, careful not to pop the blisters on my heels. The shoes don't fit right. They'd probably belonged to someone else—maybe a few other kids, judging by the smell of them—a revolving door of foot sweat, recycled through Social Services and passed down to me. I stretch out my toes and let them breathe for a while. Guess I'll have to get used to them.

My head hurts and I'm hungry. I need to find something to eat before sunset—before it's dark enough outside for someone to notice if I turn on a light—but I'm too worn-out to move. My legs ache after the long walk from the hospital. I'm not as strong as I used to be. I lie back on the hospital pillow, even though I'm not tired. It smells like Mercy, safe and secure, and I let myself close my eyes and leave.

My muscles are heavy and my body falls away easily, like stepping out of a thick coat. I leave it lying on the blanket on the floor. It feels good to be free of the pain and fatigue. In this form, I'm tireless. I don't get weary or slow. I look back at my body before wandering away, still fascinated by this strange mirror that isn't. The boy on the floor is pale and thin—too thin. The tan line on my forehead where the mile-high sun used to darken the skin just below my Highland Waste cap is faded, and the calluses on my hands have gone soft. I barely recognize myself, even without the scars. I linger for a minute out of habit, just to make sure my chest rises and falls, and I wonder if this weird need to check for signs of life will ever pass, or if one day I'll just stop caring.

I walk through the wall, trying to ignore the tiny sting of pops and snaps. Trying not to count the threads that break each time I let go.

A woman's voice stops me cold. It echoes through the halls. I can't tell from which direction.

"John!"

Ms. Cruz's voice is clear and insistent, and growing louder.

She came back for me.

"John!" The voice is not in my head. Not a memory. It's coming from the hall outside.

I rush through the wall out of the boiler room, leaving Pink scrambling to follow. I fly around the corner and skid to a stop. A pale mist of long hair and skirt hovers by the spot where the police found me, beside remnants of the dark stain that's discolored all my memories of her. Ms. Cruz turns slowly, like a swirl of dense fog, and seems to blink her blank black eyes. Pink catches up, jerking to a halt beside me. Her heavy breath crystalizes in white puffs. Frost crackles and spreads over the floor, leaving a frozen film on the walls and the lockers, as a chill consumes the hall.

Ms. Cruz is walking fast. Calling my name.

She came back. She's looking for me. She's heading toward the boiler room. I should get back to my body before she finds me.

Then suddenly, she stops, her heels midstride, her skirt midsway. Voices. People talking down the hall. She hears them, too.

She changes direction, following the sound. She turns down a dark hallway to her right.

"John, is that you?" she calls out.

Two figures lean together at the end of the corridor. Their heads snap up when they hear her, their hands concealed behind their backs.

"Who's there?" she calls to them.

They stand in the shadows. They're barely illuminated by the red exit sign above their heads. They don't answer and she stiffens.

"You aren't supposed to be here. The school is closed. You're trespassing," she warns.

Pink and I gape as Ms. Cruz's lips part slowly. Her mouth hangs open, as if the words are stuck. I hear them inside my head, a hoarse rasp. Pink's eyes meet mine, and I know she hears it, too.

"You aren't supposed to be here." Ms. Cruz points to the stubborn stains still lingering between the tiles on the floor, smoky tendrils trailing from the indistinct shape of her fingers. "This wasn't supposed to happen."

The guilt that knots my throat is thick and suffocating. She's right. I wasn't supposed to be here that day. I was supposed to wait in the hospital. I was supposed to go home with her. I threw her books and her generosity back in her face, and she came looking for me anyway. She died looking for me. She died trying to give me a life.

"I can't do this."

Pink's strong, clear voice rings out beside me. "What wasn't supposed to happen?"

Ms. Cruz's form swirls and coalesces. Her wild smoke hair billows around her. She tangles her fingers in it and pulls, and I barely recognize the woman I knew. She's shaking her head, like she's agitated or confused. An agonizing wail rises from inside her. "You weren't supposed to be here! You were my responsibility!" I crush my hands over my ears. Her screams echo every accusation in my head. It's deafening, almost more than I can bear. Suddenly, she crumples. There's a hitch in her breath. "I was supposed to take care of you."

"I'm sorry," I cry out. "I'm sorry I didn't wait for you. I'm sorry I didn't believe—"

"We never should have seen them," she says, cutting off every thought inside my head. "We weren't supposed to see them."

"Who?" Pink asks urgently.

"That man, and the boy. The man was angry. His head was covered. They were in the dark. I shouldn't have seen them."

Lights flash in my head, scenes flickering like an old movie. I remember rounding the corner behind her. I remember seeing the man's hood. And the boy—Cameron Walsh. Their heads were bent together. Something changed hands between them. They turned at the sound of her voice.

They're walking toward her now. The man's wearing gloves. He holds something in his hand. It's tucked in close to his side. As he nears, the blade shimmers in the dim light.

"What happened?" Pink urges her on. "What did you see?"

Ms. Cruz doesn't answer. She stares at the stain on the floor. But I know. I remember. She had startled them. The man and the boy had jumped apart when she stumbled upon them in the hallway. I remember now. I remember what was hidden in their hands. What they traded that no one was supposed to see.

"Weapons," I say. "For drugs." Ms. Cruz had seen too much.

He descends on her, his hood pulled low over his eyes. He swears as she digs a sharp heel into his shin and swings her bag of books into his side. The bag hits his wrist and the knife clatters to the tile. Ms. Cruz swoops down and grabs it.

I move fast, sliding through the boiler room wall and throwing myself into my body. But it's too fast. My nerve endings scream as I jerk myself to my feet and stagger for the door. I lurch into the hall almost blind, my eyes slow to adjust to the semidarkness. I hear them before I see them. She's grunting. Putting up a fight.

I run toward the sound, tripping on myself and pushing off the walls. My muscles are clumsy and slow, my breath ragged.

I skid into the fray and try to pull her behind me. I aim for her arm. Instead, I catch the wide strap of her messenger bag, and my books tumble out, throwing me off-balance. I grab her arm just as he punches her stomach, doubling her over. She looks up into his face. Then down at her belly.

She is dead weight, sliding down, taking me with her. My fingers dig into her skin as I ease her to the floor. Footsteps pound fast in opposite directions. I spare a look over my shoulder. The man in the hood sprints one way, the kid who'd hung back in the shadows throws open the emergency door. All I see is his back tearing through it.

I turn back to Ms. Cruz, waiting for her to say something. The man must have knocked the wind out of her. Her breath comes short. It sounds all wrong. Wet somehow.

I look down at her shirt, at the dark stain spreading over it.

I let go of her arm and it falls limp. Her eyes flutter and close.

"Oh, shit. Oh, fuck, no!" The knife is still inside her, buried in her belly to its dull black hilt. I jerk it out of her. It makes a terrible sound when it hits the floor, echoing in the vast, silent space. We are alone.

"Help me!" I scream. "Somebody, help!"

I wipe her hair back from her forehead, leaving sticky red trails over her face.

"Stay with me! Don't leave," I'm begging. But she's not breathing, and the smell of death is overpowering. Hot and suffocating and familiar. My knees are wet. I look down at the creeping stain, the blood coming faster without the knife to dam the flow. "Come back," I plead, wiping away my tears with wet hands. But she's already gone.

I slide down the wall, the bricks scraping my spine until I'm sitting beside her in a warm pool of her blood. It clings to me. All I can see is her death on my hands and the red light over the exit door. I try to stand, but my knees won't hold me up, and I slide back down. They can't have gotten far. I want to find them. I want to kill them. But my body won't move.

I remember everything, all of it coming back in angry flashes of red. Ms. Cruz had backed away, but the hooded man lunged with a knife.

I remember how she struggled. Fought back and knocked it away. But somewhere between the time she discovered them and the moment he stabbed her is the hole in my memory. The gap in time when I ran back for my body. In those moments, I'd missed something. Something important.

"He dropped the knife," Ms. Cruz says, startling me. My mind reels to the last thing I remember before I left her there to fight him alone. The knife hitting the tile floor. Ms. Cruz bending to grab it.

"Then what?" I ask, desperate to fill in the gaps.

Her arm slashes the air, mimicking the attack. A single swiping stroke, level with her head. "I picked it up." Her head rolls toward me, lips unmoving. The words pass from her eyes to my mind, a key sliding into place. "I cut him."

Time stands still as my mind connects the pieces. The hooded man is tall. Ms. Cruz slashed him, high, a sideways motion. He'd been wounded. Probably scarred. It would have been a clean cut, maybe in the shoulder . . . or high across the chest.

It's like someone's pulled the hood from my mind, and suddenly I can see.

Monetti. Standing in Warden Somerville's bathroom. Wearing nothing but a scar on his chest.

"What did he look like?" I hear myself ask, but I already know the answer.

Ms. Cruz's face twists and stretches. Her lips peel back, and her teeth extend into fangs.

Pink shouts, "John! Behind you!"

Ms. Cruz scales the wall and darts past me. I turn to see her hunched and growling, face-to-face with another ghost. He is smaller—a wisp of smoky gangly legs and unruly hair and vacant black eyes. They circle each other, snapping and snarling—Ms. Cruz and the ghost of Cameron Walsh.

"You leave him alone!" she bellows, stretching herself taller until she is towering over him. The boy gnashes his teeth at me, then takes off running. He disappears through the boiler room wall.

Pink looks on, colorless and shaken, as Ms. Cruz shrinks down to a gentle mist. She smooths her skirt, and the wild tendrils of her hair drift and settle against her shoulders. Her shape clarifies, and in it I see the vague semblance of the woman who was once my teacher—my friend. But this apparition—this muddled and twisted thing—isn't Ms. Cruz anymore.

"You shouldn't stay here, John," she whispers in my head. "Cameron is angry. He's been here too long. He's changing. He doesn't see himself clearly anymore." She shakes her head, massaging her translucent temple. Her face is puckered and confused. "Why are you here?" she asks in a small voice, tipping her head curiously, as if we only just arrived. "You shouldn't be here."

"Neither should you," I manage to whisper. I look to Pink, and she nods gently. I reach for Ms. Cruz's hand. It feels almost solid in mine, but I'm afraid of what she might become if she binds herself to this place much longer. And I don't want to remember her this way. "You've done everything you can for me."

"But you were my responsibility. You were my—" Her voice is rising, and I smile because I should know that Ms. Cruz never takes no for an answer. It's why she's held on so long. Because she's determined. Because she's strong. But I can be strong, too.

"Feeling responsible isn't the same as being guilty. None of this was your fault. Go. I'll be okay. I can take care of myself now."

Relief washes over her face. Her mist seems to sparkle with it. She squeezes my hand, strong enough that I can almost feel it, and lets go. Splinters of light radiate around her, prisms catching her face and illuminating her with color from within. Gold glasses, black hair, her gentle brown eyes, and her warm pink smile. The way I want to remember her. Her face turns upward and her lips part with a look of wonder.

I feel a pang of loneliness as she's gathered up in a million pinpricks of light, like stars sifting backward through an hourglass.

"Don't be afraid," Pink whispers. A tear falls down her cheek, and she rests her hand close to mine.

"I'm not afraid," I tell her. Sometimes, it's just hard to let go.

TWENTY-NINE

I sit for what must be a long time, holding that knife, watching Cameron's blood spill out in a wide arc from his body. It mixes with Ms. Cruz's and soaks through my pants. I sit until I am cold and shaking. Sirens wail in the distance, but I am somewhere else, my mind lost in the memory of my father's kitchen.

I am awake when the exit door swings open and flashlights carve slices of red through the darkness. I can just make out Ms. Cruz's pale, blue face, her empty messenger bag, and the tumble of books across the floor before I am blinded by white light. It shines like a tunnel, getting bigger. Voices call out from behind it. I know the light's coming for me.

I am yanked up and dragged away from Ms. Cruz's body. I look over my shoulder. All of it—the blood, the bodies—growing farther and farther away. It's like I am watching from someplace else.

Like I'm not really here.

I can't feel anything, not the tug at my back as the handcuffs click shut. I don't feel my feet touch the ground as they lead me from the school. I am numb.

Muffled voices ask question after question, but I don't speak. I'm pulled toward the flashing lights. Shoved down by my head into the backseat of a car. I have the right to remain silent.

I walk Pink home. Pink and I say weary good-byes. Neither of us has enough strength to acknowledge it may be our last. I have to go back to the Y and solve this on my own. Alone. I have to keep quiet about what I know now. I can't risk involving Vivian. She's too close to Monetti. She'd be too easy for him to silence if he thinks she knows too much. I don't even tell Pink the name of the man behind the hood. The less she knows, the safer she is.

Then I head south to the Y. I run the whole way, trying to figure out exactly what I'll do when I get there. Confronting Monetti under his own roof will only force him to kill me quicker. But he doesn't want to kill me himself, or he would have done it already. He wants someone else to do it. He's setting up Six and Verone to take the fall so he can keep his own hands clean.

It makes perfect sense. He steals the knife to get rid of the evidence and sabotage any shot I have at a retrial. He marks it up with Six's name and sells it into the general population in the Y to get it out of his own hands and, in doing so, incriminate Six. Then he positions Six to kill me. Six and I have a history of fighting. So he gives Six just enough wiggle room to pick one more—like this morning in the showers. If he'd managed to drown me before Ben stopped him, no one would have thought twice about his motives.

Then Monetti covers his trail on the outside. He hires Verone to get rid of Pink and shut her up for good, just in case she knows something, probably using a disposable cell phone number to communicate with all his players. Probably, he passes money and messages anonymously, using a lawyer as a mule, so Six never has to know who sold him the knife and ordered the hit.

Simple.

The hard part is knowing what to do about it. If Monetti has his way, Six will kill me. Verone will kill Pink. And Monetti will answer to no one.

I pause outside the gate, looking in on the Y. The sun beats down on its high white walls, glistening off the razor wire. Could I survive out here, on the outside? Do I even have a choice when the enemy's inside the gate? Monetti won't let me have a life—not even this one—because he's afraid of what I might remember. That one day, it'll be me holding the key.

One thing's certain. I can't stop him alone.

I pass through the wire and walls and head straight to the infirmary. It's always a strange feeling, coming back to myself. I'm hard to look at from the outside. It's easier not to remember the pain when you never stop to look at your own scars. But here I am, on a cot in a cell. My hands are balled into fists, and I am asleep in my clothes on top of the covers. I circle the bed as my threads wind tighter, nothing but a length of fraying twine in my hands. I can't stop thinking about what Pink said. About not being afraid. My head's wrapped in metal. But that other thing, the part that beats beneath my ribs, feels so damn fragile.

I think about what the warden said, about how we all have scars. How as long as we're breathing, we all have choices left to make.

The nurse checks his watch and heads toward my cot. I shrug back into myself, stretching to fit all the guilt and fear I've brought back with me. Every inch of soft tissue is aching and stiff with it. But I'm breathing. And for now, that's enough.

I sit up before the nurse turns the lock. "I want to see the warden."

Ten minutes later, Officer Brooks is escorting me to administration. He doesn't sing as we make our way down the hall, but he doesn't cuff me, either. His breath smells like turkey sandwiches and shame when he knocks on the warden's door. Warden Somerville stands with his back to us, hands on his hips.

"Sit down," he says. "Officer Brooks, you can wait outside."

I don't look at the pictures or smell the books. I know by the warden's posture, this won't take long. I sit on the edge of the big leather chair, not letting my back touch the cushion.

"I'm disappointed in you, son," he says when he finally turns around. He thinks, rocking his jaw back and forth as if I've hit him. "Vivian's never been one to sneak around and do things behind my back. I'd like to know what's going on between you and my daughter."

"I don't know, sir. I mean, there's nothing going on. Nothing I know of, anyway." I don't dare tell him about the kiss. It didn't mean anything anyway. And her hand touching mine through the glass had been an accident. I clear my throat of any uncertainty. "I was working in the yard, and Officer Brooks told me I had a visitor. So I went."

"What did she want?"

"She wanted to know what it feels like to die."

Warden Somerville slumps into his chair, the anger draining from his face. He loosens his tie and stares at his picture frames. After a moment, he reaches into his desk drawer for a bottle of antacids and shakes a few into his hand.

"She took her mother's loss very hard. We both did. What did you tell her?"

I told her the same thing he would have wanted me to. The same thing he wants me to tell him right now. His face wears the same expression Vivian's did. And Simpson's. And Rickers's. The pain of knowing the answer but not being able to live with it. Desperate for someone to tell you you've had it all wrong, so you can finally give yourself permission to move on.

"I told her it didn't hurt. That her mother wasn't afraid. That she was still here with her."

The warden's shoulders shed some invisible burden.

Until I say, "I lied."

The second hand on the brass clock ticks. I don't breathe. Don't dare disturb the ghost in the room, the one that's haunting the warden's eyes.

"Vivian was here earlier," he says, quietly. "When I asked her why she wanted to see you, she told me a different story. She's hell-bent on this notion that you're innocent. That you deserve a retrial. She wants to help you file for an appeal."

An appeal. It's a word I've never spoken out loud. Not to anyone. It reeks of false hope and makes no promises. But I can't help feeling like maybe there's a chance if the warden is behind me.

"Vivian and I made a deal. She will not see you anymore, and if you can look me in the eye and tell me you're innocent, if you can give me one scrap of evidence to go on, I will do what I can to help you prove it."

And just like that, all that hope bleeds right out of me.

We can't build a case around a suspect who doesn't exist! It's all in your head!

She cut a deal and moved on, leaving me with the burden of proof for a crime I've already been convicted of.

I will do what I can.... No commitment, no terms, no binding contract. This isn't a deal. It's a placation. It's a handoff. It's bullshit. Not a single person in this place is going to believe me.

"Sir," I say, feeling the static and anger welling up inside me, "I've been looking cops, lawyers, jurors, and therapists in the eye for fourteen months. All that time, I've *been* telling the truth. But it seems to me, no one's satisfied unless they hear what they want to hear anyway. You can lie to your daughter if that makes you feel better, but you don't have to lie to me. You and I both know you made your choice about me a long time ago."

I stand, not particularly caring whether I've been dismissed or not. I've got nothing further to say.

THIRTY

I get a pass on Saturday afternoon group because Dr. Manning is on vacation. I spend the hour huddled in bed. The pages of Ben's magazine crinkle in the bunk above me.

"You gonna show me that trick sometime?" For once, the quiet is too much, leaving me too alone in my own head. Ben leans over the edge and hangs upside down to look at me, his car magazine fluttering from his hand. He glances cautiously at the cell door, then jumps down, quiet as a cat, and slides into my bunk. He opens the magazine, flips to a random ad for engine oil, and drags his index finger over the crease, catching something under his nail. A wiry stick of metal, not much wider than a toothpick and no longer than a child's finger, pops out of the spine.

Ben holds it out. "I've been making them. They're thin enough that I can bend them back and forth a few times and snap them off at the right size. Don't even need wire cutters."

The tip is sharp against my finger. Sharp enough to draw Six's blood. And small enough to stash most anywhere if no one's looking for it. But it's no shank.

"A little small, isn't it?"

Ben shrugs. "It ain't supposed to be a weapon. But Six was gonna kill you, and I didn't have a better idea. The tip feels like a blade if you don't see it."

I roll it between my fingers. Nothing in the Y is only what it's supposed be. Toothbrushes aren't just toothbrushes, pens aren't just for writing, and soup cans and fruit cocktail aren't just a lunch. "If it's not a weapon, what is it?"

"It's a lockpick."

I turn it over, seeing it new, catching a thin slice of Ben in its reflection. "Breaking and entering?"

He snatches the pick and slides it back into the crease of his magazine, pouting like I insulted him. "I never broke nothin'."

"So why'd they arrest you, then?"

"I picked the lock and sneaked into that big garage over on Downing. The one that restores old cars. I was just . . . looking, is all. And I was hungry, so I helped myself to the vending machine. But I never broke nothin'," he grumbles.

I can't rein in my smile. Ben definitely isn't what he looks like on the surface, either. I kind of like that about him. "Simmer down. I'm not accusing you of anything. What were you looking for anyway?"

"My brother." It takes him a minute to open his mouth again. Like he's afraid something too big might leap out of it. "He'd be about twenty now. I was twelve when we got separated. The State put us in different foster homes. My mom's cousin took me in, but Davey . . . he was into a lot of trouble. She didn't want any part of him. But I did." Ben unravels a loose thread on my blanket, picking at the memory. "He always liked cars. A guy we went to school with told me he'd heard Davey was fixing up cars downtown somewhere. But no one was real sure where. No listed number—I checked. But I figured if I hit enough garages, I'd find an address or a phone number. Something." Ben balls up the thread and plucks it away. “Never did find him. The silent alarm brought the cops down on me just as I had my hand halfway up the damn vending machine.” He shakes his head. “I would have paid them back for the chips if they hadn’t arrested me first. I was only reaching for my wallet. But they figured I was reaching for something else. After that, everything went a little crazy.”

He’s so earnest. I don’t doubt him for a minute. I wipe the smile off my face. “I believe you.”

That kind of knocks Ben back a bit. He sinks against the wall with his magazine in his lap. “Yeah? Well . . . I believe you, too.” He looks in my eyes when he says it, and that kind of knocks me back also.

“His name is Davey?”

“David Edgar Haggett.” He speaks his older brother’s name with a quiet reverence.

I commit it to memory. No due date to worry about. No trade to square up. Just a soft, internal pressure to find him, to wrap up Davey Haggett and put him in Ben’s hands.

THIRTY-ONE

The library cart squeaks down the pod about an hour before third chow, its left rear wheel spinning out to the side, not quite hitting the ground. Martín eases it to a stop outside my cell door and hands a Sherlock Holmes mystery through the opening.

"I thought I told you, I don't want to read these anymore." I try to stuff it back through before he wheels it away.

Martín doesn't take it. "As your trusted youth offender librarian, I'm telling you to read this. Reading is fundamental." Martín lowers his voice. "And in this case, it's good for your health."

Ben glances up from his magazine, and I wait for his pages to start turning again before I take the book.

I blow out an exasperated sigh and open the back cover—due tomorrow.

The buzzer sounds and the guards shuffle us out for our daily ration of fresh air. I leave Ben in a bright corner of the yard, hanging out with his new friends. Holmes isn't far, his leg propped against the wall and face raised to the afternoon sun.

"I guess Martín didn't tell you, I'm not taking any new jobs," I say, handing him the book.

"This isn't a job."

"You want me to arrange to have someone pick up a package at the club. By tomorrow. If that's not a job, what the hell do you call it?" I struggle not to raise my voice. Try to keep relaxed to avoid notice by the guards or anyone else who might take a sudden interest in our conversation.

"I call it payment rendered." He holds the book toward me. I don't take it.

"What's that supposed to mean?"

Holmes raises an eyebrow and inclines his head to his buddies. They're kicking around a homemade Hacky Sack with Ben. Ben looks up, the smile sliding off his face when his eyes find mine. He looks away.

"I don't get it. Payment for what?"

"Haggett and I made a deal. He supplies me with some of his shiny little lockpicks, and in exchange, I do everything I can to keep you alive. This"—he shoves the book back at me—"is my side of the bargain. I had my brother put together a little something for you. Your outside man can pick it up at the club. Six is in the hole tonight for that stunt he pulled on you in the locker room. You've got one night till he's back in the pod and shit hits the fan again. So get to work."

Holmes pushes off the wall. I clutch the book and follow him. "How is this supposed to keep me alive? I don't understand."

Holmes pauses to look at me over his shoulder. "You understand better than the rest of us, Smoke. Sometimes it's not who you know but what you know that will save you. The way I see it, you're the only person who can."

Ben is unusually quiet in his bunk that night. No rustling of magazines or sheets. Neither of us speak about his deal with Holmes. The words *thank you* are two hard pills to swallow. Almost as hard as *I'm sorry.* Tonight I feel like I'm choking them down by the handful.

The lights snap off and I ease out of my skin with more care than usual, breaking as few threads as possible. I don't have many left.

I head left at the end of the pod, rather than straight through the wall. The mess hall is dark except for the dim glow of the emergency lights. I enter cautiously. Silently. A pit opens inside me at the thought of what I'm about to do. But I am the only one who can fix this.

I creep past the serving station and can almost hear the crackle of frost blooming over the metal as I slide my hand over it.

"Simpson," I call out.

I wait. No answer, except for the hum of a freezer coming to life.

"Matthew Simpson," my voice echoes back. "I know you're in here."

A serving spoon skitters across the tile and clatters at my feet. It's chased by another.

"I know you're listening, Simpson. And there's something I need to say."

Something shifts in the air. His anger is palpable, a cold I can almost feel. A gray mist swirls nearby, watching, listening.

"I'm sorry."

Pots and pans begin to shiver. A serving tray vibrates, rattling on a high shelf.

"I made a mistake."

The tray flies off the edge. Crashes to the floor. Three metal bowls leap off a rack, their clangs echoing through the kitchen.

I shout as four more pans hit the floor. "Your mother is okay! I was wrong! And I'm sorry!"

Simpson's features twist with grief and rage. He curls in on himself, wailing, dragging his smoke fingers down his cheeks, and shredding the flesh from his face. He flings his arms wildly, throwing pots and pans across the room and scattering a box of plastic spoons to the floor. A tray slides fast down the serving station, hurtling toward me. I slam down my fist, stopping it in its tracks.

I will not let Simpson haunt me.

"Go away!" His black eyes pierce me across the mess. He paces in tight, agitated circles, watching me over the cold steam table.

I am determined to finish this. Determined to make him forgive himself, to set what's left of him free. "There's nothing I can do to make it right or take it back. I can't fix what happened to you. And you can't change the decision you made. But you can't stay here punishing yourself." I can feel his black eyes following me. "You belong somewhere else."

"I have no place else! She was my home!"

The steam table rattles and Simpson's fists shake. The emergency lights begin to flicker. Frost creeps and crackles over the metal surfaces, and pockets of steam rise as if the kitchen is alive.

"You made a choice. It wasn't the right one. Now you have a chance to make another. If you stay in this kitchen—if you stay here, in the Y—you'll become something you never wanted to be. Someone your mother wouldn't want you to be." The memory of Ms. Cruz's wild hair and bared teeth comes unbidden to my mind. "But you're the only one who can make that choice."

Simpson collapses to his knees, pieces of him billowing up and spilling around him. The shaking pans fall still.

I pass through the steam table and step cautiously toward him. He looks so transparent, so insubstantial. Like the slightest breath or a word might scatter him. I kneel across from him. He stares down at the pile of plastic spoons, looking defeated.

"You can wait for her there," I whisper, afraid to disturb the fragile silence. "But you have to let go of this place. You have to make peace with what happened here so you can move on. So the light can find you."

Walkie-talkies squawk, and the mess hall doors crack open. Flashlights swing back and forth over us and pause at the mess on the floor.

"Fucking rats," the guard mutters, and storms out.

Simpson sighs, deep and tremulous.

"What if the light never comes?" he asks. "Because of what I did."

"It will." I'm sure of it for some reason that I can't prove. No evidence to back it up. Just my word against a world that has already condemned him.

"How do you know?" His cavernous eyes are wide and vulnerable. I look straight into them.

"I don't."

He thinks about that for a minute. Truth is, I don't know what'll happen to Simpson once he finally lets go of his grief and his rage. I can't say for certain where he'll end up when he decides it's time to go. I can't say for either of us.

"But I do know the only thing holding you here is you."

He stretches his neck to an unnatural length, studying me, his head tipped skeptically. "Then what's holding *you*?"

I must look like a ghost to him. A dead man. A hypocrite. I look down at the mess on the floor. Who am I becoming, the longer I stay? "That's a damn good question."

I linger in the mess hall long enough to say good-bye. Long enough to watch Simpson close his eyes and make his choice. Relief floods through me as those first fingers of light consume him. That I was right about this. That there's hope. That maybe there *is* another side for boys like Simpson—and like me.

THIRTY-TWO

I poke my head through the wall of the break room, just long enough to make sure she's decent. Pink's shift starts in ten minutes. She hovers in front of the mirror, tugging her wig into place and wrestling her unruly curls up inside. She reaches for her mascara, brushing it on in short, rushed strokes.

"Knock, knock."

Pink jumps and pokes herself in the eye. She swears and squeezes it shut while the other one waters blue gunk down her face.

"Jesus, John! What the hell are you doing? You must have a death wish!"

I can't help but smile, watching her stomp her feet and throw a fit. "Why? Are you gonna kill me?"

"No! You are! You aren't supposed to do this anymore! Hand me a tissue, will you?" She reaches out, snapping at the empty space between her fingers and squinting at me. Then she snatches a tissue from the box and mumbles, "Sorry. Sometimes I forget you're not really . . . you know . . . here."

"You want me to go?"

"No," she says quickly. Her eyelashes are wet and it makes her look like she's been crying. And something about that makes me wish I could hand her that tissue worse than anything. "I thought you were going to talk to the warden. What happened?"

"He won't help me."

"So we'll talk to Vivian."

"No. I can't risk involving anyone else."

"Oh," she says softly. She pivots slowly toward the dressing table. "I thought maybe you'd already talked to her. I figured someone would be coming to pick this up. Some guy dropped it off earlier. He told the bouncer it was for me. But it's got your name on it." She holds up a large manila envelope. "Do you want me to open it?"

I almost reach for it, forgetting myself. Holmes didn't tell me what's inside. Or whose secrets might come spilling out of it. But there's no other way, and Pink already knows all of mine. "Would you mind?" I'm ashamed for having to ask.

Pink tears through the tape and pulls out a stack of photocopies.

"What is it?" I lean over her shoulder, almost brushing against her. She shudders and goose bumps race up her arms, but she doesn't push me away. I have a fleeting urge to wipe the blue smudge from her cheek. To press my lips against it. Just to see if I can.

She flips through the pages. "Copies of arrest records. And probation reports. For Anthony Verone, and someone named Tyler Garrison," she says.

Verone and Six. A file full of dirt on the two people who've been trying to kill us.

Sometimes it's not who you know but what you know that will save you.

Holmes must think I'll find something in their files I can use. Some bit of information I can barter with.

"What's all this for?" She bulldozes her cosmetics out of the way, toppling her hairbrush and mascara to the floor. Then she fans the first few pages across her dressing table so I can get a better look.

"Tyler is an inmate in the Y. The one who's trying to kill me. I guess I need to go through these and look for anything I can use. Anything that might keep Tyler and Verone off my back—"

"Or maybe a connection." Her eyes flash back and forth between mine. If there's any shared history between Six and Verone—any common thread between them—this file might be a paper trail back to the person who hired them both. Tangible proof that Monetti's trying to get rid of me.

The break room door cracks open, and a frazzled blue wig appears through it. Pink shuffles all the papers back into the file and stuffs it inside the envelope.

"Candy, are you coming to work anytime this century? These dogs are barking, and I'm ready to cash out."

"I'll be right there," Pink calls out. She waits for the door to close and looks apologetic when she sets the envelope down on the table. She shakes her head and backs out of the room, as if she's torn. "My shift's starting. I can look over the papers tonight and come see you in the morning."

"Wait. There is something else you can do for me," I say, rushing after her. "A phone number. I need it traced. Do you think your sister's friend... the one who helped you find Verone... could he do you one more favor?" I don't want to think about what that kind of favor might cost her. Instead, I picture her hauling trash bags in her big, ugly coat. I remind myself she's smart and strong. That she can take care of herself.

She pulls a pen from her apron, darting a hurried glance at the door. "Sure, he's probably here tonight. What's the number?"

I recite the number. She scribbles it on her palm, then flashes it with a wave good-bye. I bite my tongue as she runs out the door.

Pacing, I look from her coat to the envelope to the tube of lipstick under her mirror. She forgot to put it on and I wonder if she feels as naked out there without it as I do here without my skin. I wait around for a few minutes, thinking maybe she'll come back for it.

I stare at the tube, trying to pinch it between my fingers, but they slip right through. Then I reach out and nudge it with my mind. It wobbles and topples over. Seems like all I ever manage to do is push. Why can't I grab onto anything? Pull it toward me and just hold on to it?

I give it another aggravated nudge. It skips over the table and lands on the floor. I bend down and find it lying beside a business card. It's the business card Pink wrote Anthony Verone's information on before she was attacked.

Only now the card is faceup.

JAMES C. MONETTI

SECURITY SPECIALIST & CORRECTIONS OFFICER

COLORADO DEPARTMENT OF CORRECTIONS

I bolt for the door and dive through it. Heart pounding, I scour the bar and the tables around the room. No sign of Monetti. Maybe he isn't here yet. I can stop her before she talks to him. Stop her before she can ask him about the number.

Because that number has to be one of his.

I spot Holmes's man sitting alone at a table by the door. I follow his line of sight to a group of tables in the back, where I catch a glimpse of Pink's hair.

"I need to talk to you," I say, close at her heel as she sets an order of drinks on the table.

She gives an imperceptible shake of her head and grits her teeth as if to say *Not now.*

"It's important."

"Busy night," she says loudly, plastering on a phony smile. "Can I get you gentlemen anything else?"

"Please."

"Not now, John," she whispers.

I chase after her to the bar. "That number I gave you—"

"I already took care of it!" she snaps. "James was already here. I gave it to him and he left." She refuses to look at me as she loads her tray with a fresh round of bottles and returns to her section.

What have I done? I stand in place, arrested by the blaring music and the flash of the strobes. She gave him one of his own cell numbers and asked him to trace it. She's as good as dead. He doesn't have to trace it. He already knows every call he's ever made from that number. Every hit he's put out, every piece of stolen evidence he's sold. He has a record of every outgoing and incoming call ever received. . . .

Or ever missed.

My mind races backward. I'd called that cell number twice. Once from the desk in visitation. And once from . . .

The warden's house.

A hot wave of panic rolls through me. I crane my neck in both directions, scanning the room for Pink. Holmes's man is at the other end of the bar, doing the same. He pushes off his stool and walks toward the hallway, pausing near the restroom, looking both ways before pushing open the door to the ladies' room. Empty.

I beat him to the break room and slip through the door.

Her backpack is right where she left it, but her chair is empty.

A breeze rustles her coat sleeve.

The back door is hanging open. The frame is dented and scratched, like someone pried it from the outside. I sprint through it, landing in the alley beside an abandoned crowbar.

Pink is gone.

THIRTY-THREE

I don't know where Monetti is, but I have a pretty good idea where he might be going. I race through Capitol Hill toward Cherry Creek, through alleys and front yards, until I'm standing on Vivian Somerville's front porch. The warden's car is gone—the driveway's empty. I pass through the wall into the soft, warm light of her living room. Vivian's curled on the couch with her laptop in a faded T-shirt and flannel pajama pants. Her stockinged feet poke out from under them. Brow furrowed, she studies a news article, trailing a finger down the screen. The headline is a kick to the gut:

TEACHER AND STUDENT FOUND DEAD AT LOCAL HIGH SCHOOL

Beneath the headline are two photos: one of Ms. Cruz I recognize from my freshman yearbook, and a class picture of Cameron Walsh. No photo of me, the unnamed student found at the scene who had already been taken into custody when the article was written.

What's she doing? She made a deal. She told her father she wouldn't see me again. But here she is, trolling through the murky waters of my past, making me think she might actually care. Vivian's lips move in sync with the words under her finger. Then she pauses, her face crinkling.

We both jump at a knock at the door. Vivian stretches on her toes to look through the peephole, then flips the lock.

"Hey, Charlie, what a coincidence!"

Officer Rickers stands in the doorway with his knit cap in his hands. Relief washes over me. Vivian won't be alone if Monetti comes for her, too. I just have to find Pink. "Hi, Vivian. Can I come in?"

"Sure, but Dad's not here." She crosses her arms against the cold. "He left a few hours ago for that conference in Texas."

"Yeah, I know. He was worried about leaving you alone. He asked me to check in on you."

"Sheesh. He'll only be gone two nights. I keep telling him I can take care of myself. Really, I'm fine. And if I know Dad, James will probably come by in a while to check on me, too." Rickers frowns, like he's as disturbed by this as I am. "But you're welcome to come in and warm up if you'd like. Can I take your hat and gloves for you?"

Rickers shakes his head. He stuffs his hat in the pocket of his coat. "No, thanks. I can't stay long. I'm on my break. I just saw your lights on and figured you were up."

"That's sweet of you. I couldn't sleep so I've been up reading." Vivian gestures to the laptop on the sofa. "About you, actually."

Rickers's eyebrows pop up. "About me?"

She points to a photo on the screen—a cluster of police officers warding away the media with outstretched hands. "I didn't know you and John knew each other before he went to the Y."

Rickers's eyes skim over the article, and his smile fades.

"That's you in the picture, talking with the police, isn't it? It says here you were one of the first responders on the scene. Here, look." A chill races through me. I lean in to read over his shoulder, feeling the hairs lift on his neck and his spine stiffen.

Rickers was there. At the scene. Why hasn't he ever told me?

"Oh, I wasn't working for the police then." Rickers runs a finger under his collar. His face is ruddier than usual, and sweat beads on his neck. "I was doing surveillance . . . running a probation investigation. One of my kids was involved."

Vivian seems to prickle with curiosity. "You mean, Cameron Walsh. The boy John killed. He was on probation?"

Rickers gives a noncommittal shrug, and shakes it off like it's nothing. "My team watched a lot of kids. I don't remember them all."

"But surely you'd remember this one," she says, handing him the open laptop. "You probably knew a lot about him. If he was on probation, he probably hung out with a pretty bad crowd. Maybe you know something that could help John?"

He sets her laptop on the coffee table, closing the browser as he does. "Why do you care about helping John?"

"Because he was in my house and ate dinner at my table. And he was nice. I can't make myself think he murdered those people in cold blood. I don't want to believe that he'd lie about that. He says someone else was there—a man no one else saw—and I want to find a reason to believe him." A silence passes between them. "Don't you?"

Rickers hesitates. "Sure I do." His forehead's shining, and he wipes his upper lip with a gloved finger. I don't like any of it. It all feels wrong. "How about we hit the all-night diner and talk about it over coffee?"

"Really? I thought you said you had to get back to your shift?" She points to the kitchen. "I can put on some water for coffee here. It'll only take a minute."

He folds back his sleeve and checks his watch. His smile is weak, distracted. "Sure, that'll be great."

Vivian disappears into the kitchen. From the living room I hear water filling the kettle, and the quiet hiss of the burner as she sets it on the stove. I watch Rickers pace the living room, still wearing his coat and gloves. Why has he kept all this a secret from me? That he was there at the school when I was arrested? That he knew Cameron Walsh?

A phone rings deep in Rickers's pocket. He digs it out and inspects the number.

"Fucking Monetti," he grumbles, and flips it on. He puts the phone to his ear but doesn't speak.

A faint *"Hello? Hello? Who is this?"*

Rickers doesn't answer. Just listens as he walks to the window, pulling back the curtain and looking both ways down the street.

There're no cars parked outside. Not even Rickers's old blue Crown Vic. He shuts the phone off and pulls his gloves on tighter.

No. This is wrong. This is all wrong.

The kettle screams, and we both look at the closed kitchen door.

No, no, no!

I dive for it, landing in the center of the kitchen. Vivian bustles around me, digging in cupboards and arranging cookies on a plate, readying mugs and creamer and spoons. Trusting him the way I had trusted him.

"This isn't right. Something isn't right. He shouldn't be here. You have to run!" I say frantically. "Get out the back door. Just go!"

She shivers as if shaking off the cold.

"Go! Go now!"

She rubs her hands over her arms and stands in front of the dulling orange coils, warming herself before she reaches for the kettle. The microwave door fogs as she presses the latch on the kettle and pours out two steaming cups.

I focus all my energy. I push with everything I have, drawing three bold letters in the condensation.

RUN.

Vivian's hand trembles, and the kettle rattles as she sets it back on the coil. She watches the letters trickle like blood down the glass. Her face pales, and she backs away from the stove. I round on her, hoping instinct will push her away from the cold spot and toward the back door.

"Go!" I will her.

"Vivian? You need a hand in there?"

Her eyes dart toward Rickers's voice. She snatches the plate of cookies off the counter and lunges for the living room door.

No!

A spark of anger ignites inside me. I push a chair back from the table. It screeches across the floor, blocking her path. I change direction in my mind and push again, shoving it against the door and wedging it under the knob. Vivian stumbles backward, dropping the plate. It shatters, spraying glass over the floor.

"Viv? You okay?"

The doorknob rattles.

"Vivian? What's going on in there?"

She stands paralyzed, staring at the chair.

"Vivian!" Rickers bangs with his fist. "Open the door!"

In a minute, he'll break it down. I search the room. There's a knife block on the counter, but it's no good. I can't grab, only push. All I see on the table are salt and pepper shakers and a sugar bowl.

"Vivian!"

I push the bowl hard, flipping it on its side, spilling a pool of white granules over the surface. Vivian yelps and turns at the sound. I focus, pushing the sugar with my mind. She watches in horror as I carve a warning.

BAD MAN.

"Vivian. Open this goddamn door!" It bows as Rickers puts a shoulder into it.

Vivian lunges for the rear door to the alley, ignoring the glass under her feet. She fumbles with the dead bolt.

"Hurry!" I shout.

The living room door splinters and cracks, loosening the knob. Rickers wedges himself into the opening, crushing glass under his boots. He grabs her by the elbow just as she works the locks free.

No!

I shove him, but it only makes him come at her harder. She's fighting. Kicking. He covers her mouth and pushes her to the floor. I shove canisters off the counter, aiming for his head, but they shatter around him, and he hardly notices for all her thrashing. Vivian's feet bleed through her socks, trailing red smears, the room taking on the color of a crime scene, as Rickers struggles with a roll of duct tape stuck in his pocket. He loosens his grip and Vivian screams, her eyes wide and terrified as Rickers pulls back and hits her in the face, knocking her silent.

I cry out, helpless, imagining what he must have already done to Pink.

Rickers works fast, taping her mouth shut and binding her wrists and ankles. He heads to the bathroom and pulls the plastic shower curtain off the rod. I shut my eyes, digging my hands into my skull, my scars. Vivian is going to die. Pink is going to die. And I can't do anything to stop it. A static hum fills the air. Vivian's hair lifts in a halo of strawberry strands, tiny pops of dry air crackling as Rickers drags her over the floor and wraps her loosely in the plastic.

No, no, no!

Rage crests inside me. I grab my head and scream. The overhead lights flicker and burst, plunging us into darkness.

Rickers pauses. He stares at the ceiling. Then he tightens his grip before dragging her out the back door. His car is parked in the alley, backed tightly to the rear of the house. I panic as he pops the trunk and rolls Vivian on top of Pink's still body.

I look from house to house. The coach lights are all off. The windows are all dark. The power is out down the entire street. I need a witness. Anyone other than me. Someone the cops would believe. But the shades are all drawn. The alley is empty. Rickers's car starts and rolls out into the street with its headlights off. I chase after it, but it only gets smaller and smaller until I can't keep up and it's gone.

I stand on the dotted line in the middle of the road, screaming.

And then I feel the first tug.

THIRTY-FOUR

Ben jumps back. I suck in a sharp breath and fly out of my bunk. I'm cold all over and shaking. My jumpsuit is soaked to my skin. The cell is dark, slivers of light creeping in at the edges. The boys in the pod are stirring and muttering. I choke back the urge to vomit and hold the wall until the dizziness passes. Deep inside, everything hurts.

"Sorry, Smoke," Ben whispers, giving me a wide berth. "You were hollering and thrashing around. You woke up the whole pod. Bumper got pissed off and started yelling for an officer to come shut you up. Figured I'd better get you up before the guards did."

I nod, unsteady and still trying to make sense of my surroundings. Pink is gone. Vivian is gone. Rickers has them.

And I'm here. Locked down. Almost daylight.

I ease onto my bunk, listening as the pod quiets again. A night duty guard makes a slow pass and peers in our cell. Bumper gets back to snoring. I lie awake until the predawn light begins to filter through the slats in the cell door.

I need to get out of here. Not part of me. All of me. Today.

"Ben," I whisper, hoping he's as good at breaking out of things as he is at breaking into them. "Do those picks work on handcuffs?"

Ben thinks for a minute. "I guess so."

"How long would it take you to teach me?"

Ben and I get up early, make up our bunks, and do our morning routine before the lights come on in the pod, buying us a few free minutes before our group gets called to first chow. We huddle on my bunk with a piece of paper and a small pencil while the other cells are shuffling around, getting ready for the day. Ben sketches a picture of a lock mechanism, using the pencil to demonstrate the technique for springing the latch.

"Not planning on going anywhere, are you?" Ben's only half joking. His eyes are creased with concern.

A few weeks ago, I'd have asked myself what it'd cost me to confide in Ben. Now I wonder how I can afford not to. "I'm leaving. Today."

He scrutinizes my face, clutching the pencil tight in his hand, as if waiting for the catch. The trade. The deal. But I share this information without conditions. Without expectations. I don't need or want anything in return.

"Here," he says, tweezing a pick from the folds of his magazine and swapping it for the pencil. "Take this one."

"How many more do you have?"

"Got three more. What else do you need?"

I think about that for a minute, mapping out a long shot in my mind.

I count on my fingers. "I need Oscar, I need Martín, and I need Holmes."

Ben's face falls, almost imperceptibly. His need to be needed doesn't escape my attention.

"Think you can manage a trip to the infirmary for me?"

He brightens, ferretting two more picks from his magazine and adding them to the one already in my hand. He sucks in a sharp breath and uses a third to carve a long, deep gash across his palm. I cringe and reach to stop him, but Ben quickly slips his hand in mine, grabbing it and holding on tight. His palm is warm and slick, but his grip is solid. He doesn't flinch.

He's giving me more than his word. He's giving me his blood. A vow.

A knot gathers in my throat. Instinct's telling me I shouldn't... can't accept this. But a soft ache inside me is telling me I don't want to say no.

I let Ben break away first. He leaves the last pick in my hand. Then I whisper a list of things I need in his ear. He strides to the bars, his back straight and his head high. He reaches his bleeding hand through the opening.

"Guard!" he shouts. "I need to see the nurse."

THIRTY-FIVE

The door buzzes open. After a few minutes of third degree, Ben is escorted to the infirmary. All the other podmates filter out of their cells, trying to make the most of the few minutes of free time we have before morning chow. I find Oscar sitting on the floor of the pod, glassy-eyed and looking bored.

I gesture to the space beside him. He narrows his eyes and nods, probably wondering what the hell I want. We don't talk much outside of group.

"Someone told me you're a real Boy Scout," I say, gauging his reaction.

He doesn't look at me. His dull gaze trails up and down the pod.

"Personally, I've never been much good at starting fires. Never quite got the hang of it." I'm talking too fast. I should slow down, but I'm feeling anxious and rushed. All I need to do is light a spark. To breathe some air into the dry tinder inside him. But if I'm not careful, I'll spook him.

"I like to watch them," I keep on. "I like it when the match takes and the flame comes out of nowhere." A light flickers behind Oscar's eyes, making him twitchy. "I like the smell. Woodsmoke and gasoline. That crackling sound it makes and the heat on my face."

Oscar shifts uncomfortably. He massages his forearm, at the hibernating need stirring under his skin.

"Ever thought of starting a fire in here?"

Oscar's eyes skate to mine, sweat beginning to shimmer on his forehead. "I can't."

"It'd be easy," I say.

He wipes his palms on his jumpsuit, looking everywhere but my face. "You know as well as I do, nothing's easy. Not in here."

I uncurl my fist, revealing the two paper matchsticks I took from the warden's bathroom. Oscar licks his lips. He reaches for them as I close my fingers and snatch them away.

"Where'd you get those?" He's hoarse with wanting, and I know I have him. He's ready to deal.

"You want them? You can have them. But you've got to do something for me."

I whisper the terms. Then we shake on it. When he breaks away, my palm is empty.

I find Holmes in the locker room in line for the showers. He stands a few inches taller than the rest of the line, and the black crow on his neck is easy to spot. I pull him aside with a nod.

"Your boy didn't come through last night," I say, boldly positioning myself for a list of demands. "Someone took my girl on your watch, right out from under his nose."

Holmes shrugs, making it clear he doesn't much care. "I don't guarantee anyone's safety."

"Maybe not, but now you owe me." A week ago, I would have been more cautious. I would have weighed my words more carefully. But right now I don't have the time or the patience.

He must see it in the set of my face. He studies me from scar to shoes. "What do you want, Smoke?"

I take a quick look around to make sure no one's listening. The showers are running and people are talking and every sound echoes off the tiled walls. "I want a pair of street clothes delivered to Mercy Hospital. Today. Your man will know what room. And I want a car and driver waiting in the patient pickup lane by noon."

"That's less than five hours."

"It's plenty of time to make a few calls." I let my gaze slide to the loose tile on the wall where his cell phone is hidden, leveraging my offer with a not-so subtle threat. "Can you do it or not?"

Holmes scratches his neck, calculating. "I can get you the clothes. The ride's gonna cost you."

"How much?"

"Depends on who's riding and how far they need to go."

"Not far. Less than ten miles. Something low-profile but quick."

A smile stretches over his face. "If I didn't know better, I might think you're a flight risk, Smoke."

I don't answer. It's better for both of us if he doesn't know.

"What's it worth to you?" he finally asks.

"Three of Ben's picks," I say, hoping it's enough. He shakes his head and turns away.

"And a personal-safety tip."

He raises a brow. "I'm listening."

"Stay clear of the mess hall at the end of first chow. I hear it's gonna get messy. If someone were looking for an easy time to get away with something, I'd say every guard in the house will be tied up for at least thirty minutes. The pod should be empty."

Holmes nods. "I'll talk to my brother. Give me until noon. You'll have your clothes and your driver."

"And Ben?" I need assurance that someone will look after him when I'm gone. Negotiations aren't over until I'm sure he'll be safe.

"He'll be all right."

I turn to go, eager to tackle the few remaining items on my checklist so I can get out of here and find Pink.

"Hey, Smoke," Holmes calls after me with a sly smile. "It's been nice knowing you." I watch Holmes disappear into the showers, wondering if he thinks I'm going to die or if one of us believes I might actually make it out alive.

The clock reads 7:15. I find Officer Brooks arriving in the pod to start his shift. Like clockwork, he's exactly fifteen minutes early.

"Officer Brooks?" I call out when he reaches the end of the sally port. I'm coming out of the showers wearing the same sweaty, bed-wrinkled jumpsuit I woke up in. He raises an eyebrow. Officer Brooks is big on hygiene, timeliness, and perfectly made bedsheets. Lucky for me, he's also big on initiative. "I was up late studying for this big exam I've got tomorrow. Only I'm missing a book. Since you're early, would you mind taking me down to the library? It'll only take a few minutes. I promise to be quick." I don't hold back any of the urgency I'm feeling. Brooks calls out to the guards in the control room, and I brace for the buzzer when they let us through.

Brooks is feeling better today. His baritone fills the hall, and I wonder if some of the lift in his spirits is because the warden is away. Brooks waits outside the library, watching me through the window. When I get inside, I'm not surprised to find Martín already bent over a book. I slip into the stacks, feeling his eyes on my back, too. I scan the shelves quickly. I grab a biography about Harriet Tubman and a worn copy of *Auto Repair for Dummies* and walk them to the checkout desk in front of him. Without a word, I take a pencil from his wooden holder and scribble the address of Matthew Simpson's old apartment, my name, and tomorrow's date on the card in the back of the first book. In the second book, I write David Edgar Haggett's name and a message in the margin for Ben. I sign it, *Your friend, Smoke.*

Quietly, I push both books toward him, trying to figure out how to say what I need to say. I check over my shoulder. Brooks checks his watch and motions for me to get moving. So I take a long, slow breath, ready to empty the last few coins from my pocket. "Your parents' neighbor has been talking to Immigration."

Martín's head is down, but his eyes stop moving over the page. The fact that he is alert and afraid isn't something I can see. It's just something I know. Something I feel through the fragile threads that connect us.

"Immigration has officers watching your house. They're waiting for your cousin's van to come back. They know about the families in your basement. Tell your cousin not to bring anyone else to the house. They'll arrest them all on sight."

Martín nods tightly, his knuckles white on the book.

"Why are you telling me this?"

Because I'm leaving, and I might never see Martín again. These tokens—this currency that bought me a life here—are no good where

I'm going, and for reasons I can't put into words, I want to give him this one thing. But the rules of unconditional friendship are foreign here. Trades keep us balanced. Favors tip the scales. If I don't ask for something in return, he'll doubt my motives.

"Have your cousin go to this address tomorrow. After dark. I'll show him a safe place where the families can stay for a few days until your dad can figure something else out." I shut the book on the Underground Railroad and leave it in his safekeeping. Then I show him the other. The trade.

"Haggett's brother has been missing since 2008. He'd be about twenty years old now. He might be a mechanic or work in a garage. Last warm lead was a shop on Downing. Ask one of your sisters to check the Internet and call around. If you find him, put his address and phone number in here and make sure Ben gets this book."

I snatch a random paperback from the return bin and head for the door.

"What's in it for you?" Martín asks.

I don't have the right words to answer. And I'm not even sure I could explain. I just hope he understands that what I need most isn't something I can frame in the context of a deal. Trust is something that can only be freely given. And I believe in Martín. I trust him.

"Those books you wanted to trade for? They're in my footlocker," I say. "Tell Ben I said you can have them. *Adiós,* my friend."

His chair scrapes the floor.

"Smoke." He leaps to his feet. His face struggles to hide emotions I've never seen him wear before. He walks around the desk and stands in front of me. Looking up at me. "No. I keep telling you, your Spanish sucks. You and I? We don't say good-bye. We say *Nos vemos.*" *We see each other.* Martín grabs my hand, pulling me into a firm embrace. He slaps my back and says quietly, "My cousin will meet you tomorrow night. I'll make sure. Be ready. It's a long road, but he'll get you there safe. I'll know where to find you."

It's almost eight o'clock when I find Ben in our cell with his hand bandaged in gauze, sitting beside an arsenal of medical supplies he's laid out on my bunk.

"What do we do next?" Ben rubs his hands together, forgetting his injury. "Build a bomb?"

A smile twitches its way to the surface. "You think we're going to make explosives with antibiotic ointment, two aspirin, cotton balls, and a medicine cup of rubbing alcohol?"

Ben looks offended. "Well, if those dumbasses in B can make margaritas out of fruit cocktail, and god-only-knows-what out of Nilla Wafers, why the hell can't I make a rocket launcher out of this?"

I laugh in spite of myself. "Sorry, Ben. No rocket science today. Just a little minor surgery."

His eyebrows shoot to the ceiling. "Excuse me?"

I check the clock on the wall. Our group will be cycled into the chow hall in ten minutes. We'll have to work quickly. I unzip my jumpsuit, pulling the orange fabric down to my waist. Then I drag a chair to the bed and sit beside him. All the humor drains from his face.

"I don't understand."

I grab his hand and pull it to my head, guiding his fingertips over my scars.

"Feel that?" I say, pressing his fingers into the tissue and rocking them back and forth over the seams. "That's a metal plate. It's about three inches long. You're going to take this." I pluck the pick he gave me from the inside of my shoe, wet a cotton ball with alcohol, and wipe the metal clean. "You're gonna grease it with this," I say, shoving the tube of ointment in his hand. "And you're gonna slide it into my scar, between the skin and the plate."

Ben turns a strange color and sits down hard on the mattress.

"I can't hide it in my clothes. If I'm stripped, I might lose it. And last time I left, they wanted to put me through a scanner. They can't put me through a regular full-body scanner when they take me out of here. I set their alarms off because of all the metal in my head. They'll have to use a hand wand, and if they're in a hurry and not paying close attention, they won't bother to notice the pick. It's small and it'll be sitting right up against the plate. The scar tissue will hide the swelling."

"What do you mean, when they take you out? You think they're gonna let you waltz right out the front door?"

"No, they're gonna wheel me out. On a gurney."

Ben shoots to his feet, hitting his head on the bunk frame. "Nuh-uh. I don't like this. I voted for the rocket launcher, remember?" He paces the short cell, raking a hand over his shaved curls. I'm grateful I've been here long enough to grow mine back. If Ben's careful inserting the pick, it'll go in straight and lie flat against the plate, and only bleed for a minute or two. My hair and my scar should hide any trace of it.

"Come on, Ben. This is no different from hiding a pick in a magazine." I swab my scalp with alcohol. Then I use a fingernail to bend a one-millimeter lip on one end of the pick. I dip the other end in the tube, coating it thick with ointment, and hold it out to him. "I don't have much time left. I need your help." If I miss this window, I might not make it to Vivian and Pink in time. I just hope they still have time left.

Ben grabs the pick with shaking hands, grimacing as I hold the hair away from my scars and guide him to the entry point. He breathes hard and fast while he works up his nerve. I feel a pinch and a sting, then a chill sliding under the skin like a cold finger. I grit my teeth as metal grates metal, like nails on a blackboard inside my head.

"You're doing good, Ben. That's it. Keep going. Almost there," I soothe him as the pain sinks deeper and deeper. When he's done, he lurches to the trash can and vomits.

I press cotton to the wound, igniting shooting pains through my skull, while I wait for the bleeding and ringing in my ears to stop. Then I pull on my jumpsuit, ruffle my hair to cover the bruise, and pat Ben's shoulder.

"Come on. Time to eat."

THIRTY-SIX

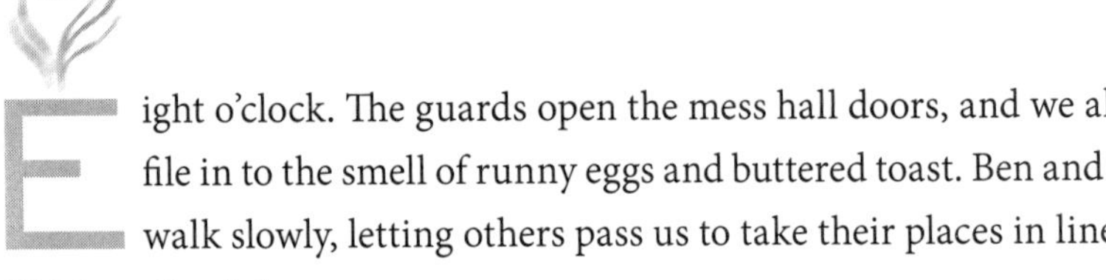

Eight o'clock. The guards open the mess hall doors, and we all file in to the smell of runny eggs and buttered toast. Ben and I walk slowly, letting others pass us to take their places in line. Neither of us is hungry.

"Who's it gonna be?" Ben asks.

Bumper's sitting on the far side of the room. Normally he'd be a good candidate for a fight, but I'm not sure if he'll bite after our conversation during mop detail a few days ago. I only have one shot and I have to be sure he'll hit back hard enough to make it convincing. Rico sits with him, but I'm not sure if his religious convictions—or his fear of me—would hold him back. No, it has to be someone who hates me. Someone who'll put everything he has into that hit. Besides, Rico's too short to land the target.

Ben jabs me with his elbow, inclining his head toward the serving line.

Six. He's out of Segregation.

I turn to Ben and try my best to smile. "Take care of yourself, Ben."

"You too, Smoke."

Ben's standing real tall and I'm glad for it, even if his eyes are shining, and his voice sounds strange because of the lump in his throat. It bobs as he chokes it down. "Send me a postcard, okay?"

"You bet." I hold out a fist, and he taps it with his own. The only good-bye the mess hall will afford us.

I wait until Six is through the line and setting his tray on a table. Then I cross the room against the flow of bodies, attracting the attention of a guard. I smile a little. Just enough to confirm that something isn't right. Then I come up behind Six. Just as he's getting ready to sit down, I put a hand between his shoulder blades and push.

Six turns around with a contemptuous smile.

"You have no idea how long I've waited for this." He winds back. I drop my arms and turn slightly, offering him a clean shot at the side of my head. His fist strikes with the force of a bulldozer. I drop, unconscious, sliding free of my skin before I hit the floor.

Side fights break out, orange suits falling into the fray like dominoes in every direction. Ben rushes to me and falls on his knees, covering me like a living shield. He whispers something I can't hear over the din, and runs his hand under my hair, checking to make sure the pick's still in place.

I drift backward, out of the chaos, searching the crowd for Oscar. He stands alone in the far corner, cupping something in his hand. When he lights the first match, no one's paying attention. He raises it to his face, smelling the flame, then he drops it into a metal trash can. He ducks, darting under a table and crawling under the maze of chairs, plugging his ears a second before the blast. Black clouds billow through the room. Orange jumpsuits drop low to the floor, everyone covering their heads. A second blast follows close behind. Oscar rocks back and forth under a table, his eyes closed and his head thrown back, high on the rush and breathless from the smoke.

Guards storm the hall with gas masks and fire extinguishers, spraying white powdery fumes into the haze. I drift back to Ben. He clings to my body, waiting for the guards to make it through the mass of brawling orange jumpsuits and smoke-blackened faces. The air thickens, dense and unbreathable. Ben starts coughing. Inmates gag and run for the exits back to the pods, hunched low with their hands behind their heads, past masked guards brandishing Maglites and pepper spray. The crowd parts for two guards carrying a backboard and medical kits.

It's time.

The guards peel Ben away from me and drag him out by his elbows.

"Don't you die on me, John Conlan! You hear me? Don't you die!" Ben's screaming as they pull him out the door, smoke-black tears streaking down his face.

I ignore the crushing pain in my chest, the knot in my throat. I let go of this place. I let go of this life. I let go of the choice I made before, until I feel my threads snapping.

The medics check for a pulse. Listen for breath. A white light shimmers warm above me. It brightens and spreads, and I begin to feel its pull. I close my eyes. I let go of my fear, slowly disconnecting, drifting away from myself. And I hold on to the one thing that might be strong enough to keep me breathing. I hold on to the four tense and fragile threads that keep me tied to myself—Ben, Martín, Vivian, and Pink. I cleave to my memory of their faces, hoping that when the time has come, those memories are enough to guide me home.

The guards work fast, walkie-talkies blaring for an ambulance. I'm light. Disoriented. Floating away from the pain, until the room is muted and my awareness of it is hazy and distant.

One. Two. Three. They haul me onto the backboard and strap an oxygen mask on my face. I drift behind myself, holding fast to four threads, only now beginning to understand the risk. I'm maintaining the barest of vital signs. If I let go completely, if my heart or my lungs stop, I'll have no way to pull myself home. I fight to stay alert and connected. I'm frighteningly aware that part of me, some part I locked away a long time ago, *wants* to let go.

The backboard and medics race through gate after gate. Each time, the buzzers crush my soul. Each one reminds me I can let go. I can choose not to hear them anymore. I cover my ears, grit my teeth, and clutch desperately at my last four lifelines. I hold on to my self.

We come to the final gate. Cuffs and shackles snap around my wrists and ankles. We're clear. Then out, and the sunshine's blinding and the wind should be blistering, but I don't feel it. The ambulance is just ahead. They lift my body inside. I stay close beside myself. The light is determined to take me. It yanks me off my feet. I grab my shoulders and hold on, resisting the pull at my back. I am face-to-face with my scars—the ugly memories they grew from. I think about letting go. Instead, I close my eyes and picture Pink's face.

The ambulance door slams shut. Sirens scream and we clear the fence. I focus on the barest of breaths, the shallowest of heartbeats. I fight the light until it dwindles and fades away. And I hold on.

THIRTY-SEVEN

My body is stable. I'm still clinging to it when they roll me through the back doors of the emergency room. The light is gone. I no longer feel its pull, but the fight has left me weary. My threads are thin and brittle, and every passing moment makes it harder to hold on. I back away from myself and check out my surroundings. My body lies on the gurney in a curtained room. A guard stands against the wall, trying to stay out of the way as a doctor and nurse come in. The doctor asks the guards to remove the cuffs from my hands. The nurse hooks me up to monitors and an IV bag. The doctor shines a penlight in my eyes and repeats my name loudly, a gentle tug at my consciousness.

I look at my self. My face is covered with a dark smoky film. A large black bruise spreads over my cheek, stretching up to my scar. I sneak in close, checking that the pick is still there, but it's buried under swelling and bruising and hair, and I'm grateful when I can't easily find it.

The doctor frowns at the paramedics and the escorting guard. "He's stable now. But based on his medical history, I'm going to keep him overnight for observation. We'll be moving him upstairs to a room. I've ordered some scans just to be safe."

“He’s high security,” the officer says. “We’ll need to post a guard at the door to his room. After he’s moved, I’ll need to secure him.”

The doctor looks from my sleeping, smoke-stained face to the guard. “Ankles only. I need access to his hands, and I need to be able to move him. I wouldn’t worry. He’s not likely to wake up for a few more hours.”

When the doctor leaves the room, the guard picks up a magazine from the wall rack and waits. I study the shackles, hoping Ben’s pick will be strong enough to get the job done.

A few minutes later, I’m wheeled into an elevator and transferred to a room. The guard hovers just outside the door, watching as the nurses cut off the remains of my jumpsuit and shut my shoes and socks inside the wardrobe against the wall. They tie a hospital johnny loosely around me and take notes on a clipboard. My name is on the whiteboard by the door. After the nurses leave, the guard checks in once, then takes a seat in the hall.

I drift around to get my bearings. I know Mercy Hospital inside and out. I took long walks during the weeks I lived here, exploring behind open doors so I could pass through them at night while everyone else was sleeping. This time, my room is on the second floor, on the rear side of the building facing the green space.

A few minutes before noon, my door cracks open and a candy striper enters with a stack of fresh linens and towels. Her long hair is pulled forward to conceal a black crow tattoo on her neck, and the photo on her lanyard doesn’t quite match her pierced and heavily made-up face, like maybe she stole it from someone else.

Holmes came through.

The girl deposits the stack of linens inside the wardrobe and leaves. The clothes must be buried inside. It’s time. I’ve got everything I need.

I drift to the nurses' station, eavesdropping on phone calls and conversations, garnering enough to know I've only got twenty minutes before they move me to Radiology to take pictures of my head.

I glide back to my body, as close as I can get. I close my eyes and grab those last four threads, and I pull with my mind. I pull harder, clinging to their faces. I'm sluggish and tired, and the effort of holding on is like swimming upstream. Pain blooms in my skull, pushing me back. My body is stiff and sore. My stomach is empty, my chest is tight, and my throat is burning dry. It would be so easy to let go. But I think about Pink, and I pull myself home.

I suck in a smoke-ragged breath. The pulse monitor accelerates with erratic peaks. I grab myself one last time by the shoulders and heave myself into my skin. It fits like cold leather, reluctant to warm or bend to me.

My heart skips once, twice on the monitor, before settling into a rhythm. The plastic mattress creaks as I shrug myself into the last of my fingers and toes. I pluck the oxygen tube from my nose and cast it aside. I'm tied up and connected and tangled everywhere. Carefully, I reach over and switch off the IV and oxygen monitors. I pop the clip off the end of my index finger, rip the IV tape off, and extract the needle from my hand. When my hands and face are free, I feel under my hair for the pick. My scar tissue throbs where the pick is still buried inside. Breaking the soft scab that binds it, I ease it out like a hot thorn and wipe it clean on my bedsheet.

Careful not to rattle the cuffs, I draw my feet toward me, and slide the pick into the keyhole. I close my eyes, picturing Ben's drawing, seeing his pencil moving in the air. Then I feel it—the click and release. I shed my restraints and ease off the bed. Quietly, I open the wardrobe and dig around in the pile of linens. A pair of jeans and a shirt are wrapped inside, along with a baseball cap and an insulated flannel. I slip on the clothes, pulling the bill of the cap low over my eyes. Something crinkles inside it, but I don't have time to look.

I put on my socks and shoes, and crank open the window. I pop the screen free and lean outside. A drainpipe hangs to my left, and a thin brick ledge to my right.

Voices carry in the hall, coming closer.

I scrape the hospital johnny off the floor and drop it out the window, letting it float down to the grass. Then I knot two bedsheets together, tie them to the window crank, and toss them out so they trail over the sill. The window, I leave wide open. I've learned a thing or two since the last time I left this place. People only see what they want to see. What they expect to see. They search for proof that supports their established belief systems, even when the truth is hiding right under their nose.

So I climb into the wardrobe, hold my breath, and wait.

From inside, I hear the door open to my room. Then arguing, followed by the heavy fall of the guard's boots as he rushes to the window. I listen for the squawk of his radio as he calls in a missing patient, possibly dangerous, fleeing the rear of the building.

I wait until the room is empty. Until the voices in the hall fade toward the elevators and the nurses' station. I climb out of the wardrobe and check that the coast is clear. Then I sneak down a back stairwell, and walk out the front door.

Holmes's man is waiting in the patient pickup lane on a glossy black street bike. He holds out a motorcycle helmet with a dark-tinted full face visor. I pull off my ball cap and slip the helmet over my head. Inside the cap's rim is a crisp twenty-dollar bill and a note.

Smoke,

I won this in a bet over breakfast.

If you're reading this, I guess I picked the right horse.

—Holmes

I smile to myself and tuck it into my pocket. My fingers bump against something cold and smooth. A pocketknife. Two things I didn't ask for. And can't pay back. Making me wonder if maybe the rules I've learned to live by aren't as hard and fast as I thought.

I jump on the bike behind Holmes's man.

"Where to?" he asks.

"Athmar Park," I say over the rev of his engine and the wail of approaching sirens.

We're going to Rickers's house.

THIRTY-EIGHT

Holmes's man drops me off a few houses away. Rickers's blue Crown Vic is in the driveway, and I hope like hell that means Pink and Viv are there, too. I duck through the neighbor's side yard, crouching low as I skirt Rickers's fence. Then I vault over it into Rickers's backyard. Like most houses here, his basement window is recessed into the dirt, framed by a metal escape well and topped with a grate.

I creep low to the ground, coming up behind his kitchen and peeking in the back door. The lights are off. A cell phone rings inside. It glows on the kitchen counter. Five rings. No one answers. A minute later, it starts ringing again.

I drop off the back step and squat by the window well. Silently, I lift the grate and lower myself into the hole, careful not to crunch the gravel under my feet. I try the window. It doesn't budge, and I can't see inside. It's blacked out by heavy drapes.

Popping my head up, I spot a large river rock in the landscape bed and I carry it down with me into the hole. I slip off my flannel and wrap the rock inside it. Then I wait for the first ring. On the second ring, I smash the rock into the glass, splintering it and making a small hole.

On the third ring, I kick the window in. I use the fourth ring to swipe away the shards from the frame.

I push back the drape and look inside. The unfinished basement is dark, a gray concrete hole, empty except for some cardboard boxes and exposed beams and plumbing. Something rustles on the floor. I sink cautiously inside, broken glass crackling under my shoes. The drape falls back over the opening, and I wait for my eyes to adjust.

Movement draws my attention deep into a corner. The clank and rattle of chains.

Pink's eyes are wide over a strip of silver duct tape. She makes muffled noises through her nose. Her cuffed wrists clink against a set of copper pipes. Vivian is curled beside her, unmoving except for the shallow rise and fall of her chest. I drop to my knees, overcome with relief. They're here. Alive.

I hold a finger to my lips and pull the tape from Pink's face, listening to her breath rush in and out of her. Silently, I roll her sideways and dig the pick from my pocket. When the cuffs are free, Pink leaps for me, wrapping herself around my neck and breathing hard into it. I shush her, pulling her tight to my chest. I press my lips to her cheek and whisper, "I'm here."

Together, we free Vivian and pull away the tape. I cringe at her bruises and her swollen face.

"How long has she been out?"

"Since she got here. She put up a fight while he was cuffing her, and he hit her pretty hard."

"Her pulse is steady and she's breathing. I think she's just passed out. But it's not going to be easy getting her out of here."

Upstairs the phone rings again. This time, Rickers picks up. I climb the stairs on my toes, careful not to make a sound, and listen through the door.

"No, Verone! I need this taken care of now!"

Rickers paces. The floor creaks beneath him.

"I don't care what you do with them. Just get them the hell out of my basement. Dump them in the reservoir. Bury them in the desert. I don't care!"

More stomping.

"Not your responsibility? Of course it's your responsibility. You were supposed to get rid of her the first time. That was the deal."

Silence.

"You'll do this in an hour or you can kiss your probation good-bye." Something hard, probably the phone, hits the floor.

Vivian stirs and whimpers. I whip my head around, knocking heads with Pink, and the stairs creak as we both steady ourselves. She scrambles down the stairs to quiet Vivian, too late. Vivian sits up and screams. The basement door flies open just as my foot hits the bottom step.

A soft click stops me cold.

I can feel the gun aimed at my back.

Pink wraps Vivian in her arms. They crouch in the corner, terrified.

"How the hell did you make it out?" The top step groans, then another, as he slowly makes his way down. He presses the cool steel to the back of my head.

"I've got friends. More than you can quiet." I fist my hand at my side, concealing Ben's pick between my fingers. "Why'd you do it?" The question burns under my skin. "You got away. You had me behind bars. Why'd you take the job in the Y? Why bother trying to kill me? Why not let me rot there?"

Rickers thinks about that. Maybe wondering if it's worth his breath to explain.

"Dr. Manning and I go way back. She worked with a lot of my probation kids. So after your trial, we're out having a few beers after work, and I ask her about you. She says you're making progress. But you won't stop talking about the man in the hood. To the point where you even have her second-guessing her evaluation. After a few beers, she starts babbling, wondering if she should recant her testimony, and I start wondering who else you might be talking to. So I make sure Six gets a phone, and I tell him to keep an eye on you."

"The laundry," I say, remembering my conversation with Bumper. That's how the knife got in. He could have passed a phone through the same way.

Rickers chuckles darkly. "You've got eyes and ears everywhere, don't you? That's exactly what Six says when he calls me. He starts calling you Smoke, spewing off at the mouth about how you have all these connections outside. How you're dealing information in and out. And it gets me a little worried. So Lisa and I start hanging out in the bar down the street from the Y after work, so I can keep tabs on Dr. Manning and make sure she isn't planning to do something stupid."

"Why? Because then you'd have to get rid of her, too?"

Rickers is quiet for a moment. "So that's where I meet Monetti. He and Lisa hit it off playing pool, and next thing you know, I've got her asking him to hook me up with the job in the Y. I figure, I'll watch you from the inside, and then I'll know who you're working with, who you're talking to."

"So you were using her just like you used Dr. Manning? Just like you used Monetti. And me." I can see the chain of events roll out in my mind, even as I say it. "You practically pushed Lisa and Monetti together. Then you set me up to catch them, so you could go straight back to Monetti and make sure he knew that I was the one who ratted him out. So he'd be mad enough to want to kill me."

"I wanted to see how you operate, Smoke. I needed to see how you're passing information. And if Monetti decides to get rid of you in the process, then I'm just killing two birds with one stone, aren't I? But see, even after all that, I still couldn't figure out how you were doing it. You never had a visitor. Never made a phone call. I couldn't find a single trace of a letter or note in your cell. Until the day Candace here shows up in visitation, and suddenly, I know who your source is." I can practically hear Rickers shaking his head behind me. I can hear the sigh as he takes in the scene that's unfolded before him—an escaped convict and a kidnapped girl in his basement, the warden's daughter bleeding in the corner.

"I thought it'd be easy to take care of you, Smoke. I could let Six take you out. Or Monetti. Both of them hate you enough to dig their own grave. But then Vivian throws herself into the mix, talking to Daddy about how you're innocent. How she's going to help you find the man in the hood. Things get complicated. And now I've got a fucking mess on my hands."

"You have no idea how big this mess is." Monetti's voice is close behind Rickers's. "Put the gun down, Charlie."

The barrel leaves my skull, and I'm light-headed without the pressing weight of it.

"Set it down nice and easy," Monetti says. He must have a weapon. A gun. Otherwise, Rickers wouldn't be so quick to cooperate.

I want to turn, to see the picture I can't piece together in the silence that follows. But I don't. I hold perfectly still, seeing everything play out in Pink's eyes. Her lids drop slowly as Rickers lowers his weapon.

She looks to Monetti, relieved. Until Monetti bends to pick up Rickers's gun and points it. At me.

"You tell me, Charlie." Monetti's shaking with adrenaline and rage. "Tell me why there's a cell phone in your kitchen with a call history that reads like a prison intake roster."

"It's none of your business. Those numbers belong to kids I used to work with. Before the Y. I was running surveillance teams—"

"That was a long time ago, Charlie. These calls are from last month, last week . . . Hell, some of them are from today! Anthony Verone? Ring any bells?"

Rickers is quiet.

"Funny. I was at Verone's house a few days ago. I'm investigating a little corruption problem we've got in the Y. Seems Anthony Verone has been bribing the officers at the visitation desk to let him in to see an old friend of his . . . Tyler Garrison. Wasn't Six one of yours, too, before he got arrested and sent back to the Y?"

"What's your point? I worked juvenile probation. I ran surveillance on a lot of kids."

"That doesn't exactly explain why I confiscated a disposable phone from Six's cell this morning, with your number in it."

Rickers doesn't answer.

"So help me understand what's going on here, Charlie. Tell me why one of the kids on the phone in your kitchen is stalking a seventeen-year-old girl in a nightclub. Why is she in possession of probation records with your name on them? Why is Tyler Garrison trying to kill Smoke on my watch? You tell me, Charlie! Why's the warden's daughter cuffed in your basement? What are you mixed up in? What's the connection, 'cause I'm not seeing it, man!"

Monetti can't see it, but I can. The pieces are finally snapping together. Rickers has been supplementing his income, using kids who are on probation to do his dirty work. Dealing drugs. Selling confiscated weapons. Killing witnesses. He's holding their freedom over their heads. It's why he was in an empty school with Cameron Walsh. It's what he was doing when Ms. Cruz found them there. He was one of the first on the scene because he was already there, wearing a hoodie and gloves. He wasn't doing surveillance on Cameron Walsh. He was exchanging drugs and knives with a kid who was probably too afraid to say no, because he'd rather live in an old boiler room in an empty school than go back to jail. Ms. Cruz saw them—witnessed a transaction that could expose an entire ring of crimes Rickers was involved in. So he killed her. And I inadvertently eliminated the only other witness. Rather than kill me, Rickers patched himself up, changed his shirt, and reported me, knowing I'd take the fall for both crimes. Framing me was cleaner, less risky than leaving behind three bodies and no suspects. And framing kids was something he'd already become good at.

I turn around, one inch at a time, hands up where Monetti can see them.

"You did it," I say to Rickers. "And then you were the one who called it in. You reported me." Monetti's eyes skip back and forth between us, confused. "I didn't kill the teacher at the high school. Rickers did. The kid I stabbed, Cameron Walsh, was on probation. He was one of Rickers's assignments. Rickers is dirty. He's using the kids on probation to move confiscated weapons and drugs. Ms. Cruz was at the school that day looking for me and accidentally walked in on a deal. Rickers killed her, and I killed Cameron Walsh in self-defense. And now Rickers is using Verone and Six to take care of anyone who can connect him back to the crime. He's afraid someone might actually believe me." I hope that someone is Monetti.

Monetti stands at the base of the stairs, blocking the exit. He holds the guns level on both of us.

"Tell me the kid's lying, Charlie."

Rickers looks at me with a twisted smile, probably wishing he'd gotten his hands dirty and killed me while he had the chance.

"It's true," Vivian says. "I saw Charlie's picture in the paper. He was there the night of the murders. He was the surveillance officer assigned to Cameron Walsh."

The gun on me slips lower in Monetti's hand.

"Candy, you know I can't let him go." Monetti sounds almost apologetic, like he can see the next question written on Pink's face. "I'm going to call this in to the police. We'll get this all straightened out."

"But—" Pink argues, tears swelling in her eyes.

"I don't have a choice. Conlan's an escaped felon—"

"And you're an ass!" Pink snaps. "It's no wonder my sister won't go out with you!"

"It's okay," I say, hyperaware of the barrel that's still pointed at me and wanting only to defuse the tension in the room. "I know the truth. And you're both safe. That's all I wanted." I lace my fingers behind my head in a show of good faith. If he's going to take the gun off one of us, I'll be damned if it's Rickers. I kneel down slowly, ready to be cuffed. When I do, I see a pair of feet standing behind Monetti at the top of the stairs.

"Behind you!" I shout.

Anthony Verone aims his gun at Monetti and descends the stairs. Monetti turns, drops to his knees, and fires. Verone slumps and tumbles the rest of the way down.

In the chaos, Rickers scrambles for Monetti's hand, desperate for his gun. With Ben's pick wedged between my fingers, I leap at Rickers, hurling a punch into the side of his neck. Rickers screams, the pick is lodged deep in the skin.

I roll away, reaching for the knife in my pocket, scooting on my back across the floor. Rickers charges after me, neck bloody and teeth bared. I snap the knife open just as Rickers drives his knee into my chest and clamps his hands around my throat. I shut my eyes, ready to thrust.

A deafening shot tears through the room.

Rickers's eyes fly wide open. He falls slack and drops sideways to the floor. Monetti stands behind him with his gun raised. His eyes are like dark mirrors as the shock settles on his face. I look down at the clean blade in my hand.

"In sixty seconds I'm calling the cops. Then it will be my duty to come after you." Monetti is shaking. I can hear it in his voice. The barrel is trembling in his hand. It's not quite pointed at me. "Or you can turn yourself in. I'm not making any promises. You still killed that boy, engineered a prison riot, and fled custody. I will tell them what I know—what you and Vivian told me, and what Rickers said. But there'll still be consequences to pay if you come back. Do you understand what I'm saying, Conlan?" I understand that Monetti is giving me a choice. Run, or give myself back to the Y and take my chances on a retrial.

I look to Pink, but she's hugging herself, and her eyes are glued to the floor.

Sometimes they just need someone to tell them it's okay to move on.

"I'll take care of them," Monetti says. Then, slowly, he lowers his gun and turns his back on me. He checks his watch and unclips his phone.

"Stay, John. Turn yourself in. We can prove you're innocent. I can help you. We can fight for a mistrial." Vivian looks like her father, her gray eyes full of hope. But hope and faith aren't the same thing, and I'm done trying to prove myself. The people who matter already believe.

Pink looks up when it's clear I'm not leaving.

"What the hell are you still doing here?" she says softly as a tear slides down her cheek. She wipes it away and takes a steadying breath. "Go."

Monetti starts dialing.

Sparing one last look so I'll remember Pink's face, I pull the drape from the basement window and climb up the ladder through the grate. Launching myself over the fence, I take off running. I sprint toward the sunset, then south, dodging fenders and trash cans, ticking off the seconds in my head. I can make it. . . .

Heavy footfalls close in fast behind me. I pump my legs harder, madder than hell. Monetti lied. It hasn't been sixty seconds.

"Wait!" cries a shrill, pissed-off voice behind me.

Winded, I pull to a stop and spin around just as Pink dives into my chest. She throws her legs around my waist and holds on. I wrap my arms around her and squeeze her tight. She's light enough to carry with me. Strong enough to make me stay. The one thread I can't imagine breaking. She takes my head in her hands, trailing wet tears over my scars, down my cheeks, sliding her lips over mine and kissing me hard. I grab on tight, pulling her into me, holding her close, until I'm all tangled up inside.

She breaks away, shaking, and whispers, "Go."

Behind her, Monetti's closing in fast. I grab her face, pull her in for one more kiss. Memorize her lips as she backs away.

Monetti clears the next corner. I let go of Pink's hand and look both ways. A trash truck barrels down Mississippi Avenue, and I dart through the intersection and cut in front of it, close enough for the bumper to graze my leg. I grab the handle and jump onto the platform, letting it carry me away. I look back and see Pink and Monetti, frozen at the corner, staring at the empty sidewalk where I just disappeared.

EPILOGUE

I wipe the sweat from my eyes and swat a mosquito. It's summer in the jungle, and the air is hot and thick. I set my tool bucket inside a makeshift shed beside my camper and head for the sand. I've been living in the little trailer park for six months, since Martín's cousin dropped me off at the end of the long dirt road just north of Tulum with a note in a language I couldn't read and an envelope full of pesos. A man put me to work that same day—collecting trash in the morning, hacking weeds in the jungle, painting and repairing stuff—and gave me a small run-down trailer to sleep in. I've learned enough Spanish to hold up my end of a conversation and to count change. I don't talk much anyway. And I don't need much to get by.

I pass friends along the way. They call me *Juan Humo*, John Smoke—the name Martín's cousin had written in his note. Today they call me *gringo* and laugh at my mess of blond hair. It's sun-bleached and long now, hanging almost to my chin. Long enough to cover my scars, though I don't much notice them anymore. They've faded with time and the sun. Maybe that's what Dr. Manning meant by distance. That it softens the jagged, ugly parts of our past, until our scars aren't so hard to look at anymore. Until they're just another piece of our skin.

I rake the sweaty tangles out of my eyes, roll up my cargo pants, and wade out into the bath-warm water. The sun is sinking lower. I think it might be Tuesday. Maybe the second Tuesday in June, but time is hard to hold on to here.

The sky is turning pink. I count four early stars in the sky. I find the brightest one and think of her. I hope she's graduating.

A calm surf licks at my toes, pulling the sand out from under my feet. I've grown used to the feeling. The slip of the earth beneath me. I picture Pink's hand on the wood floor of the club, that night she told me why the ground was always solid beneath me . . . because I believed it would be.

The places you can go, the things you haven't figured out how to do yet . . . it's all in your head.

I press my own hand into the wet sand and watch the sea rise up to fill in the hole.

I know I can't go back.

I walk for a while. Until the sky is dark and full of stars. More than I've ever seen. I'm looking up when I trip on something in the sand.

A book. I pick it up and thumb through it.

Travel to Mexico with a handful of dog-eared pages. Out of habit, I flip to the back cover and pause. The pocket is stamped GREATER DENVER YOUTH OFFENDER REHABILITATION CENTER. It's checked out under my name. No due date. Just numbers. Latitude. Longitude. Martín's handwriting in the margin.

I'm light. My mind travels someplace else and something tugs deep inside. The tide pulls at my feet and I look down to see I'm standing beside a pair of footprints. Not my own. The water surges over them, stealing bits and pieces of a message left in the sand.

I'M HERE, it reads, deep enough to linger.

Down the beach, I see her. Pink looks up at the stars and starts spinning.

AUTHOR'S NOTE

"The Good, the Bad, and the Uncertain" by Elle Cosimano, posted 10/3/14 on *Huffington Post*

The first time I stepped foot in a prison, I was four years old. I grew up just outside Washington, D.C., the daughter of a warden. My father ran facilities that housed some of our nation's most violent offenders, like the D.C. Jail and the Maximum Security Facility at Lorton, and I still remember holding his hand, my black Mary Janes tapping a happy rhythm down the corridors to the squawk of radios and buzzing sally ports on those days when I visited him at work.

You might presuppose certain things about me, knowing I'm a warden's daughter. You probably assume that my father was strict (he was), that he had very firm ideas about right and wrong (he did), and that the lessons he taught me about the differences between good people and bad people are as concrete as the walls we use to keep them apart.

But here, you'd be wrong.

If anything, my filtered, watered-down child's understanding of my father's job created a very muddy lens through which I learned to see the world. The stories I heard and the people I met in my youth blurred the lines between criminals and heroes, making them harder to define.

Take George, for instance.

My dad brought George home from work one Thanksgiving to share dinner with our family. George was a quiet man with a warm smile—a decorated war veteran like my father, except George walked with the aid of a cane because of wounds he suffered while serving in Vietnam. And though I was only eight years old at the time, I recall his polite and genuine appreciation for the meal and for my family's hospitality. You see, George didn't work at the prison with my father. George was an inmate there, doing twenty to life for Murder One. He was a decent man who'd made a terrible mistake—a mistake that cost him the rest of his life and took another. In the blink of five courses, I learned something I would never forget. That good people sometimes make bad choices.

Then there was Duffy.

Duffy was a murderer. Not a situational offender, like George. Duffy had killed several people and continued to do so without remorse behind The Wall. I never met Duffy. I never even knew his name. But on the day of my fifth-grade school play, when I looked into the audience with shaking hands, my father's seat was empty. There was a situation at work, my mother explained, and Dad might not make it in time for the play.

Duffy had decided he didn't want to go back to his cell block after recreation that day. He hunkered down in The Yard with a brick in his hand, and threatened to brain anyone who tried to make him come inside. My father knew it would take half a dozen officers to forcibly remove him, and, inevitably, someone would get hurt if they tried.

But something unexpected happened when my dad approached The Yard. He told Duffy, "I promised my daughter I would go to her school play, and I'm missing it because of you."

Duffy thought about that. He put down the brick and returned to his cell.

I never knew Duffy was a murderer—that he'd committed heinous acts of violence against inmates and officers, and had once threatened to kill my father. I was too young to hear this kind of backstory. Instead, I would remember him as the inmate who'd chosen peace over violence so that my dad could make it home in time for my play. Back then, I embraced Duffy's act as selfless and heroic. I wouldn't understand until years later that Duffy was no hero. He had just made a choice to do one good thing.

People like George and Duffy rise to the surface of a collection of images from my childhood. Of the high school field trip when my father invited my U.S. government class to visit the D.C. Jail, and we all crammed into a Plexiglas-and-steel sally port in a housing unit, looking hard into the faces of bad people. One of them looked just as hard at us. He pointed to a confident, good-looking boy in my class—a kid most people never knew was broken inside—and told him, "I know you. You're me. That thing you're thinking about doing? That road you're thinking about walking down? It leads right here."

Later, I would realize the greatest lesson my father taught me is that we are not one-dimensional. That we can't be singularly defined by our last victory or mistake. We're human and complicated, and we all have a backstory. Like the scary-looking six-foot-four bearded, tattooed biker who lived in the house across the street—who happened to be an undercover narcotics officer for the District of Columbia police department and a close friend of my father's. Or Dr. Elizabeth Morgan, the Ivy League–educated plastic surgeon who spent almost two years in the D.C. Jail for civil contempt because she refused to produce her daughter for nonsupervised visitation with a man she suspected was sexually abusing her.

Complexity of character makes a crime drama more compelling and a mystery more difficult to solve. If readers are spoon-fed watered-down versions of heroes and villains, the answers become obvious and they're left with nothing to chew.

When I sit down and write a mystery, my goal is to make readers think. I want them to question their presuppositions. I want them to doubt themselves until the very last page. Sometimes, that means turning our universal belief systems—right and wrong, good and bad, wicked and just—on their heads.

These are the lessons, the images I carry with me as I develop characters for my stories. Orange jumpsuits do not define our whole person any more than a judge's robes or a shiny badge. We are deeper than our tattoos and piercings. We are more than the diplomas we hang on our wall. When we all strip down to what makes us universally human, telling the good guys from the bad guys isn't always so clean-cut.

ACKNOWLEDGMENTS

Sarah Davies, my agent and dauntless champion, this book would not be a book without you. Thank you for your wisdom and your vision, for taking my stories to places I never dared dream of on my own. You've taught me that words are like threads—I don't need a lot of them—I only need the right ones. Thanks for holding on to this story and guiding it to a loving home.

I am grateful to my editor, Emily Meehan, and everyone at Hyperion who fell in love with Smoke Conlan and offered him a voice. Thank you to the following people who gave his story a place in their hearts and on their shelves: Hannah Allaman, Maria Elias, Christine Ma, Sara Liebling, Jamie Baker, Frank Bumbalo, Jackie DeLeo, Holly Nagel, and Dina Sherman. Thank you for your passion and enthusiasm for Smoke's story, and for all you've done to share it with the world.

This story was born as a writing sample—an application to the 2012 Nevada SCBWI Mentor Program—and found its legs the night Ellen Hopkins called to tell me I'd been accepted into the program as her mentee. I am beyond privileged to have worked under the guidance of Ellen Hopkins and Holly Black on various elements of this story. I am grateful to them both, and all of the participants of the 2012 Nevada SCBWI Mentor Program group, for their wisdom, encouragement, and feedback. Smoke's voice and his story are more powerful because of all of you.

I am thankful for so many things in my writing life, but none more so than the companionship and camaraderie of my critique partners, Ashley Elston and Megan Miranda. Thanks for being my partners in crime, for helping me dispose of (fictional) bodies and giving me the insight to write better books. You make this crazy roller coaster a lot more fun. I'm so lucky to share this ride with both of you.

While the Y and all the characters inside its walls are products of my imagination, this book required the help and expertise of many very real people. Immeasurable thanks to Lee Lofland and the entire staff of the Writers' Police Academy, which I annually attended from 2012 to 2014 in order to conduct hands-on research for my books. Special thanks to Sgt. Catherine Netter, for her class on Jail Searches, and for sharing insights into the world of corrections.

I am especially grateful to retired Deputy Director for Institutions of the District of Columbia Department of Corrections William Plaut (I also call him Dad), for answering my multitudes of questions about prison culture, processes, and terminology. Thank you for helping me "capture the flavor of the joint," and for helping me find the right balance between fiction and fact. And most important, for bringing George home for dinner.

Special thanks to Dr. Lydia Kang for answering my medical questions, to Kathleen Murphy-Morales for assisting with Spanish translation, to Emily Hainsworth for fact-checking my memories of Denver, and Kate Bassett for being Smoke's first and biggest cheerleader.

Last but not least, my family makes great sacrifices in support of my dreams. Thank you to my parents, who made this journey possible. To my children, who fill both my heart and my creative well. And to my husband, the thread that guides me home.